THE GRUDGE LIST

THE
GRUDGE
LIST

THE GRUDGE LIST

CHRIS BRYDA

PALMETTO
PUBLISHING
Charleston, SC
www.PalmettoPublishing.com

Copyright © 2024 by Chris Bryda

All rights reserved.

This book or any portion thereof may not be reproduced or used in any manner whatsoever without the express written permission of the publisher except for the use of brief quotations in a book review.

Hardcover ISBN: 979-8-8229-5697-1
Paperback ISBN: 979-8-8229-4720-7
eBook ISBN: 979-8-8229-5743-5

Author's Note

This was my very first book written so I have made a lot of mistakes. My apologies in advance to the readers. The Grudge List has been a book I wanted to write but never had the time to complete. All the people in the book are fictious and do not resemble anyone from my childhood. The place Dickens Ave exists, and I grew up there on the near Northside of Chicago. I did have a paper route as a sixth grader at St. Hedwigs Grade School. I did in fact deliver the Chicago Today newspaper when it was in existence. Street ball and street hockey were two sports we played as kids on the surface streets of the Bucktown neighborhood. The year 1970 was an interesting year as a kid growing up and I will never forget it. I hope the readers enjoy the story that is a complete fabrication of fiction and is in no resemblance to anyone living or dead. Enjoy the read. Thank you in advance for spending time with Mike Peters the paperboy.

Chapter 1

Michael Peters was just an ordinary boy. At twelve years old, he was the middle child in a five-kid package. His father was a draftsman by profession but rarely worked a day in his life. Dad had come home from the Second World War with what would be described today as PTSD. This was rarely diagnosed during that era. Now, however, it is quite a common situation. His mother was a registered nurse. She had obtained her degree and skill during the wartime drive for nursing students. During the war, training programs were offered that included a twelve-month guaranteed hitch at the local hospital. This was a war-effort program that helped to train and employ as many nurses as possible to take care of wounded soldiers who were being shipped back from the European and the Pacific theaters. Michael lived in a small four-bedroom house on the north side of Chicago. The three-story building had a basement that had been converted into a two-bedroom living arrangement for the younger kids, including Michael. There were bunk beds to accommodate the fourth and fifth children of the family. The second floor was the main part of the house and had the other two bedrooms, a living room, and a kitchen. The third story had been converted to an attic. This was where some mischief always took place from the oldest to the youngest of the five kids. The old neighborhood was referred to as the Bucktown area of Chicago. Michael never knew why Bucktown was the name, but when you are a twelve-year-old kid, not a lot of things make sense. Michael was named after his maternal grandfather, who had come to the United States from Germany around the turn of the twentieth century. Good Catholic mothers always named their children after the prior parents and gave them middle names after saints of the Catholic Church. Michael's middle name had been selected in honor of St. John, which was Mom's thing. Michael John Peters was his name. But he always preferred to be called Mike.

Chapter 2

Mike motored his 1970 Schwinn Junior Sting-Ray men's twenty-inch bike toward the newsstand distribution office located on the corner of Hamilton Avenue and Webster Street. Mike's house was on Dickens Street, so it took him only a few minutes to pedal over to the office, which was always a hub of activity. Other boys were already there in the office, rolling the newspapers up and then affixing a rubber band to each rolled paper. Each rolled newspaper was placed in a news bag pouch and then mounted to the front handlebars of a paperboy's bike. Mike didn't care that his Sting-Ray was well worn and had a lot of miles on the frame while most of the other boys had newer bikes. He liked the beat-up look of his bike and knew he would not be a target of a theft if a bigger boy wanted his bike. Mike finally rolled the fifty newspapers that composed the total for all the customers on his route. He then stuffed them into the standard news bag pouch that all the boys had. The news rolls were placed in such a way that Mike could grab them one at a time and throw them into each customer's doorway. Once balanced and ready, he left the office to ride his route.

***

Mike always started his route on Webster, then went on to Shakespeare, Charleston, Dickens (his home street), McLean, and finally a few houses on Hoyne. When he had finished with his route, it was a short ride back to his house, where he would start his chores and homework. The paper route usually took one hour from start to finish and could usually be done by 4:30 p.m. This was an hour after school during the week. Since the customers were being delivered the afternoon edition of the *Chicago Today*, the paper office guaranteed delivery before dinnertime. There had been an attempt by the newspaper a few years back to deliver the papers in the morning, but this did not work out because all the paperboys ranged in age from ten to fifteen. The workforce would clearly not work out. So, the paper decided to use the afternoon door-to-door delivery by young boys to undercut its rivals. A morning edition of the paper was left to rival newspapers such as the *Chicago Tribune* and the *Chicago Sun Times*.

***

Mike arrived home on Monday after his delivery of papers.

"Do you have one for us?" his mom asked.

Mike had a few leftover papers and handed one to his mother. She unrolled the paper and gasped at the headlines.

"Another murder. Did you see this, son?"

"What are you talking about?" Mike replied.

"It's in the paper, Michael Peters."

Michael's mom would always use his full name and middle name when she wanted to make a point and get his immediate attention.

"Michael John Peters, did you not see this on the front page of the newspaper?" his mom said.

THE GRUDGE LIST

"No, Mom, I did not," Mike replied.

"There has been another murder. A man by the name of Wally Bass was murdered, and the news was on the front page. Did you not notice this on the front page, son?" his mom said again. It was Monday, June 1, 1970.

"No, I did not, Mom," Mike replied. "Who is Wally Bass?"

"The paper says he was the guidance counselor at Gordon Tech High School. He appears to have been found murdered in his home on the Northwest Side of the city. He lived alone, so no one noticed he had died until he did not show up for work at the local high school. A police officer went to do a wellness check and found the TV on and saw the body in the recliner through the window. His throat had been slashed from ear to ear, and he appears to have bled out in the chair while watching TV. No other details are available. The police are baffled. You really should take some time to read the newsprint you're delivering, son," Mike's mom said.

"Mom, why should I? It changes every day; I just deliver the news," Mike replied. "I don't write it."

"This is true, son," his mom answered.

"I will try to read some news later. On the next ride." Mike left, irritated by the constant badgering from his mom. It felt like the third degree from the Spanish Inquisition.

Chapter 3

The paper office was a busy place on Tuesday, June 2, 1970. The boys were busy rolling and stuffing the papers into their news pouch bags like they had done so many times before, preparing for the paper routes in the Bucktown neighborhood. The boys were giving grief to Mike because he was reading the front page of the newspaper. The front page read, "WALLY BASS MURDERED IN HIS HOME ON THE NORTHWEST SIDE ON SUNDAY." There were no added items on the murder other than that the Jefferson Park precinct police were completely baffled by the murder. No cause or reason was forthcoming in the article. The police said there would be a briefing later in the day but did not say the time or place. As Mike skimmed the pages of the *Chicago Today*, there were other stories that sparked his interest. There was an advertisement for *Kelly's Heroes* to be released in the local theater soon. There was a follow-up article on the Apollo 13 launch and safe landing following the near disaster of the liquid-oxygen tank. There was an article on the breakup of the Beatles. There was also an article on the four students killed at Kent State by the National Guard. But what really piqued Mikes curiosity was the article on Casey Kasem, who syndicated the *American Top Forty* program. This article was by some journalists who commented that this was an enormous success for Casey Kasem and the music industry. The boys continued to tease

Mike about being a slacker as they all left the newsstand office. Mike needed to roll and rubber-band his fifty papers and get going. The office was empty except for him.

The manager came over to the area where Mike had started to roll the papers.

"What's wrong, Mike?" said Larry, the newsstand manager. "Why aren't you done rolling the papers?"

Mike explained to Larry that his mom had questioned him yesterday about not knowing anything about the news articles in the paper that he was delivering. She'd implied that he was not interested in knowing about the news of the day.

"That must be a mother thing," Larry retorted.

"My mom says I do not take an interest in anything I do. I just deliver the newspapers. I don't read them."

"Maybe just read one or two articles before you hand it to your mother. That way she will think you have taken an interest in what is going on in the world."

"That's not a bad idea," replied Mike. "Then maybe she will think I am interested in the world."

"Wouldn't hurt. Now get those papers delivered to your customers," Larry said as he pointed to the door.

"Will do."

Mike started his route about fifteen minutes later than his normal time at 4:00 p.m. He wondered whether his customers even cared if he was a few minutes late in the afternoon.

Mike liked to listen to music while he delivered his newspapers. The radio of choice was the General Electric GE7 handheld set that was tied to the frame of the Sting-Ray. As he pedaled and threw his rolled papers at the doorways, hallways, and porches, he listened to WLS 890

AM, his favorite station. The DJs Bob Sirott and Larry Lujack were the main guys who would flip the vinyl and broadcast to the neighborhood during the daytime hours. Rock and roll top forty was the mainstay of the airwaves, and Mike was happy to have company from the radio station. There were contests that the DJs would advertise, but Mike would always miss them because he was not at home waiting for their call. The DJs would call listeners who sent in postcards with their names and phone numbers, and they would win prizes. But Mike was always on his bike when the DJs were calling the contestants. *Never in the right place at the right time,* Mike contemplated.

***

The paper route this day was a routine milk run, and all fifty deliveries were made with no problems. Mike got home a little later than normal, and his mom was there waiting for her copy of the Tuesday edition of the *Chicago Today*. This time Mike was determined to be well informed if his mom asked any questions about the news articles on the front page.

"How was your day, Mike?" Mike's mom greeted him as he walked in the door.

"Ok. I guess nothing exciting today. The Wally Bass murder was still on the front page. The Jefferson Park police said they do not have any new developments on the murder or suspects. That would not be a good thing to know if I lived in that area of town. I am sure the neighbors would feel a little bit uncomfortable if a murderer were living among them," Mike said with a quick tongue.

"I am sure they will figure out who killed Wally Bass," his mom replied.

The Wally Bass murder remained on the front page of the newspaper for three days in a row. No added information was forthcoming from the police. Mike wondered whether this lack of new facts would increase the circulation of newspapers by creating lots of press and coverage of the event.

Chapter 4

The detectives assigned to the Wally Bass murder scene were Abbey Cato and Rick Douglas. They arrived at the house where the bloody body of one deceased male was stuck to a La-Z-Boy. Coagulated blood had nearly frozen the skin to the chair material. Even though the temperature in the house was seventy degrees, the deceased was attached to the chair and needed to be detached. The detectives had never seen a body in this state of deterioration and rigidity. Detective Abbey Cato found the ME on the scene and started to discuss the next steps of how to process the crime scene.

***

The ME was a seasoned pro. Michelle Lynn had been in this position for the last ten years for the Cook County Medical Examiner's Office and was well versed in these types of extractions. She had mentioned to the detectives to take as many crime scene pictures as possible before she tried to remove the victim from the chair. Once removed, the victim would in most cases bleed out more because the chair material would no longer be sticking to the flesh. The time of death appeared to be at least two days ago, probably on Saturday afternoon. The body was completely cold, and rigor mortis had set in at least twenty-four hours ago. The ME would not know for sure until the body was processed down at the county morgue. The apparent cause of death was a knife wound. The victim had been slashed from ear to ear with a very sharp hunting knife, with at least a six-inch blade, by a right-handed assailant. Based on the position of the body, the victim had to have known the murderer because of the lack of defensive wounds. The deceased may have been sleeping or drugged when the crime took place, but that was only an educated guess.

Chapter 5

Ray Chambers was a struggling newspaper reporter with a mediocre career with the *Chicago Today*. He was fresh out of college this past year and had considered himself lucky to land a gig with the newspaper.

He was given assignments that were not liked, and he considered the tasks beneath him as a reporter. Reporting on the car break-ins in the Loop area of Chicago was not his cup of tea. But he dug up whatever he could find. Ray dreamed of covering murder investigations and writing some newsworthy stories. But his editor had pushed him down the list of assignments doled out to the reporters on staff. He was disappointed and needed a way to figure out a reporting angle to propel his name to the top of the list of reporting hotshots on the team.

Ray decided to abandon his assignment of car break-ins in the Loop area for the Wally Bass murder investigation. He would make up the report on the break-ins and send it in, knowing that the editor would not figure the story was fictitious. He visited the police district in the Jefferson Park area to see what he could dig up. The detectives assigned to the case were at the crime scene and were not in the district's headquarters, so he made a decision to go to the scene, thinking the detectives would still be on-site. Lucky for Ray, they were. Ray traveled to the murder site of Wally Bass and stumbled onto Detectives Abbey Cato and Rick Douglas.

"Are you Abbey Cato and Rick Douglas, the detectives assigned to the murder investigation?"

"We are. What can we do for you?"

"I am Ray Chambers, a reporter with the *Chicago Today* doing a story on the Wally Bass murder. Can you provide me any information regarding the murder?"

"No comment" was the reply from Abbey Cato. "The watch commander, Dane Hoy, has published all the information pertaining to the crime scene and the murder details. Please contact the Jefferson Park police district for any updates."

Ray tried to ask more questions, but the detectives would not answer any questions.

"Stay behind the yellow tape," said the beat cop on the scene.

Ray walked away dejected from not getting any information on this murder investigation.

***

Ray returned to his home on Hoyne Avenue after the visit to the murder scene of Wally Bass. The name Wally Bass was familiar to Ray, and Ray thought he might have gone to school with him, but it was just a passing thought. He needed to write up a story on the murder of Wally Bass and was determined to write up a creative news article so he would get noticed by the editor. He poured himself a cup of coffee. It was late in the afternoon on Wednesday, and he had to write a news article with substance. He started the article with "Who Was Wally Bass?" A high school guidance counselor who was murdered in his home for no apparent reason. His throat had been slit from ear to ear, and the police department had no idea who had done it or why it had happened. Ray typed up the news article on the comments from the detectives, which were zero. Added to the details was the fact that the victim had been drugged and sedated before the slitting of the throat. This detail had not been known to the public, and Ray took a chance and embellished this fact. This juiced up the article and made it more interesting to read. Ray wondered whether this stretching of the truth was going too far, but it was worth the chance in his mind.

Ray walked into the editor's office the next day and dropped off the article. Lew reviewed the scrap of paper that Ray handed him.

"Lew, this is details on the Wally Bass murder."

"What murder?" Lew yelled.

"I did a report on the Wally Bass murder."

"What the hell is this?" Lew said. "I did not ask you to do an article on this."

"Well, I did not like the car break-ins assignment you put me on."

"You work on the assignments I give you. Otherwise, you can find another job elsewhere. Understand?"

"Yes, Lew, I understand," said Ray in a low, burly voice.

Ray walked out of Lew's office and went to his desk, dejected, and annoyed at the response he'd gotten from Lew.

The editor, Lew Kelly, printed the follow-up article on the Wally Bass murder despite his yelling at Ray. Lew had a hard deadline and needed a small spot on the front page. The details of the murder victim's having been drugged and sedated were included in the story.

Chapter 6

He got in his blue '66 Chevrolet Chevelle SS and drove to the Northwest Side of Chicago, which was just a short drive from Bucktown. Taking the Kennedy Expressway and getting off at Foster Avenue would be the most direct route for the next intended victim. Cruising down Foster to Harlem and then to North East Circle Avenue took only about twenty minutes.

***

The house was near the Norwood Park neighborhood, so parking on the opposite side, next to the tennis courts, would not engender any suspicion. The final walk up to North East Circle Avenue, where Kevin Burger resided, was only a block. As he exited the car, a full moon was rising in the starry sky, which was in full bloom on this beautiful June evening. A short walk up to the house, and he would be back in the car, driving back home. As he exited the Chevy, he grabbed a backpack with some tools that was on the passenger seat.

As he walked through the neighborhood, there appeared to be a lack of people milling around. It was only about 10:00 p.m., and the streets were not rolled up yet. The neighbors were home, asleep or watching television, and were not out enjoying the warm summer night. As he got closer to the house, he got nervous. What if someone saw him walking through the neighborhood late at night with the backpack? He could say that he was coming home from a late class at the nearby high school. This was a chance that had to be taken. Get in, do it, and get out.

***

Kevin Burger lived with his parents at the house on North East Circle Avenue, on the second floor. A large walnut tree would provide access to Kevin's room from the south side of the house. All he had to do was climb up the tree, pry open the window, and sneak inside. The climb was easy, and someone had raised the window slightly to take advantage of the cool air wafting into the house. But Kevin was still downstairs. So, a little wait in the closet before Kevin arrived was necessary. It was only about a fifteen-minute wait before Kevin entered the second-floor bedroom. He had prepared a rag soaked with chloroform. He'd placed a mask over his mouth so as not to breathe in the obnoxious odor of the chloroform. As Kevin went toward the bathroom, the killer jumped from the closet and placed the chloroform-soaked rag over Kevin's mouth. The chloroform was a fast-acting knockout agent that could immobilize someone in ten seconds. Kevin was subdued and immobile in eight seconds flat. So far so good. The victim would be out for about thirty minutes. He placed Kevin on the bed against the wall, sitting him up in the middle of the mattress. He slit Kevin's wrists with the six-inch hunting knife he'd pulled from the backpack. A large amount of blood started to gush all over the bed. He applied more chloroform to Kevin's mouth just in case. A walk to the bathroom to find a pair of scissors so they could be planted on the victim's person was now needed. He placed the scissors in Kevin's right hand and smeared them in blood to make it look like a suicide. Kevin's body fell forward and nearly rolled off the bed. That would have made a loud thump had he not caught it. The body was folded toward the right side of the bed. It looked like the way a body would fall naturally.

He placed the knife in the backpack and made sure the chloroform was secured. No one noticed him gently slipping out the window and onto the walnut tree like a cat in the night as he left the now-deceased Kevin Burger's house. A brisk walk to the car, and then he would be on the road home.

***

The walk back to where the car was parked was dark and without people. He had survived another killing and was almost giddy with delight. *Get into the car and just drive,* said his inner voice. A few minutes later, the Chevy purred onto the Kennedy Expressway, headed back to Bucktown. The radio was turned on, and once again WLS 890 AM rock and roll was blasting through the car speakers. He would later notch the hunting knife with a second kill when it was safe to do so. Another successful retaliation.

Chapter 7

Today was Friday. Collection day. This was when the boys would deliver the afternoon paper and try to collect the money owed by the customers on the paper route. Most of the boys liked to work on Friday. If they had done an excellent job all week, the customers would tip them in time for the weekend.

***

The bike ride to the newsstand would be short, only a five-minute ride from the house on Dickens. It was a wonderful day, sunny, seventy-five degrees, and dry. Lots of neighbors were out and about this afternoon. The streets were clear of most car traffic, and riding down the center of the street was always a little bit risky, but it felt like Mike owned the road. Mike stopped at Skippy's on Hoyne Avenue for a fountain Coke. This was his favorite soda, and he felt it gave him the energy he needed for the Friday ride. The Coke was all syrup and sugar but tasted so good going down.

When Mike arrived at the newsstand, the place was buzzing with boys coming in and out, because they all knew it was payday. It meant that the boys would have a few dollars in their pockets for the weekend adventures.

"Tommy, what are you going to get with your tips?" said Mike.

"I think I'll buy a new hockey stick. I really need one; the one I have is broken and falling apart. I tried to tape it up several times, but it is still bent. What about you, Mike?"

Mike turned his head and said, "I really would like to buy a new catcher's mitt. I like playing street ball, but I keep dropping the balls because of the hole in the old one."

"Street ball," Tommy said. "What's that?"

Mike explained. "Street ball is where you strike a rubber ball off a ledge on a building and the ball crosses the street. If the ball travels to the first lane of the road and hits the ground, and the fielder does not catch it, it is a base hit. If the ball travels to the second lane and it bounces, it is a double. If the ball travels across the road onto the sidewalk and bounces, it is a triple. If the ball travels over the sidewalk and onto the grass across the street and is not caught, it is a home run."

"Now I get it."

"If you want to play sometime, just let me know," Mike said.

"Why don't you try street hockey with me and the boys sometime, Mike?"

"I don't have a hockey stick, Tommy."

"I can get you one when you're ready."

"Ok, thanks. I'll play hockey with you, Tommy, if you play street ball with me sometime."

"That's a deal, Mike."

Mike went back to rolling his papers to get ready for his route. *I cannot be late today*, Mike was thinking. *I will read the paper after I collect and deliver the papers today.*

***

Mike started the Friday delivery and collection. His route would take him to fifty houses, and most of the occupants would not be home until at least 5:30 p.m. The collection effort on Friday usually took a delivery/collection visit, then a separate collection visit Friday night, and then a follow-up visit on Saturday morning to collect from the ones not home on Friday. Sometimes this was a smooth event with no hitches, and other times this was a time for the customers to complain to the paperboy and reduce the tip for the delivery service the paperboys provided. When a customer complained, Mike knew that the tip would be light. He would have to make a special effort to provide a little better service for that customer in the next week. One customer complained and requested that the paper be delivered between the door and the screen. Another customer wanted the paper delivered in the mailbox. Another customer wanted the paper stuffed in the package slot of the door; this way he did not have to go outside to retrieve the paper. Mike did not appreciate special requests. He would have to get off his bike and accommodate these customers in many ways. He could not sling the paper and ride on. This slowed down the delivery process and made the paper route a lot longer. Some paid handsomely for the extra service, and some did not. *All just part of the job*, Mike thought.

Mike continued his route with his GE pocket radio playing rock and roll from WLS 890 AM radio. He stopped at each address, knocked on the door, delivered the paper, and tried to collect the money due. The newspaper cost was $0.15 per day Monday through Saturday and $0.50 per day on Sunday. That was $1.40 per week from each customer. Most customers would have the money ready when Mike tried to collect it. The tips would range from $0.25 to $0.60 per week per customer. It was easy for the customers to just hand Mike two one-dollar bills and be done with the amount they owed. Occasionally, a customer would be mad, and there would be no tip.

One of the last customers on the route for collection was Ray Chambers on Hoyne Avenue. Mike rang the bell with the paper in hand, ready to deliver it to the customer.

Ray answered the door and said, "Hang on just a minute. I need to get my wallet. You're welcome to come in and wait while I get it."

Mike said ok.

Mike was standing in the living room and saw a corkboard full of pictures and news articles from the *Chicago Today*. He was familiar with the newsprint because he had delivered many papers. There were clippings on the corkboard about the Wally Bass murder and some notes about Kevin Burger. Mike was not sure what that meant, but he did not want to pry into the private doings of his customers.

Ray came back from the kitchen with his wallet in his hand. "How much do I owe you?"

"It's $1.40 for this week," said Mike.

Ray handed Mike two dollars and said, "Keep the change."

Mike said, "Thanks. I appreciate the tip."

Ray turned to Mike just before he left the doorway and said, "We are in the same business. I report on the news for the *Chicago Today*, and you deliver it to our readers."

Mike looked at him funny and said, "Oh, I get it. Thanks." Then he walked out the door.

Mike had put two and two together but wanted Ray to think he was not that sharp. *Oh, Ray is a newspaper reporter for the* Chicago Today, *and he lives in the neighborhood on my paper route*, he thought. *He is working on the Wally Bass murder and other related stories, and he tips good. What a cool job.*

Chapter 8

The Sunday delivery for Mike was always a challenge. He had to get up early, at 6:00 a.m., and deliver the papers to the customers' homes by 7:00 a.m. The *Chicago Today* prided itself on the fact that Sunday home delivery always arrived by the paper's advertised and agreed-to time. This was a policy that Mike did not like because of the super early start time. The paper could not be rolled and rubber-banded because of the one-inch thickness. All the boys in the office knew that the delivery was not fun. Sunday deliveries meant at least three return trips to the newsstand office to pick up the papers. About twenty newspapers could be stuffed into the news pouch bag at any one time because of the weight and size of the paper. The Sunday paper sometimes weighed two pounds. No slinging today.

***

As Mike left the newsstand office, he once again turned on the radio he had attached to his Schwinn Junior Sting-Ray bike. Today would be the Casey Kasem top forty rock and roll songs during the paper route delivery run. The normal DJs on WLS 890 AM radio were off today. As Mike started his route, he had to stop at each house, put the kickstand down, pull the paper from the canvas pouch, and then drop the paper at or near the doorway. This took a tremendous amount of time but was expected by the customers. Most would be in their bathrobes and did not want the neighbors' nosy eyes upon them as they retrieved their Sunday papers. For those who complained that Mike should place the paper between the doors, the Sunday paper would not fit. Mike was glad it was not raining today because then the paper would be even more work to deliver. When it rained, the papers had to be wrapped in plastic sleeves so as not to get wet. This was the last thing Mike wanted to think about today.

Mike made a total of three trips back and forth between the newsstand and the customers' homes delivering the papers. He delivered a total of fifty papers on a Sunday morning. The very last delivery was handed to Mary Crystal, a widow.

She had seen Mike coming down the street and was waiting to intercept her paper.

"Good morning, Mrs. Crystal. How are you today? Here is your Sunday paper."

"Thank you, my dear. You are such a nice boy."

Mike handed her the paper, which weighed two pounds, and she nearly dropped it in the handoff. Mike caught it as it was about to fall out of her hand.

"Did you see this? Kevin Burger found in his home. Dead of an apparent suicide," Mary said to Mike.

"No, I did not have a chance to read the paper this morning."

"This is awful. A young man commits suicide on the Northwest Side of Chicago."

"Northwest Side, Mrs. Crystal?" Mike asked.

"Call me Mary, please!"

"Ok, Miss Mary."

"You are such a polite young man. Thank you. This makes two deaths this week on the Northwest Side of the city. Wally Bass and now Kevin Burger."

"What is going on?" replied Mike.

"Sure, don't want to be anywhere near that area of the city."

"That's why we are here in Bucktown, Miss Mary," said Mike.

"Thanks for the paper. Now go home and be safe, my boy."

"I will try."

He was not sure when or where, so he passed on the thought of a connection. It dawned on Mike that he wanted to be a detective when he grew up, like Dick Tracy was back in the thirties. He was always figuring out who had done it and saving the day. Or like Mikey Spillane with his signature Mike Hammer character just recently released in January 1970. Either way Mike was moving toward being a "dick." He liked the idea. He would have to do some digging on this occupation. This was not a schooltime activity being taught in the sixth grade at St. Hedwig's Catholic School. Mom would never approve, so he would need to keep it secret from her and the rest of his family.

Chapter 9

Detectives Cato and Douglas arrived at the residence of Mr. and Mrs. Burger, who had found their son dead in their house on the second floor and called it in to the police department. This was the morning after the apparent suicide, and the parents were beside themselves with grief. The house had been taped off by a sergeant with the customary yellow tape that read, "Police Line Do Not Cross." Now the investigation would start in earnest.

***

The ME, Michelle Lynn, had beaten them to the crime scene and was already processing the site.

"Looks like a suicide, Michelle," said Detective Cato.

"Yep. Looks like it indeed," Michelle said. "The young man has bled out fast for a one-inch pair of scissors found in his right hand. The slits in his wrist look a lot deeper than that."

"Do we have a suicide or a murder here, Doc?" Cato asked.

"I'll know more when I get the body back to the office to do a full autopsy on him," Michelle replied.

"What shall we tell his parents?" Cato asked.

"Nothing, Detective Cato," Michelle replied.

"Ok. You're the boss," Cato replied.

"Thanks," Michelle said.

"We do not want to mislead the parents on this in any way," Cato said.

"Cato, do you see a suicide note anywhere?" Douglas asked.

"No, I do not," said Cato.

"Well, we'd better look around and make sure there isn't one," Douglas replied.

"We don't want to come to an inaccurate conclusion," Cato said.

As the detectives searched the second-story bedroom for any information or a suicide note, they noted there were no signs of a distraught young man. The bedroom was neat and orderly. There was no mess except for the extensive blood pools on the bed. The bathroom was neat and tidy. The room appeared too clean for a man who wanted to commit suicide. The closet had his clothes hanging up straight and orderly. Something did not add up.

"Hey, Rick, does this look like suicide?" Cato said as she turned to him.

"No, it does not. Two and two are making five, and the little voice inside me is screaming that this was a murder," Rick murmured back to Cato.

"My thoughts exactly."

"Let's get down to the ME's office for the autopsy before we turn in our report to the watch commander."

"Sounds good."

***

Back at the Cook County Medical Examiner's Office, in the morgue, Michelle Lynn was just starting the autopsy when Detectives Cato and Douglas arrived. Dr. Lynn started the autopsy by talking into the microphone.

"This is the autopsy of one Kevin Burger, deceased Friday evening, June 5, 1970. Age twenty-two, male, white Caucasian, approximately 170 pounds, five foot ten inches. Died of an apparent suicide by slicing his wrists with a pair of one-inch scissors found in his right hand."

"Michelle, can I interrupt you for a minute?" said Detective Cato. "The slits on the wrists appear deeper than the length of that one-inch pair of scissors. Can you look at this first rather than the body parts like you normally do?"

"Sure, I know you guys do not like the smells in this room. Got a hot date today?" said Michelle.

"No, I do not, but I have a hunch that this was a murder based on those gashes on the wrists," said Detective Cato.

"Ok, give me a second." Michelle shot a glance at Cato. Speaking into to the microphone, Michelle said, "The slit wrists appear to have bone fragments in the bloody messes on both wrists. This result would be inconsistent with a one-inch blade. The depth in each arm appears to be at least three inches, and the slit has partially severed the wrist bone from the hand."

"In layman's terms, Doc?" Detective Cato asked.

"Looks like the blade used to slit the wrists of Kevin Burger was a substantial blade in size and width and could not possibly have been the one-inch pair of scissors."

"Thanks, Michelle," said Detective Cato.

"So, this was a murder?" Rick chirped in.

"I believe so," said the doctor.

"We will let you do the rest of the autopsy and wait for your report, but the two of us will operate on the premise that this was a murder," Detective Cato said.

"Your call, Detectives."

"Thanks, Doc," Detective Cato said as she grabbed Detective Douglas, and they left the examining room.

***

Later that evening, the ME's report came out. Dr. Lynn had labeled Kevin Burger's death a homicide. The cause of death was the slitting of the wrists with a hunting-type blade of at least four inches in length and a quarter inch in width. The knife was not found at the scene, only a pair of scissors that was inconsistent with the wounds. There were four other pages of facts and measurements, but none of them mattered to the detectives. They had what they needed and knew their hunches were correct.

Another murder on the Northwest Side of Chicago. The neighbors were restless, and the detectives needed to figure this one out—quickly.

Chapter 10

The phone rang, and Ray did not want to talk tonight. Probably a wrong number or a sales call. He was tempted to let it go but instead picked it up.

"Hi, this is Patrick Duffy. I work at the Cook County Medical Examiner's Office with Michelle Lynn. I have a report on one Kevin Burger, who was brought into the morgue on Friday night. An autopsy was done on this male victim, and the details of his death have not been made public. Are you interested?"

"Sure, I am interested."

"It will cost you fifty bucks," Patrick whispered into the phone. "Meet me in the cafeteria on the main floor of the Cook County building at Twenty-Sixth and California in an hour. I will fill you in on the details."

"I'll see you there in an hour."

Ray could not hold back his adrenaline rush. He would receive unreleased public information on the body of Kevin Burger. This would help his editor see him as a true reporter, digging into a case and getting the facts where all others had none.

Ray arrived in fifty minutes at the cafeteria on the main floor of the Cook County building. This part of town was where a lot of Cook County business took place. The morgue was the collection point for all the bodies before they were released to their loved ones. It was also a place for the Jane Does and John Does of the world. The morgue was only one building of a massive complex of government buildings located at Twenty-Sixth and California. The ME's office was right next to the morgue on the first floor. The cafeteria was just down the way from the ME's office and was midway between the county jail facilities.

Ray bought a cup of coffee and sat down at one of the long tables and waited for Patrick Duffy. He now remembered running into the guy a few months ago at a bar in the neighborhood and on a separate occasion at a ballgame, and Ray had let him know that if in the future he had any information on any newsworthy stuff, he would pay him for it. Ray was thinking to himself, "This had better be good for fifty bucks."

"Hey, do you remember me?" Patrick said to Ray.

"Yes, I do. How are you, Patrick?"

"I am fine. I have something for you if you are interested. You still interested?"

"Yes."

"Where is my fifty bucks?"

Ray handed two twenties and a ten to Patrick. "This better be good."

"Oh, it is," said Patrick. "I have the preliminary autopsy report on Kevin Burger. You know, the guy who committed suicide."

"Yes, I heard of the suicide. That is not the latest news—it's old news," Ray retorted to Patrick.

"But it was not a suicide. It has been labeled a homicide. A key fact has been omitted from the public press release."

"What fact?" Ray replied.

"The fact that the wrists were sliced with a sharp hunting knife with a blade of at least four inches long. The scissors found at the scene under the victim's hand had a one-inch blade and could not have done the damage in the report. That is worth the fifty bucks."

"Yep, that is worth it. Thanks, Patrick."

"Do you want a copy of the ME's autopsy report summary?"

"Sure. Thanks again."

Ray took the copy of the report, which was in a small envelope, and stuffed it into his jacket. "It was a pleasure doing business with you."

Patrick got up and removed himself from the table. He disappeared into the hallway, and then Ray exited the building.

In the car, just before Ray went home, he read the report. The ME's summary report did in fact say that a hunting knife with a four-inch blade had been used to slice the wrists of Kevin Burger. The death had of course been labeled a homicide by ME Michelle Lynn. A note in the report had mentioned the fact that detectives Abbey Cato and Rick Douglas were the assigned police contacts for all further information. No release of information would be made unless the watch commander, Dane Hoy, authorized it.

Chapter 11

It was a lazy Saturday morning at the house on Webster. Ray thought about all the errands he had to do and was not in the mood to do any of them. He was thinking about the information he'd obtained from Patrick Duffy yesterday at the cafeteria meeting in the Cook County building regarding the autopsy report on Kevin Burger. Should he get a start on the article, or should he wait until Monday?

Ray decided to start the article on the murder of Kevin Burger today and then maybe take some time off on Monday when it was due in the editor's office. His editor, Lew Kelly, would not know the difference, since this information was not going to be released to the public. He knew Lew would be mad at him because the deadline on Monday was to be about the recent CTA L train graffiti crimes he was assigned to. He had no real interest for covering this assigned story even though he rode the L often enough to write some gibberish fluff piece on the topic.

Ray started banging away on the keys with his fingers one at a time, putting the information down. The writer's choice was a Smith Corona Galaxie Super 12 electric typewriter in atomic blue. This was his favorite piece of equipment for a reporter. It had been a gift from his parents when he'd graduated from college last year. Ray alternated between one-fingering and two-handing the keyboard as he pondered each stroke.

"The Suicide Murder of Kevin Burger" was the title of the article.

Late Thursday night, one Kevin Burger was reported as deceased by his parents on North East Circle Avenue on Chicago's Northwest Side. The preliminary investigation into the death ruled it a suicide. No further details were available from the press conference held on Friday afternoon. Detectives Cato and Douglas were assigned to the case to determine whether this was a true suicide or if some nefarious criminal was loose in our fair city. The victim apparently committed suicide by slitting his wrists and bled out while sitting on his bed in the second-floor bedroom of his parents' house. That the victim appears to have been murdered is a hunch that this reporter has, and no other details are available at this time. This reporter feels that the police are holding back vital information as the perpetrator goes free in the city we live in.

Ray knew these last two sentences were going to cause Lew's voice to skyrocket once he read it. How could he know this would be Lew's reaction? Lew had done this to Ray before, and it would not be the first or last bit of yelling from the editor to a reporter just trying to get ahead in a very competitive job. Lew needed to yell at all the reporters so that he would feel like he was in charge. Ray would need an answer for this if he were going to get this article printed. *What should I tell Lew?* Ray decided he would tell him that it was his investigative reporting and research on the murder that had brought him to this conclusion. It did not hurt to have an inside source at the Cook County Medical Examiner's Office, a fact that he could not share with Lew.

Ray finished banging away on his electric typewriter, completing the article on the murder of Kevin Burger. He then went to the kitchen to pour himself a cup of coffee because he felt he would need the boost to do the editing. He read through the article a second time, and one thought came to mind: *Boy I am good at this.* Ray contemplated his skills as a reporter, knowing damned well that what he had done was obtain information that could never be revealed. But he could hide behind the First Amendment as every good reporter had done before him. *Oh, the Constitution. What a marvelous founding document for the United States of America*, Ray pondered.

Ray read the draft of the article again. He did not change one word. This was ready to be turned into Lew Kelly on Monday.

Ray turned on the TV to WGN Channel 9 and just caught a glimpse of the local Chicago news. A reporter was at the Jefferson Park police precinct and was reporting on the murder of Kevin Burger. The reporter was saying in the news broadcast that Dane Hoy had given a press conference and announced that Kevin Burger had been found deceased of an apparent suicide on the Northwest Side, on North East Circle Avenue in the Norwood Park area. The watch commander said there was no additional information at this time. This case was going to be closed pending any future developments, and a future news conference would be held if any new details were available.

Ray was thinking that this was bullshit, and that the additional information would not come out unless the watch commander was forced to admit it. Dane Hoy did not mention Detectives Cato and Douglas in the press release, stating only that the police were on the case and actively pursuing all leads. Ray had to be careful not to draw too much attention to his article and cause himself to be a suspect in the case. He did not want to get into the crosshairs of the police. He would be in the crosshairs of one Lew Kelly on Monday when he turned in the article.

Until then, Ray could relax and enjoy the show.

Chapter 12

Ray went to work on Monday as if it were a normal day. Taking the Armitage Avenue bus to the downtown office building on Wacker was the quickest way to get to the office. The CTA bus was full of workers going to the downtown office buildings as on any other workday. Ray hated driving his car down to the Chicago downtown area because parking was always at a premium and so expensive. So, the bus was the poor man's choice for traveling to the office.

The *Chicago Today* offices were located at the corner of North LaSalle and West Wacker Drive in the downtown business district. The news division was on the thirteenth floor, and that was where Ray had a desk. Lew Kelly's office was also on that floor but was a nice corner office with lots of glass windows and a view of the Chicago River.

Ray went to his cluttered desk when he arrived at 9:00 a.m. and putzed around his desk pretending to author his assigned article. The assignment about graffiti on the L was not on his mind. He was wondering when Lew would yell from his office, "Where is that damned article, Ray?" This was Lew's normal method of controlling his staff of reporters. The reporter would yell back in a low and demurring voice, "I will bring it to your office, Lew!"

At 10:00 a.m. sharp, Lew yelled, "Where is that article, Ray?"

Ray replied, "I'll come to your office with the article in just a minute."

"Well, hurry up; we have a deadline to meet today."

Ray walked into Lew's office. "Here is the article on the L graffiti," he said, knowing that the article was completely made up. "Here is the article on the Kevin Burger suicide/murder from Friday night."

"What the hell is this Kevin Burger bullshit?" Lew barked.

"I did some investigative reporting on the Kevin Burger suicide and found out that this really was a murder made to look like a suicide."

"Did I assign you this article?"

"No," said Ray. "I took it upon myself to investigate and do some substantive reporting on my own time."

"Your own time?" Lew yelled.

"Yes, my own time."

"Let me read this," Lew retorted.

Lew took the pages from Ray and started to read them with a scowling look of intensity. "Looks good. How did you come to that conclusion, given the fact that the police have not released this as a homicide?"

"Just uncovering the facts of this case," Ray said.

"Are the police covering something up?"

"Maybe," Ray replied.

"Then how do you know it's a murder and not a suicide, as was reported by the watch commander?"

Ray replied, "Because I did some investigate research and found out that the police are misleading the public."

"What facts are you using to base this conclusion on?"

"I have a tip that I paid for. And I will submit an expense report for this information."

"Was this information illegally obtained?" Lew barked.

"No, it was in the normal course of a question-and-answer session with an informant."

"This had better not get us in trouble with legal or the police, or you will be looking at a criminal offense here."

Ray said, "No, this is all on the up-and-up, Lew. I have a summary report with some details on the deceased. This will protect us."

"Let me be the judge of that," Lew yelled at Ray. "Go back to your desk and give me a chance to read the submitted article a little more carefully. If I want to review that report then, you better have it handy."

A few minutes went by and nothing from Lew. Twenty minutes went by, and finally Lew said something.

"We are going to run this article on the Kevin Burger suicide/murder angle but lighten up on the conclusion that this was a murder. I do not feel like sparring with the police department and fighting with the legal department today."

Ray's article would run in the Monday afternoon edition of the *Chicago Today* with the headline "KEVIN BURGER, SUICIDE OR MURDER? ARE CHICAGO'S FINEST HOLDING BACK?" all in bold black letters and all in caps on the front page.

Lew knew this front-page article would draw a lot of attention from the brass in the office, the police department, and the legal team from the newspaper. The *Chicago Tribune* and *Sun Times* were kicking their butts on circulation this year, and Lew was determined to do everything in his power to increase circulation. His job was riding on resurrecting this paper's news department to be a competitor of the other two papers. Lew could remember when he was a reporter and the chances he took to get a story. Lew had a thought: *Is Ray the reporter I once was?* Lew wished for a moment that he had stayed a reporter instead of taking the editor's position and getting nothing but grief from everyone who tried to tell him how to do his job. Lew played the memory of being a reporter once again.

***

The Monday edition of the *Chicago Today* was printed, distributed, and ready for circulation.

The paperboys of the Bucktown office would be rolling, rubber banding, and delivering the paper to the neighborhood by 4:00 p.m. that afternoon.

Mike was at the newsstand office as on any regular afternoon. He read the front page and was aghast at the headline. *Another murder on the Northwest Side*, he thought. *What is going on? Is there a murderer loose in the neighborhood? Do we have a serial murderer in the city? I need to figure this out and solve these crimes. Is this what I want to do with my life?* Mike was full of ideas. But none of them mattered for now.

"Hey, Mike, get those papers rolled and get out of this office and get them delivered," Larry said as he pointed to the doorway. "And don't let the door hit you on the way out."

"Yes, I know," said Mike.

Out the door he went to deliver the Monday edition of the *Chicago Today*.

Chapter 13

This was Tuesday, June 9, 1970, the day after school was done for the summer. Everyone at the St. Hedwig's grade school was excited about three months of no more homework. The penguins—the nuns and teachers at the school—would get a rest from the kids.

***

The Bucktown neighborhood was bustling, with kids all over the streets and sidewalks. The Creedence Clearwater Revival song "Looking Out Your Back Door" could be heard on Mike's GE radio as the boys were playing their favorite game, street ball.

Mike and Tommy were teamed up against Johnny and Danny in a nine-inning game of street ball on Dickens Avenue. The game was a poor kid's version of baseball that could be played across the street with a rubber ball and a mitt if you could afford one. Those kids who could not afford mitts used their bare hands. Hitting the rubber ball against the ledge of the school building to ricochet up into the street was the objective. If one of the other two players caught it, this would be an out. If not, a single, double, triple, or home run was tallied.

"Hey, Mike, turn it up," said Tommy. "I really like that song."

"Looking Out the Back Door"—he wondered aloud what this band was thinking of when they wrote the song.

Mike yelled to Tommy, "Don't know, but it's a good tune."

Tommy whacked the ball against the ledge.

"Back, back, back, it's a home run," Mike shouted. "Nice hit."

That made three runs scored in the first inning for the Cubbies. That was the team's name Mike and Tommy had selected. Johnny and Danny had picked the Sox this time. Street ball was always the Cubs against the Sox, the North Side against the South Side. After the bottom of the first inning, Johnny and Danny were up to bat. They did not score any runs. Three straight outs.

"Bummer," said Mike. "Better luck next inning."

As the game progressed and the boys took a break in the seventh inning, Mike said, "What do you all think about these murders reported in the newspaper?"

All four of the boys had paper routes in the Bucktown neighborhood and delivered papers from the same newsstand. So all the boys had seen the front-page news in the *Chicago Today*.

Tommy said, "It does not matter to me. They are not happening in our neighborhood. Why should we care?"

Johnny and Danny just shrugged their shoulders, and both said in unison, "Can we get back to the game?"

"Sure," Mike replied. "Your team ready to lose again?"

"We'll see about that," Danny replied.

"Ok, top of the eighth inning. The score is the Cubs 10 and the Sox 9. Here we go," Mike said as he slammed the ball against the ledge.

Tommy yelled, "Home run again. Nice hit, Mike."

Mike tossed the ball to Tommy for the next at bat.

Tommy hit the ball against the ledge, which resulted in a fly ball to the outfield. Johnny caught it to rob Tommy of a triple. Mike took another at bat that turned into an out.

The bottom of the eighth produced no runs for the Sox. The top of the ninth inning produced no runs for the Cubs.

"Ok, last chance. The Cubs have eleven runs and Sox have nine runs," Mike shouted.

Johnny and Danny needed two runs to tie and three runs to win.

The three at bats ended in three straight outs.

"It's over. The Cubs win. The Cubs win. The Cubs win," Mike proclaimed.

"Just as Harry Caray would say it," Tommy proclaimed.

Mike and Tommy were razzing and barking at Johnny and Danny for losing the ballgame once again.

"We want a rematch," Johnny said.

"How about tomorrow?"

"Sure. The summer has just started. It will be a long season." Johnny shot a glance at his teammate, Danny.

Mike pulled Tommy aside, and they both sat on the stoop of the building they were playing street ball against.

"So, what do you really think of these two murders on the Northwest Side?"

Tommy said, "Somebody needs to figure this out, or there will be more murders in the city."

"You really think so?"

"Yes, I do."

"We need to solve these murders," Mike replied.

"No way. I am not getting involved in this."

"Come on, Tommy, I can't do this alone. I need help."

"Not interested, Mike. You're all alone on this one. This is your thing, not mine."

"You're a buzzkill, Tommy. I'll figure this out with or without you. I just thought it could be a fun game to figure out who did it before the police concluded something."

"Again, I'll pass on this, Mike."

Mike left Tommy on the stoop and said he was headed home. He had to get his bike and get ready to start the Tuesday afternoon paper route.

As Mike walked to his house, he pondered how he would start his investigation into the murders of Wally Bass and Kevin Burger.

Go to the library down the street and do some research by reading all the news articles?

Talk to the detectives, Cato, and Douglas, about the crime scene?

Talk with his big brother, Henry, about the bodies?

Talk with Ray Chambers, the reporter who was authoring the articles for the *Chicago Today*?

It made sense to use the library as the first source of information. This way no one would know what he was doing. This was the safe method for a twelve-year-old boy to use to play detective on a murder case. No one would suspect a paperboy of being a reporter or even give him the time of day.

Mike had a plan, and he was going to start with the library. But not today.

He had to get his paper route started.

Chapter 14

Mike was planning a visit to the Chicago public library Tuesday evening after dinner to start his research on the murders of Wally Bass and Kevin Burger. He needed to figure out a way not to tell his mom where he was going so as not to tip his hand on what he was up to.

"I'm going out to play, Mom, if that's ok."

"Sure, go ahead, son. Just be back by 8:00 p.m. and stay on the block so I can keep an eye on you."

"Will do, Mom," he said as he exited the front door and went down the stairs.

When he knew his mother was not looking, he would head to the library on the corner of Dickens and Armitage, just a short walk to the end of the block.

When Mike walked into the library, he noticed that there was no one in the building. Just one librarian at the main desk. He approached the frail old woman.

"Can I help you, sonny?"

Mike looked at her. "Where can I find the local newspapers?"

"That would be in the news area of the library in the back corner over there." The librarian pointed to the location.

"Thanks. I need to do some homework," Mike replied.

As Mike walked away, the librarian thought to herself, *That's funny. I thought school was out for the summer. Why would this little boy be doing homework for school late at night?* The thought crossed her mind and then was replaced with *Only one more hour to go.* The library closed at 8:00 p.m., and then she would be done for the evening.

Mike found the news area of the library and looked at the shelves where the newspapers were. The cubicle had only the previous seven days of all three major papers: the *Chicago Tribune*, the *Sun Times*, and the *Chicago Today*. Mike thought to himself, *How am I going to do research when there is only seven days' worth of newsprint to review?* Mike picked up the papers one at a time. First the *Chicago Tribune*. The seven days of news had the murders of Wally Bass and Kevin Burger on the front page. So, it was easy to read and do the research on the murders. Next was the *Chicago Sun Times*. Same thing: seven days of news on the front page. Then he went to the *Chicago Today*. Again, seven days of news on the front page. There did not seem to be any difference on the Wally Bass murder among the three papers. But there was one difference on the Kevin Burger murder. Both the *Chicago Tribune* and the *Chicago Sun Times* said this was suicide. But the *Chicago Today* speculated that this was not a suicide and that the police were holding back on releasing the real cause of death as a homicide. Mike thought this was an interesting difference and did not know what to think of it.

Did the *Chicago Today* know something about the deceased that the other two did not?

Was the reporter who had authored the article better at investigating what was going on?

Was there something nefarious going on?

Mike had lots of questions he was asking himself, and he had no answers for the little voice inside him. Mike went back to the librarian's desk to ask a question.

"The library will close at 8:00 p.m." the librarian mumbled in a deep voice to Mike before he could say a word.

"Thanks, I'll be out of here in few minutes," Mike replied. "Can I ask you a question?"

"Sure," the librarian replied. "You're my only customer tonight."

"Where can I find more information on these murders in the paper?"

"Why would you want to know about that stuff?" said the librarian.

"I am just doing some homework on the current events of the day." Mike returned her stare.

"The only other news would be from the detectives, or I believe the watch commander of the police department. But all the public information would be in the three newspapers," the librarian reiterated.

"Thanks," Mike said as he walked away from her desk.

He would have to go to the police to get more information on the deaths of Wally Bass and Kevin Burger.

How would he get up to the Northwest Side?

How would he mislead his mom on his whereabouts?

His little voice was talking back to him, and once again, he had no answers.

Mike thought Larry, the newsstand manager, might have an idea. He would be well versed in how the paper was put together and where he could find out more information about the events.

***

The next day, Mike asked Larry about the newspaper and how it was put together. Mike was told there were a bunch of reporters who reported on the stories and the editors refined the stories before they placed the printed versions in the paper.

"Why are you asking me these questions about murder victims?" Larry said to Mike.

"I am just trying to read a little bit about these events, even though they are gruesome," Mike replied.

"Death in this world is not an easy thing to deal with, but it sells papers. The *Chicago Today* needs to sell papers to increase its circulation. This paper is having a hell of a time competing with the *Tribune* and the *Sun Times*," Larry replied.

"Thanks. I want to be a detective when I grow up and solve murders like the ones in the paper."

"You will need to go to detective school for that," Larry replied.

"Detective school. There is a school for that?" Mike turned to Larry.

"Yep."

"Well, that's what I want to be when I grow up."

"I think you can make a great detective. But most detectives could use a little bit of luck as well," Larry replied.

"Thanks for the chat," Mike said as he left the office.

Mike was pumped up with the thought of becoming Mike the detective. *What a neat job. Solving murders. Putting criminals behind bars. Figuring things out.*

Chapter 15

Mike had decided he was going to go to the Jefferson Park police district to talk with the watch commander in charge of the Wally Bass and Kevin Burger cases. This district was over ten miles from his house, and he had no idea how to get there. There was always the issue of what to tell his mother as well. If he disappeared for a few hours, he would surely be missed. Mike was certain he would be punished by his parents if either one found out.

Mike figured out an idea of how to disappear for a few hours. He would tell his mom that the newsstand manager, Larry, wanted him to come in early one afternoon. This would be for extra work at the newsstand office before the paper route that day. His mom would never figure it out.

During his paper route delivery on Wednesday afternoon, Mike mulled over all the things he had to cover for this trip. He would tell his mom after his Wednesday deliveries that Larry wanted him in early on Thursday for some light office tasks, such as cleaning out the office and tidying up the boys' prep areas at the newsstand.

***

Mike finished his paper route on Wednesday afternoon as on a normal afternoon and then went home. His mom was getting dinner ready for the family.

"Mom, can I go to the newsstand early on Thursday?" Mike asked.

"What do you have to go to the newsstand early for, son?"

"Larry asked if I could help him with a little bit of cleaning up at the newsstand."

"Is Larry going to pay you for your effort or is he expecting you to work for free?" his mom said as she turned her head toward Mike.

"He is going to pay me extra for the cleanup at the newsstand. Larry said it was getting a little bit cluttered and some summer cleaning was necessary."

"Ok, Mike, you can help, but make sure he pays you for your extra effort. I don't want any son of mine being taken advantage of."

"Thanks, Mom, I will do that."

So, Mike's plan was put in motion. Now he had to figure out how to get to the Jefferson Park police district's office on the Northwest Side of the city.

***

Mike had looked up the address in the six-inch-thick phone directory at the newsstand earlier on Wednesday, just before he started his paper route. He would take the Damen Avenue bus to the CTA blue line at the Kennedy Expressway and then walk to the Jefferson Park police district office at the end of the line. The Jefferson Park police district office was just a block away from the end of the blue line.

Yep, that will work, Mike had thought as he hashed it out in his mind.

***

Thursday morning, Mike reminded his mom that he was going early to the newsstand.

"Mom, don't forget I need to go to the newsstand early today to help out."

"Ok, son. Just be careful and let me know if you're going to be late today."

"Will do," Mike replied.

Just after lunch, Mike left the house on Dickens and headed west toward Tommy's house on Hoyne Avenue. Mike was going to leave his Sting-Ray bike at Tommy's house as part of his plan. Tommy thought Mike was crazy but was in on the plan. Mike pedaled to Tommy's house, left his Sting-Ray bike, and walked east on West Charleston Street toward the Damen Avenue bus stop. Mike waited about ten minutes until the bus came to pick him up. Mike got on the bus and dropped his coins into the fare box before the driver could say anything.

"Aren't you a little bit young to ride the bus?" said the driver.

"No, my mom lets me ride the bus to go to my grandparents' house. That's where I'm going today," Mike replied.

"Oh, ok," said the driver. "You put your money in the box already?"

"Yes, I did," said Mike.

The trip to the Kennedy L train was quiet and uneventful. No one talked to Mike, but people gave him a couple of strange looks.

"Why is that kid riding the bus without his parents?" one rider said.

Mike just kept to himself and kept his head down so as not to make eye contact with any of the riders on the Damen Avenue bus.

Mike got off at the Kennedy L stop and proceeded through the turnstile. He dropped his coins into the slot and pushed the lever, and he was on the platform of the Kennedy L train. He looked around for the Jefferson Park stop on the overhead map above the sign to figure out which way he needed to go. He needed to be on the west side of the tracks, headed northwest toward the O'Hare Airport direction. Mike waited only a few minutes, and the train pulled into the platform. Once the train departed, the conductor announced the next two stops. Mike was sure he was on the right train because he could see the overhead sign with the stops in big white letters. It was seven stops until the Jefferson Park exit. Once the conductor mentioned Jefferson Park as the next stop, Mike got closer to the doorway.

"Jefferson Park this stop," said the conductor.

Mike got off the L train. Now he would need to walk one block to the Jefferson Park police district.

***

As Mike walked into the police building, he got a little bit nervous.

"I am here to see the watch commander," Mike said to the police officer at the front desk.

"Can I tell the watch commander what this pertains to?" said the big burly officer behind the desk.

"I need to talk to the watch commander about the Wally Bass and Kevin Burger cases. I am doing a homework assignment on how the police department process works for getting news to the public about deceased people."

"Little boy, do you have an appointment with the watch commander?" said the officer.

"Well, no, I do not. I thought he would talk to me for my school paper at St. Hedwig's Catholic School," Mike replied.

"Give me a minute and let me see if I can reach the watch commander, Dane Hoy," the officer said as he got on the phone.

"Officer Hoy, do you have a few minutes to talk with a little boy about the cases on Wally Bass and Kevin Burger? He is doing some homework assignment on how the process works as to how news gets to the public."

Mike heard the other end of the phone call. "Sure, I can talk with the little boy in a couple of minutes. Just tell him to have a seat and I'll be right out there. What's his name?"

"My name is Mike," said Mike to the desk sergeant.

"Officer Hoy will be out to see you in a couple of minutes. Just have a seat over there," the desk sergeant said.

Mike sat down to wait.

An officer came out of the back office and approached Mike.

"Are you Mike?" said the officer. "Hi, I'm officer Dane Hoy, the watch commander."

"Yes, I am Mike Peters. I am doing a story on how news gets into the newspaper from the police department for my grade school assignment."

"What grade school are you attending?"

"I am in the sixth grade at St. Hedwig's Catholic School on Webster Avenue," Mike replied.

"Aren't you a little bit far away from your parents? How did you get here?" said Officer Hoy.

"I took the bus to the L this time. My parents encourage me to do it."

"Are you sure?"

"Yes, I am," said Mike with a quiet voice.

"Well, what do you want to know?" Officer Hoy replied.

"I would like to know how the suicide cases of Wally Bass and Kevin Burger got into the newspapers from the police department. My summer project is to author a story on the process of how gruesome details get from the accident to the police to the paper."

"That's a tall order you're requesting."

"But Officer Hoy, I need this for my summer report. It's an extra-credit assignment," Mike said.

"Ok, I'll tell you how this works."

Officer Hoy described how the public contacted the police office or how an officer started the process. "If a crime is committed, then there are a crime scene, a report, and an ME report if there is a death on the scene. The watch commander then determines what is released to the public."

He said not all crime scene or ME information hit "the street." Certain information was sometimes left out just in case the detectives had to use it to figure out who did what.

"Sometimes the detective and sometimes the watch commander decides what gets released. Then there is a press conference for the reporters. This is where the information is released to the public. Detectives Abbey Cato and Rick Douglas have been assigned to the cases you're referring to."

"So, Officer Hoy, not all the information from the crime scene reports gets published to the papers?" Mike asked.

"Nope. This is on a case-by-case basis. Why are you persistent about asking this question, Mike?" said Officer Hoy.

"I read it in the papers early this week. The *Chicago Tribune* and *Sun Times* say that the Kevin Burger case is a suicide. The *Chicago Today* says it is a suicide/murder and the police are hiding something."

"Let me stop you there, Mike. The newspapers are free to publish whatever they think is newsworthy for their readers. But they need to report the truth, or they can be sued for false reporting and manipulating the news while standing behind the First Amendment, which gives everyone the right to free speech. Anyone can say anything they want within reason. But if a newspaper goes out on a limb, there can be financial consequences in the courtroom," Officer Hoy said.

"Thanks, Officer Hoy. I have enough for my story."

Mike had hit a nerve with Officer Hoy. Mike knew he'd hit a bull's-eye on the topic.

"Is that all you need for now? I need to get back to my cases," Officer Hoy said.

"You have been extremely helpful, Officer Hoy. Thanks again, and I'll get out of your hair," Mike replied.

"If you need anything else, here is my card. You can call me at any time," Officer Hoy said as he handed a business card to Mike.

"Thanks."

Mike walked out of the police station thinking he might have something on the investigation of the Kevin Burger suicide. But he was not sure.

***

Mike walked the one block to the Jefferson L and dropped his coins in the slot where the arms of the turnstile allowed him to get to the platform. He was headed toward the city of Chicago, toward the Damen Avenue stop of the blue line CTA train.

Mike would get on the Damen Avenue bus once he was off the L train and head to Tommy's house to retrieve his Sting-Ray bike. Then he would go to the paper route office, rubber band his papers, and deliver them to his customers in Bucktown for his Thursday paper route, just as though nothing were different that day.

Mike would not tell his mom or dad of what he'd done today. But Tommy, on the other hand, would want to hear all about it. So, Mike decided he would share what he'd learned today with Tommy and keep it between the two of them.

Chapter 16

He got in the blue '66 Chevrolet Chevelle SS and drove to the west side of the Chicago Loop. Heading toward the city's west side from the Bucktown neighborhood was again a short drive. Cruising down the Kennedy Expressway would take only twenty minutes. He would take the Kennedy Expressway and get off at the West Lake Street exit, then proceed to the parking lot on North Union Avenue. This was where the next one would happen.

He pulled into the parking lot of the five-story office building and parked the car. It was almost midnight on Thursday, and his car was the only one in the lot. Within ten minutes, a security guard came up to the car and instructed him to get off the lot.

"Hey, you can't park here," said the security guard. "It's after hours, and no one is to be loitering around the construction site while this building is being completed."

"Sorry, Officer. I drove here as a practice run to see how long it would take me to get here. I have a meeting in the morning with the superintendent of the building for a maintenance job. I just wanted to see this area ahead of time."

"Well, you can't park here," said the officer, Joe Dirt. "I patrol this construction site and parking lot for the Chicago Security Service after hours."

"Sorry. I'll get out of your hair. Do you want some coffee? I have a thermos full."

Joe got into his car and accepted a cup of coffee from the thermos that he'd carefully prepared. It contained enough knockout drops to stop an elephant.

"This is good coffee." Joe smiled.

"It is Colombian dark roast, my favorite."

It took only a few minutes, and Joe Dirt was completely knocked out. The coffee had done its job of immobilizing one security guard; now the hard part would take place. He pulled the car closer to the stairwell on the side of the building, where no one would see what was going on. He wrote a note and stuffed it into Joe's pocket: "Life is not worth living. I no longer want to live." It was signed "JD."

He carried Joe's body over his shoulder up the construction staircase. At each floor, he had to stop and catch his breath. By the time he got to the fifth floor, he stopped to place Joe's lifeless body at the top of the edge. He carefully stuffed the suicide note in the right pocket of the coat and zipped the zipper up. This way, the note would not fly out once the body descended to its hard landing. He shoved the body of Joe Dirt off the fifth floor, and it landed on the ground in only a few seconds. No one in this general area noticed the thud it made upon impact. Since this was a construction site, there was no one around, except for one deceased Joe Dirt on the ground and one killer on the fifth floor.

He descended the construction staircase slowly so as not to make any unnecessary sounds. He stopped at each floor to see if anyone was around and to listen and count *One one thousand, two one thousand.* After he heard no sounds, the hasty retreat to the car was easy and effortless. He fired up the '66 Chevy and rolled quietly out to an escape from the construction parking lot and what would be a crime scene on Friday morning.

An earlier visit to this construction site had revealed that no cameras were installed. The one security guard was the only eyes on the site. So, no video surveillance would help the police once the crime was reported. The news of the day would be another suicide in the city of Chicago, which had a population of about three million people.

***

In the morning, the construction crews arrived to see the lifeless body of Joe Dirt, the security guard, dead and lying crushed from his fall from the fifth floor. Several workers from the morning construction crew made the initial contact with the body of Joe Dirt, determined he was in fact dead, and backed away from the crime scene. They called the police, who responded within five minutes.

***

The arriving officer immediately put up the customary yellow tape that read, "Crime Scene Do Not Cross." The first officer on the scene called in to the police station that an ambulance was not required. The morgue was notified, and an ME would be needed on the scene before the body was moved. Detectives would also be needed before the body was released.

The detectives arrived shortly after the call from the reporting officer. They took pictures and measurements of the crime scene. There was nothing out of the ordinary for the detectives to put in their report. The ME on-site was Michelle Lynn.

"Hey, guys, was the body moved, or is this how you found him?"

The construction crew guys said, "No, we did not move him. We checked his pulse and saw that he was in a spread-eagle position and blood was everywhere. We called it in right away to the local police."

Michelle thought it was a little bit strange that the body was lying two feet away from the building edge. If a person wanted to commit suicide and he jumped off the building, the body would have to be at least eight feet from the building edge on the first floor. This was the usual distance that was covered when a person jumped off a building from fifty feet up. This calculation was based on her years of covering crime scenes and experience in the trade of death. A suicide note had been found in his right pocket. The ME crime report would be written up as a tentative suicide for now. But Michelle had her doubts. She would also share these doubts with the detectives assigned to this crime scene.

Chapter 17

Ray Chambers was listening to his Electra Bearcat scanner early Friday morning. He was listening to the local police station to pick up any news about which he could write. The current story he was assigned to was about Mike the bear at the Lincoln Park Zoo. Mike was old and had been ill, so the *Chicago Today* editor wanted to know what the medical team was doing about the famous bear. This was another fluff piece that Ray was not excited about. Then the scanner came to life. A construction crew at the corner of West Lake Street and North Union Avenue had reported a body at the base of the building. The police, the medical examiner, and the morgue had been called to the site of the suicide of one Joe Dirt, the only security guard on the construction site. Ray knew this was the report he could put an article together on this morning.

***

Ray raced over to the crime scene and was on the premises in twenty minutes. Upon his arrival, there was a crowd around the scene and a lot of police vehicles. He could not get close to where the body was found splat on the ground. The yellow tape was everywhere.

Ray started to ask questions of the crowd of people around the scene.

"Hi, I am Ray Chambers from the *Chicago Today*. Did anyone see what happened?"

One of the guys from the morning construction crew said, "I found him lying there this morning when I reported to work."

"So, what do you think happened?"

"Don't know. The security guard was the only one here patrolling last night."

"How do you know he was the only one here?" said Ray.

"The construction company is too cheap to hire two. There's only one."

"What do you think happened?"

"He jumped or was pushed. Take your pick of the former or the latter."

"So, suicide or murder?" Ray replied. "Can I quote you for my paper?"

"No, you cannot. I don't want to lose my job," said the man.

"Your hard hat says 'Theodore;' is that you?"

"Yes, that's me, but as I said, please don't quote me for your paper."

"May I quote you as my anonymous source?"

"That would be fine."

Ray tried to ask a few questions of the police standing near the yellow taped-off area but was unsuccessful. The policemen just told him to move along and let them do their work. Ray could see that they were not going to give up any information on the crime scenes, so he decided to go home and draft his story with what he had gathered so far.

***

Ray raced home to his house on Hoyne Avenue so he could pound out a story about Mike the ailing bear at the Lincoln Part Zoo. He would make it up as he went along and turn it in to Lew. It did not matter what he put on the paper, but it would be short and to the point. The second article would be beautifully written and turned in to Lew. This article would be about the security guard Joe Dirt, now deceased at the corner of West Lake Street and North Union Avenue—a security guard in the employment of Chicago Security Service. The body had been discovered by the construction crew when they reported for work Friday morning. Was this a suicide or another murder? The police were holding back information on the cause of the death, but the county morgue had been called to the scene to recover the deceased. The headline of the article would be "JOE DIRT: SUICIDE OR MURDER? IS THERE A MURDERER LOOSE IN CHICAGO?"

Ray knew this was a sensational title and Lew would yell at him for it. But after Lew calmed down, Ray knew that he would get more choice assignments because of this reporting. The second article to be turned in to the editor would show the kind of energy Ray the reporter would bring to the paper. Ray hurried up and finished the story. He raced downtown to get to the *Chicago Today* office building and turned the two articles in to Lew. There was a hard deadline of noon for the Friday afternoon edition for all articles submitted. Ray made sure these two were turned in with plenty of time for Lew to proof them.

"Here you go, Lew. The article on Mike the bear and one on Joe Dirt the suicide murder victim."

"Two reports from a reporter who had one assignment," Lew barked. "What's this Joe Dirt suicide article?"

"It's hot off the press—I just found it this morning."

"How did you find this one?"

"I have a police scanner. Then I ran to the site and interviewed a few witnesses on-site," Ray mumbled.

"You're chasing murders?" Lew shouted.

"Yes, there is more meat on the bones for these stories. I hate doing those fluff pieces."

"Those fluff pieces pay your salary. Well, you need to coordinate with me on these stories. I feel like you're blindsiding me."

"Ok, will do, Lew."

"From now on, you need to communicate with me and always let me know, or I'll bust your ass out of this newspaper business. Understand, Ray?"

"Of course, Lew," Ray sheepishly replied. "I'll get your approval on all the articles on future murders before I write them up."

"You do that, Ray. Are there any more you want to tell me about?"

"Not right now, Lew."

"Ok, get out of my office and get back to work."

"Thanks, Lew."

Ray left the office of the editor and headed toward his desk on the same floor. He knew he'd pulled one over on the editor, and now maybe the fluff pieces would stop. This was the third story he had reported to Lew. He was on a roll.

Chapter 18

It was Friday, collection day, once again. Mike fastened his GE radio to the handlebars of his Sting-Ray bike and rolled out the back door of his house. As he left the house on Dickens, he turned on WLS 890 AM radio. Larry Lujack was on the radio today spinning rock and roll music. Mike really enjoyed the tune that was playing; it was "Into the Mystic" by Van Morrison. It was early afternoon, and the ride to the newsstand would be down the middle of Hoyne Avenue if there were no cars on the street. Mike liked to own the road, and some neighbors took notice of this little boy's exploits.

***

Mike arrived at the newsstand and took his place on the bench where his stack of papers was placed. The front-page article staring him in the face was "JOE DIRT: SUICIDE OR MURDER?" As Mike started to read the story, he was shocked to read the details. The security guard had been found by the construction crew who came to work on the construction site Friday morning. The story went on to describe how the man had jumped off the fifth floor in the middle of the night. But the ME had not officially deemed this a suicide. The cause of death was yet to be determined. The reporter on the story was labeled as anonymous by the editor. Mike thought this was a strange development to the story. Why wouldn't the reporter want credit for the story? *Give credit where the credit is due*, he thought.

"Hey, Mike, get those papers rolled and get going," Larry the newsstand manager yelled.

"Ok, I'll get a move on."

"We are not paying for you paperboys to read the newspaper here in the office. Get going, deliver the papers, and collect from your customers."

"Sure. Will do, Larry."

Mike finished rolling the papers and headed out the door. This was going to be a long day because it was delivery day and collection day all rolled into one. The normal route was Webster, then Shakespeare, then Charleston, then Dickens, then McLean, and then finishing on Hoyne Avenue.

Mike was daydreaming about what he would buy with his tips. He really wanted to buy a new catcher's mitt since his current one had a hole in it. This way he could play street ball better with Tommy and the boys. He remembered that last week he'd dropped a few fly balls that he would have caught if his mitt did not have a hole in it. He also wanted to buy a hockey stick so he could play with the other boys in the street. The tips were not going to be good enough to allow two purchases. He would have to wait a few weeks for the hockey stick purchase.

At the end of the paper route, Mike rang the bell of Ray Chambers's house on Hoyne Avenue. There was no answer. So, he rang it once more and was just about to leave when the door opened.

"I'm here to collect for the paper this week," said Mike.

"Come in, and I'll get my wallet," Ray replied.

As Mike was standing in the foyer, his eyes wandered around the house. He could see the corkboard in the living room that displayed several news articles. The first one was on the Wally Bass suicide. The second one was on the Kevin Burger suicide. Mike was intrigued that his customer Ray was a news reporter with his work displayed on the corkboard. He stepped into the room to take a closer look while Ray was getting his wallet. The third section on the corkboard showed a piece on Joe Dirt and had a small sentence, listed below the caption, stating that this death was not a suicide, that Joe had been murdered by someone, and that the police were not releasing the information on this crime. The ME was withholding the conclusion on the death of Joe Dirt. Mike could hear Ray coming, so he stepped back into the foyer.

"How much do I owe you this week?"

"Your bill is $1.40 for the week," Mike replied.

"Here is two dollars. Keep the change."

"Thanks. I'll put this toward my catcher's mitt."

"How much do you need for a catcher's mitt?" Ray asked.

"I have a hole in my old mitt, and I want to buy a new one."

"How much is a new mitt?" Ray asked again.

"A new catcher's mitt is $3.50."

"Hang on a minute," Ray said as he opened his wallet. "Here is three dollars. Go buy a new catcher's mitt."

"Thanks for the tip. This is generous of you."

Mike knew he could now buy his new mitt compliments of Ray Chambers, the *Chicago Today* news reporter.

Mike left the house of Ray Chambers thinking that he could go to the sports store on Saturday and buy a new mitt and throw the old one away. *What a nice guy. I'm going to make sure his paper is delivered in the slot in his door every day.* It would force Mike to get off the bike and stuff the paper in the slot. *With a tip like this, I need to give this customer great service.*

Mike forgot about the corkboard and the information he'd seen on the Joe Dirt suicide story and the two other suicide articles in the living room of Ray Chambers. He was headed home after his paper route to get some dinner and then make round two of the collection process.

Chapter 19

Mike was the first to arrive at the shed behind the house on Dickens Avenue. The shed was known as "the Boys' Clubhouse" and was used as a place where clandestine meetings could happen. The shed was a room in the back of the property and had a door to the yard and a hatchway that measured two feet by two feet wide facing the alley. On Friday nights, Mike would enter through the doorway in the yard and then unlock the bolted hatchway that faced the alley. Mike and the boys would then enter the clubhouse through the alley, and the parents would never know the whereabouts of the four boys as long as they remained in the shed.

Friday night was a hangout night in the shed for the boys.

***

Tommy, Johnny, and Danny arrived shortly after Mike had opened the hatchway that faced the alley. A knock on the hatchway was the way into the club. One knock followed by two knocks followed by three knocks was the signal to open and let the boys in.

"Are we getting beer tonight?" Mike asked the group after all four boys were in the shed.

"Yes," the gang said unanimously.

"Ok, Tommy and I will go to the liquor store and get a twelve-pack of beer. Everyone pitches in two dollars." Mike announced to the group.

Mike collected two dollars from each boy and had a total of eight dollars. The cost of the beer would be four dollars, but the local buyer charged four dollars for the service of buying at the local liquor store.

***

Mike and Tommy went to the liquor store on Damen Avenue and waited around for a buyer.

"Hey, mister, can you buy us some beer?" said Mike to a guy walking into the liquor store.

"It will cost you," the guy who approached replied.

"How much will eight bucks buy us? Two six-packs?" Mike replied.

"Ok, wait in the alley, and I'll get you your beer."

"Thanks."

Mike handed this strange guy the eight dollars as he walked into the corner liquor store on Damen Avenue. A few minutes later, the guy walked out into the alley and handed Mike two cold six-packs of Schlitz beer.

"Thanks, mister. We appreciate it."

"No problem, boys. Just don't drink it all in one sitting."

The two six-packs were in a paper bag and were cold to the touch.

***

Mike and Tommy stayed in the alleyway of Damen Avenue to Dickens Avenue as they carried their prize to the shed. They performed the ceremonial knock on the hatchway. One knock, followed by two knocks, followed by three knocks. The hatchway opened, and the boys climbed in from the alley side with two cold six-packs of Schlitz beer.

"Any change, or did the guy take it all?" Danny asked.

"Nope, he took the whole eight bucks to buy us the beer."

"Ok, at least it's cold," Johnny replied.

"Yep, it's cold," Mike said as he started to hand out the beers to the boys.

"So, are you boys interested in the news reports of the suicide murders that have been reported in our newspapers this week?"

"No, they don't interest me, Mike," replied Danny.

"There have been three suicides or murders in our city: Wally Bass, Kevin Burger, and Joe Dirt. Wally Bass had his throat slit from ear to ear. Kevin Burger slit his wrists or had them slit and bled to death. Joe Dirt jumped or was pushed off a five-story construction building. Aren't you boys the least bit interested?"

Tommy, Danny, and Johnny just turned to Mike and gave him bewildered stares.

"Who cares, Mike? They were not done in our neighborhood," said Tommy.

"Well, I am going to figure this out. I was hoping to get some help from the three of you. But I can see that this is a tall order, and you boys are not in the mood to help on this quest."

"What can we do?" said Danny.

"All I ask is that you keep your eyes and ears open for any news events on these suicide or murder reports. Ok?"

"Ok, Mike, we can do that." The other boys agreed. "Now can we drink our beers?"

"One more thing on this," Mike said as he took a swig of beer. "Did you know that Ray Chambers who lives on Hoyne Avenue is a reporter with the *Chicago Today*?"

"No, I did not know that," Danny replied.

"Yep, he is a reporter, and when I was in his house earlier today collecting the weekly paper fee, I saw a corkboard on his reports. There were sections on his board that listed Wally Bass, Kevin Burger, and Joe Dirt."

"So, he is the anonymous reporter the newspaper is referring to?" Tommy butted in.

"What do you mean anonymous reporter?" Mike repeated. "The paper is just hiding the name of the reporter, is my feeling."

"No way," Mike replied to Tommy.

"Yep."

"I saw the reports and information on Ray Chambers's living room corkboard. I thought he had his name on the story bylines."

"You must be crazy, Mike," said Danny.

"The next time you collect the paper money from Ray Chambers, maybe you should ask him about the stories," Tommy said.

"I'll ask him next week if he is home. He gave me a three-dollar tip today and said to go buy a new catcher's mitt. He is a particularly good tipper."

"Three bucks. I wish I had him on my paper route," Tommy joked.

"Can we just drink our beer?" Johnny said.

"Sure, let's drink some beer," Mike agreed with Johnny.

"Are we still headed to Navy Pier on Saturday afternoon?" Tommy asked.

"I'm in." Mike nodded.

"I'm in." Danny nodded.

"I'm in." Johnny nodded.

"Ok, meet at the usual spot. Webster and Damen around 1:00 p.m. on Saturday. Bring your bike because we will be pedaling out to the pier," Mike said as he finished his first beer.

Chapter 20

The boys met at the designated location on Saturday afternoon at 1:00 p.m. Mike was the first to arrive at the corner of Webster and Damen. This was a ride day to Navy Pier, a favorite spot the boys enjoyed biking to during the summer months. Tommy was the second to arrive with his bike underfoot.

"Tommy, where are the rest of the boys?" Mike asked.

"Danny couldn't come because he was going shopping with his parents. Johnny was cutting the grass and said he would not be able to make it today."

"Oh well, we will have a good time without them."

"Agreed." Tommy nodded.

"Let's get going. It's a beautiful day. What station do you want to listen to, Tommy?"

"WLS 890 AM radio is fine. Rock and roll songs. Please."

"I agree," Mike said as he turned on the GE radio strapped to the handlebars.

As Mike turned on the radio, the song "Border Town" by Elton John was playing.

"A great song," Mike announced.

"Yes indeed. Can we take Webster Avenue all the way this time?" Tommy asked.

"I think the construction on Stockton Avenue is still going on. We may have to detour around the Lincoln Park South Pond this time. Let's see when we get there."

Tommy and Mike proceeded down Webster Avenue east to the lakefront. Their journey would take them over the dreaded metal grated bridge above the Chicago River. It was a scary bridge because of its construction and height above the river. Sometimes their bike tires would wobble, and they felt as if they would fall over, which would hurt because the metal grates were old and worn out. The city really needed to replace that bridge work, but because of the recent budget cuts, this bridge would be left alone until it crumbled.

"Hey, Tommy, did you hear any stuff on the murders when you delivered your papers on Friday? I mean from your customers?"

"No, I did not. Most of them I talked to while I collected the weekly paper fee said it was awful."

"I got the same kinds of comments from my customers as well."

"I did want to tell you something, Mike."

"What's that?"

"I snuck over to Ray Chambers's house this morning before our ride."

"You did what?"

"I snuck over to the house of one Ray Chambers. I climbed up the tree in his front yard and peeked into his front living room. I used my Boy Scout binoculars to look into his living room. The corkboard you told us about was there plain as day."

"Tell me you did not get caught, Tommy."

"No, I did not. I waited until Ray got in his car and drove out for the day."

"Tell me—what did you see?"

"The corkboard was full of stuff on the murders of Wally Bass, Kevin Burger, and Joe Dirt. Just like you told us before."

"So, I was not crazy about this stuff."

"No, you were not."

"The one thing I did notice was that at the bottom of each column was a single word for the cause of death: 'Murdered!'"

"I did not see that when I was in his house yesterday when I collected the paper bill," Mike said.

"Well, maybe you missed it?" Tommy asked.

"I don't think so," Mike replied.

"Ray must have updated the conclusion for his news report this morning."

"Watch out for that pothole ahead," Tommy yelled.

"He could have," Mike said.

"Oh boy, here we are the bridge of death," Mike said as he grabbed his handlebars tightly. "Hang on, Tommy. We got to get over the bridge."

"I hate this bridge," Tommy said.

"Me too!" Mike replied.

As the boys crossed over the bridge, they knew it would now be a smooth ride the rest of the way to Navy Pier. The distance from their house to the lakefront was just a little over five miles. The boys did not say another word until they got to the Lincoln Park Zoo.

"Hey, Mike, can we make a stop to see Mike the polar bear?"

"Sure. Are you making fun of my name again, Tommy? Calling me a giant polar bear?"

"No. I just like to see the people throwing marshmallows to Mike as he stands on his hind legs. When he does that, he looks like he is ten feet tall."

"That polar bear can sure entertain the crowd."

"As long as there are marshmallows around, Mike the polar bear will perform."

"Agreed."

"I kind of feel sorry for the bear. They say he is getting up there in age and is not in good health. But the people who visit him still throw him the marshmallows."

"The zoo does not sell the marshmallows. The patrons smuggle them in and feed him when the zookeepers are not around."

"Like now. Here he goes. Standing on his hind legs."

"He is one big polar bear."

"Yep. He must be about one thousand pounds."

"I suppose."

"Can we continue to the pier now, Mike?"

"Sure. Let's go."

As the boys made their way to Navy Pier, they could see a lot of fishermen off the side of the landing with rods and reels. They were fishing for shad, small silvery fish that fried up nicely and tasted great, according to the fishermen.

"There are a lot of fishermen here today, Tommy."

"Every spot is full."

"I wonder if they are catching anything."

"Yep, they are."

"Look at all those shad fish in those guys' cooler."

"He must have fifty fish in that one."

"That just looks like a lot of work for a three-ounce fish."

"Hey, how do you eat those small fish?" said Mike to the fisherman.

"I just fry them up in a little bit of butter and eat them whole."

"Bones and all?" said Tommy.

"Yep. That's the best part," said the fishermen.

"Thanks," Mike said as he and Tommy pedaled on.

"Do you want to stop for a Coke, Mike?" said Tommy.

"Sure. Let's get one back at the Lincoln Park Zoo concession area."

"Ok. Sounds good."

As the boys stopped for a Coke and started to walk their bikes through the zoo, Mike started to think about Ray Chambers.

"Hey, Tommy, how is it possible that Ray knows so much about these murders?"

"He is a reporter, Mike. That's his job."

"I guess. It just seems to me that he has way more information on this than most people."

"Mike, that's his job. He is an investigative reporter for the *Chicago Today*. Why don't you just ask him the next time you see him?"

"I may have to just do that next Friday when I collect from him."

"Now can we head home before anyone notices us gone from the neighborhood?" Tommy replied.

"Yep. Let's get going back to Webster Avenue and back to Bucktown."

The boys pedaled in silence the rest of the way home. Neither one mentioned the murders or this beautiful day. *One more trip over that dreaded bridge of death to get home*, Mike was thinking to himself. Then they would be back home in the neighborhood.

"Ok, Mike, see you later," Tommy said as he headed home.

"Sure thing, Tommy. Maybe play some street ball tonight?"

"Sounds good. After supper?"

"Sure thing."

Mike pedaled home and was thinking about the murders. *I am going to solve them.*

Chapter 21

Michelle Lynn had to finish her ME's report for the crime scene of one Joe Dirt by the end of the day Saturday. Her report on the crime scene was due to her boss, and he was a stickler for details. Before she finished the report, she would make an attempt to reach out to the detectives assigned to the case. Detectives Cato and Douglas had been assigned to the Joe Dirt crime investigation by the Westside watch commander even though this was not their side of town. This was a favor he had called in from the Jefferson Park precinct. So, Michelle Lynn called the detectives at their office. Luckily both detectives were in the precinct doing paperwork, which was unusual for a Saturday.

"Detective Cato, please," Michelle said on the phone.

"This is Detective Cato. Can I help you?"

"This is Michelle Lynn, the medical examiner on the case of Joe Dirt."

"What can I do for you, Dr. Lynn?"

"Call me Michelle."

"Ok, what can we do for you, Michelle?"

"About the case of Joe Dirt. Did you two uncover anything I can add to the report? I am trying to finish the preliminary report on this crime scene."

"No, we did not, Michelle. Detective Douglas and I have come up with nothing new to add to the suicide of Joe Dirt."

"I don't think it was a suicide, Detective Cato."

"What makes you think so?" Detective Cato replied.

"The body was found two feet from the base of the building being constructed. I would expect the body to be at least eight feet from the building if the victim jumped from a fifty-foot height if this was a suicide. It's kind of a hunch. The ME inside me says this was a homicide."

"That changes our focus on this crime scene if that is the case. Is that the official report of the ME's office, Michelle?"

"No. My boss wants me to close this one off and move on. But I have a nagging suspicion Joe Dirt was murdered. What did the suicide note say?"

"The suicide note read, 'Life is not worth living! I no longer want to live!' Signed with the initials JD," Detective Cato said to Michelle.

"The words in that note don't ring true, Detective Cato."

"I agree, Michelle. This sounds staged and a bit misleading."

"So, what are you detectives going to do about it?"

"We are going to follow up on all our leads. We will interview the site supervisor when he is back in town on Monday."

"So, what you're telling me is you both have bupkis?"

"That is pretty much it, Michelle."

"If anything changes on your investigation, let me know ASAP."

"Will do, ME Michelle Lynn."

"Don't be so formal."

"Ok. Michelle."

"That's better."

"Are you free for dinner tonight?"

"Detective Cato, are you asking me out?"

"No, I am asking you out for my partner, Rick."

"Tell Detective Rick Douglas it's a date."

THE GRUDGE LIST

"Hey, Rick, Michelle is interested in you. She wants to see you tonight," Detective Cato yelled to Rick in the precinct.

"Thanks for asking her for me, Cato."

There were voices in the background that Michelle could hear over the phone.

"Rick has a hot date tonight."

"Did you announce it to the whole precinct, Detective Cato?"

"Sorry. I did not realize that all these detectives had nothing to do."

"There is a reason they're detectives; their job is to detect and figure things out."

"Again, my apologies. Rick will see you at your place at 7:00 p.m."

"Thanks," said Michelle as she hung up the phone.

Then it dawned on Michelle that Rick did not have her address. *Oh well, he will figure it out. Or maybe he will call me if he can't find my address.*

Now back to the report. Michelle struggled with the conclusion. Suicide, homicide, or undetermined? The detectives had no further information to help her on this. So, Michelle decided to run one more test: she would do a toxicology report on a blood sample from Joe Dirt. The sample took only a couple of minutes. All the readings were normal except for one. There appeared to be extremely small traces of knockout drops in his blood work. They were very minute traces, and this was kind of inconsistent with the crime scene. There was a coffee cup found on the scene—coffee was a normal drink for anyone doing this job late at night, trying to stay awake. But a person does not drink coffee if the thought of suicide is on their mind.

Michelle decided to label this an undetermined case with a footnote: "Waiting on the detectives' findings." Her boss would not like this because it meant leaving the case file open for a while. The ME's office liked to close the cases as fast as possible so as to leave no doubt in the public's eye that it was doing its job effectively and efficiently for the state of Illinois and the city of Chicago.

Michelle would bounce some ideas off Detective Rick Douglas later that night. *If Rick can find my house*, she thought.

Chapter 22

It was Saturday night, and Michelle had not given Rick her address on the Northwest Side. *Will he show up on time, or will a phone call be forthcoming?* she wondered. It was a bit of a guessing game for Michelle. At 7:00 p.m., the doorbell rang, and lo and behold one Rick Douglas appeared on the other side of the peephole. Michelle unlocked the front door and let him into the house on the corner of Nagle and Foster Avenue.

"I see you had no problem finding my house." Michelle eyed Rick.

"It is not a problem finding out where someone lives when you're a detective."

"So, you used your detective skills to find my address?"

"It was easy. I had access to the personnel files of the Cook County administration building last week, and I came across your address then."

"So, you have been stalking me."

"Well, not necessarily. I have been trying to get a date with you for a while. But I have been a little shy to ask you out."

"Well, Rick, you sly dog."

"If this counts as being a sly dog, then guilty as charged. My partner said I should just go up and ask you."

"Oh, the direct approach."

"Every time I saw you, you were knee deep in crime scenes and blood and guts. It was hard to set the mood for a date."

"I guess you're right. Our professions aren't exactly meet-cute environments."

"Is Luigi's on Harlem Avenue ok for dinner tonight? I made a reservation for 7:30 p.m. It's Italian if that's ok."

"I love Italian food. Luigi's is my favorite place. It is probably the best restaurant here on the Northwest Side."

"It should only take us a few minutes to get there."

"Can I get you a drink? What do you like to drink, Rick?"

"How about a whiskey or a bourbon?"

"Sure. I have Maker's Mark or Gentleman Jack. Take your pick."

"I'll take a Maker's Mark over ice. If that's ok."

"Coming right up."

"What are you having?"

"I'm going to wait till we get to the restaurant to have some Chianti."

"You mean you're going to let me drink alone?"

"That's fine by me. I want to soften you up a little bit."

"What's that mean?"

"I wanted to discuss a case with you," Michelle said as she poured a glass of Maker's Mark over ice.

"Sure. What's on your mind?"

"The Dirt case. I have a funny feeling that this is a murder and not a suicide."

"What makes you think murder?" Rick twisted his head and rubbed his forehead.

"I performed a last-minute toxicology report on a blood sample and found trace amounts of knockout drops in Dirt's bloodstream. Very miniscule amounts but still noticeable in the blood."

"So maybe he was drugged? Now, you're playing detective. That's my job," Rick joked.

"The case doesn't add up. The traces of knockout drops in the blood. The body's location is two feet from the building. The suicide note with initials and no signature. The coffee cup was found at the scene. It just doesn't make sense. Why would a guy be drinking coffee if he was going to commit suicide? That one does not make sense whatsoever."

"I agree with you, Michelle. But why are you getting so involved with this one? It is my job to figure this out with Detective Cato."

"I know. It's just bugging me. My boss wants me to close the case file on Joe Dirt as a suicide and move on. But I can't. The little voice inside me is screaming not to close this one. To leave it open."

"I think you should follow what your little voice says. Mine is right ninety-nine percent of the time."

"When I called Detective Cato, I was hoping for you two to have some additional information on this case. This way I could justify keeping the file open."

"As we said earlier, we have no updated information on this case. Sorry about that."

"Ok. I've already put the conclusion of 'undetermined' as the status of the death, pending the detectives' report."

"Are you trying to put pressure on the two of us for the disposition of your case on the deceased Joe Dirt?"

"No. I'm hoping the two of you find something."

"Detective Cato and I have three open cases that are unsolved and that we are actively pursuing. Wally Bass, who had his throat slashed from ear to ear. Kevin Burger, who slit his wrists in his bedroom. Now we have Joe Dirt, who appears to have jumped off the fifth floor of a construction site."

"All suicides?" Michelle frowned.

"Appears so, but we will consider them murders/homicides for now. Maybe we have someone who is killing for a reason."

"Rick, let me look into the other two cases on Monday. Maybe we are overlooking some common thread among the three victims."

"Michelle, any help you can give us would be appreciated."

"I can try to help you out within reason. I can't let my boss know I am working the cases for you."

"I will not say a word to anyone."

"Ok, I'll try to dig something up when I am in the ME's office next week."

"That sounds like a plan."

"Now can we go to dinner? I'm hungry, and I would like to have that glass of Chianti. You're one bourbon ahead of me," Michelle said.

"Funny girl. Let's go," replied Rick.

"Luigi's, here we come," Michelle said. "And we'd better get moving because Luigi's has a reputation for giving your table away when you're late."

Chapter 23

Mike arrived at the newsstand shortly after 6:30 a.m. with a Coke in his hand and walked through the doorway of the newsstand.

"Is that your breakfast, Mike?" Larry asked.

"Yep. I always have a Coke on Sunday. It's the breakfast of champions."

"Don't you eat breakfast, Mike?"

"Nope, not on Sunday. Coke is my breakfast. Don't have enough time for my mom to cook me breakfast and get here by 6:30 a.m."

"That stuff is bad for you. It will rot your teeth."

"That coffee you drink, Larry, is just as bad. You put milk and sugar in it."

"Drinking coffee in the morning wakes me up."

"Drinking Coke in the morning does the same thing for me, Larry."

"You have a point. We agree to disagree here."

"I am going to get my papers delivered," Mike said as he exited through the door.

"Happy delivery. Watch out for traffic," Larry shouted as Mike drove out toward Webster Avenue.

***

Mike started his first run of delivering the monster *Chicago Today* Sunday edition. He had grabbed fifteen newspapers to start and would come back at least three times to refill his bag. He would have to get off his bike and hand deliver every newspaper to each of his customers' doorsteps. A normal forty-five-minute route during the week would take him at least one and a half hours to complete. He started to daydream about the event that the boys were going to in the afternoon. Mike, Tommy, Johnny, and Danny were planning to go to the Cubs game later that afternoon. This would be after the boys had delivered their papers during the morning. There was a 1:15 p.m. game between the Cubs and the San Diego Padres, and Mike was looking forward to a visit to the ballpark. Mike was also wondering whether the boys had produced any added information on the murders. He had been unsuccessful in uncovering anything. Mike continued to ponder this and what Tommy had done with the binoculars in the tree as he spied on Ray Chambers's house this past week. That was a really good bit of detective work. He wondered why he had not thought of doing it. Tommy had gained an advantage over him. *Oh well, just finish the delivery of the papers this morning and go enjoy the afternoon at the ballpark.*

***

The boys met at the corner of Dickens Avenue and Damen Avenue at the prearranged time of noon on Sunday. They would take the CTA bus north on Damen Avenue and then transfer to the Addison Street bus going east to Wrigley Field. The whole distance was a little over three miles and would be a short bus ride of thirty minutes door to door. They'd picked noon because the reliability of the CTA buses was not really good. The fallback plan was to just walk to the ballpark, but then the boys would be tired and could not enjoy the game.

"Hey, Tommy, looks like we are the first to arrive today ready to go to the ballpark," Mike said as he looked around on the corner for Johnny and Danny.

"Yep. You and I are always the first to show up, Mike."

"Hey, Danny. Hey, Johnny. It's about time you two showed up," Mike shouted as they arrived.

"I know we're late," said Johnny.

"Let's just get on the bus," Danny replied.

"As soon as it gets here, knucklehead," Mike shouted back.

The bus finally arrived after all four boys had been hanging out on the corner for a few minutes.

"Here we go, off to the Cubs game," Mike announced to the boys.

The four of them got on the Damen Avenue bus headed north. The boys did not talk much until they got off the Damen Avenue bus at the Addison Street corner.

"Did any of you boys hear anything on the murders from your customers as you delivered papers this week?" Mike asked.

"Nope," Tommy said.

"Nope," Danny said.

"Nope," Johnny said.

"You boys are worthless," Mike replied in disgust.

"I really think you just need to ask Ray Chambers about this murder stuff," Tommy said as he turned to Mike.

"I will at the end of the week."

The Addison Street bus arrived just two minutes after they got off the Damen Avenue bus.

"Oh crap, the bus is full of people," Tommy said.

"You boys want to walk?" Mike asked.

"It's less than a mile to the ballpark," Danny replied.

"Yep. Let's walk. We don't want to be late. We have plenty of time," Tommy announced.

So, the four boys decided to walk the remaining mile of the journey east on Addison Street to Wrigley Field.

***

When the boys finally arrived at 1060 West Addison Street, home of the Chicago Cubs, the place was mobbed with Cubs fans everywhere. The boys walked around to the bleachers section of the ballpark. They bought general admission bleacher seats and hung out in the sunshine of the outfield. The Bleacher Bums, as they were called, consisted of a rowdy bunch of fans who always gave the opposing team a rough time. The San Diego Padres were the visiting team, and they would be the victims of all the insults today. The boys did not talk anymore to Mike about the murders but just enjoyed the day out at the ballpark. Cubs game, sunshine, summertime, Sunday, no school—the good things the boys liked to enjoy during a lazy summer.

Mike continued to daydream about solving the murders of the three victims who had been in the newspaper this past week. He knew the boys were not going to add anything to solving the crimes. Mike would have to physically ask Ray Chambers about these murders next week when he knocked on his door to collect for the weekly paper on Friday, or if he saw him during the week.

The Cubs game went four hours and one minute. The Cubs won 5 to 4 over the San Diego Padres. After the game, the boys walked home because the buses were full of fans, and they did not want to wait for an empty bus. Mike attempted no additional conversation about the Wally Bass, Kevin Burger, and Joe Dirt murders with the boys.

"I am going to have to ask Ray Chambers on Friday about the murders," Mike mumbled to himself as the boys arrived back home in the Bucktown neighborhood.

Chapter 24

He got in the blue '66 Chevrolet Chevelle SS and drove to the west side of the Chicago Loop. Heading toward the city's west side of the city from the Bucktown neighborhood was again a short drive. Cruising down the Kennedy Expressway would take only twenty minutes. Then he'd take the Kennedy Expressway and get off at West Randolph Street, then proceed to North Lower Wacker Drive. This was where the next one would happen.

This was a Monday night, late at night, and there was not much traffic on the surface streets. Cruising down Lower Wacker Drive through the bowels of the city was not what most people would do for kicks even during the day. Lower Wacker Drive was where all the homeless bums and degenerates hung out. This was a city unto a city, and the homeless were here for the world to see. But no one ever came down here. The city of Chicago ignored this stretch of wasteland. It was ignored and for good reason. None of the policemen came near the place. The homeless would not call in a crime because none of them had a phone. The nearest phone would be a pay phone on the upper streets, and most of them were out of service. So, most of the time, the residents of skid row on Lower Wacker Drive were on their own.

***

He started to drive around the streets looking for Paul Cagney, who was his next victim. With every twist and turn, he could see lots of homeless individuals who did not resemble Paul. Up and down the streets slowly he cruised, but he did not spot the victim on the street.

"Hey, you over there. Do you know where Paul is? I am looking for Paul Cagney, my brother," the killer said to the bum on the street.

"No, I don't know anybody by the name of Paul Cagney. Get away from my corner," the bum said.

The killer tried another homeless person down the street.

"Hey, you over there. Do you know a guy by the name of Paul Cagney?"

"What's it to you, mister? What's it worth?"

"I'll give you five bucks if you tell me where he is. I am trying to find my kid brother Paul. I have some hot food for him."

"I could use the money and the hot food," said the bum.

"How about ten bucks and you tell me where he's at?"

"Ok. Give me the ten bucks."

"Tell me where Paul Cagney is first," the killer replied.

"Paul is on the corner, next to the cardboard box over there."

"Ok, here is your ten bucks. Thanks," the killer said as the '66 Chevy rolled down the street.

"Are you Paul? Paul Cagney?" As the killer pulled his car right next to him.

"Who wants to know?" said Paul.

"I have been looking for you, Paul," said the killer.

"What do you want?"

"I wanted to talk to you about high school."

"What about high school? That was a long time ago," said Paul.

"Did you attend Hamilton Tech High School and graduate in June 1966?"

"Yes. I did. That was such a long time ago."

"I have been meaning to catch up with you and give you something," said the killer. "My sister had your class ring, and she asked me to return it to you. She heard you had fallen on tough times and wanted me to physically hand it to you. She also wanted me to give you one hundred dollars to help you out."

"I don't remember your sister and a class ring," Paul replied.

"Well, maybe I have the wrong Paul Cagney."

"No, I am the only Paul Cagney that went to Hamilton Tech and graduated in 1966. I sure could use the one hundred dollars."

"Well, hop in the front seat, and I'll give it to you."

As Paul opened the passenger seat to get into the car, he was reaching for the bottle of chloroform and a rag. He doused the rag with the liquid, and just as the door closed with Paul in the passenger seat, he covered Paul's mouth. Paul struggled for a few seconds but was immobilized quickly. The killer applied a second dose of chloroform to Paul's nose to make sure his intended victim was knocked out for a long time. He affixed the car seat belt to Paul's waist so he would stay secure. He handcuffed Paul's hands behind the seat to keep him immobile. No one was on the corner to see Paul abducted, chloroformed, and driven away from the skid row of North Lower Wacker Drive.

He drove away with Paul knocked out in the passenger seat. Where to dispose of the body and how to finish him off were the two immediate questions he had to answer. It did not take long to figure out how and where to finish the job. It was a short ride to Navy Pier, where the parking lot was empty and not a soul was around. He pulled into a dark section of the parking lot and placed a pillow on Paul's face. He suffocated him until all the air in Paul's lungs was gone. It took but a few seconds, and when Paul stopped breathing, the job was done. He removed the handcuffs now that Paul was not breathing.

***

He made a short drive back to North Lower Wacker Drive, where he had picked up Paul originally. A check to see if anyone was around the cardboard box that Paul had been using as a home revealed that no one was around. He got out of the car, opened the passenger door, and laid Paul's body next to the cardboard box. So far so good. No one had witnessed him depositing the deceased Paul Cagney back in the skid row of the city of Chicago. Now it was time to get out of there.

***

The drive back to the Bucktown neighborhood would not take long—just a few minutes and he would be sleeping comfortably in his own bed. *Another one dies*, he thought as the events of the evening replayed in his head.

Chapter 25

Ray was listening to his police scanner late Monday night. He was having a little bit of trouble trying to go to bed. He needed another article for Lew so as to stay away from the fluff pieces that were thrown his way.

The police scanner came to life. The *Chicago Tribune* delivery driver had called in a 911 call about a brawl on North Lower Wacker Drive with five homeless individuals. They appeared to be fighting and yelling at each other. The confrontation was violent, and the caller requested that the police investigate ASAP. The dispatcher acknowledged the caller and said they would send an officer immediately.

Ray got dressed in a hurry and bolted from the house for his car. He was thinking that he had to get there before the police broke it up. Ray raced down the Kennedy Expressway and arrived in fifteen minutes. The police had not even shown up. He had beaten them at their own game. The police did not want to deal with the skid row bums of Chicago.

Ray parked on the opposite side of the street about a half a block away from where the brawl was still going on. The fight was as plain as day. There were four homeless guys arguing and yelling at each other, and one guy was sitting there just motionless. Some articles of clothing were being pulled among the four men. The winner of the pull fell back against the curb. A few minutes had passed, and the sirens of the police car could be heard over the scuffle. The four homeless guys scattered as the police cruiser arrived. The one guy who was motionless remained on the corner of the street next to the makeshift box house. Ray stayed in his car and observed that one of the policemen put on protective latex gloves before he attempted to feel the pulse of the motionless man. He felt his right wrist, and Ray could see that there was no movement of any kind. The policeman gestured to his partner still in the car, making a horizontal motion with his hand. Ray surmised that this was the signal that the man was dead. The policeman then got in his patrol car and joined his partner. He then got on the radio, but Ray could not make out what he was saying, even though the cruiser's windows were rolled down. Ray decided to wait awhile until something more happened on the corner. He was careful to duck down in his car so as not to attract any attention from the two policemen sitting in their cruiser, which was just in front of the motionless body. About ten minutes went by, and the county morgue vehicle arrived. The two police officers were pointing at the motionless body on the corner. The morgue attendant looked at the policemen and did not say a word. He just collected the body and placed it on the gurney. The county morgue van just sped away. It was followed by the police car shortly thereafter. No one had noticed Ray still sitting there in his car. No one had taken pictures of the crime scene. There were no detectives on-site to interview anyone. *That seems odd*, Ray pondered, and then he came up with an answer himself. *Could be just a run-of-the-mill homeless death in the city that no one cares about.*

Ray would have to call his inside guy at the county morgue to see if any information was available on the death of the homeless man. This would be a Tuesday item. Now it was time to get out of this area and head back home for some sleep.

Chapter 26

Tuesday morning, Ray called his inside guy at the county morgue. The number he had for Patrick Duffy was a general number for the administrative building where he worked.

The receptionist answered the phone: "Cook County morgue; this is Angela. How may I help you?"

"I am trying to get ahold of Patrick Duffy," Ray replied.

"Who should I say is calling?"

"This is Ray Chambers returning his message from yesterday. He left me a message on my home phone, and he requested I call him specifically. I don't know what it was about."

"Patrick is on break right now. I'll give him the message as soon as he comes back."

"Thanks," Ray said as he hung up the phone.

Ray figured he would wait a few minutes, hopeful that Patrick would return from his break shortly. He was right. Patrick called Ray fifteen minutes later.

Ray answered it on the second ring.

"Hello, this is Patrick. I am calling for Ray Chambers. Is he around?" Patrick asked.

"This is Ray Chambers. How are you, Patrick? Long time since I spoke with you last."

"What can I do for you, Ray?"

"I need some information on a homeless man who was picked up on North Lower Wacker Drive last night."

"It will cost you fifty bucks. Same price as last time."

"Sure thing."

"What was his name?" said Patrick.

"I don't know his name. He was picked up by the morgue van late Monday night."

"Ok, give me an hour to locate the report. Meet me in the cafeteria on the main floor of the Cook County building at Twenty-Sixth and California in an hour," Patrick replied.

"See you then. Thanks, Patrick," Ray said as he hung up the phone.

***

Ray arrived in less than an hour at the cafeteria on the main floor of the Cook County building. He grabbed a cup of coffee and waited for Patrick to join him. A few minutes later, Patrick arrived and sat down across from Ray.

"So, what do you have on the homeless guy they brought in last night?" Ray asked.

"I got a copy of the report right here in my pocket," Patrick replied.

"Let me see it."

"First things first. My fifty dollars, please." Patrick extended his hand in front of Ray.

"Oh, that's right. Here you go." Ray placed the rolled-up fifty dollars on the palm of Patrick's hand.

"Thanks," Patrick said as he curled the bills up into his hand. He quickly stuffed the money into his pants pocket.

"The report, please?" Ray said.

"Here you go."

Ray unfolded the report and started to read it.

"Put it in your pocket. Don't let anyone see I gave you this copy," Patrick murmured.

"Tell me what I just bought for fifty bucks, Patrick."

"In a nutshell, the guy's name was Paul Cagney. He was a homeless individual living on North Lower Wacker Drive. He was found dead of causes unknown late last night. There were four other homeless individuals around the crime scene, but they all vanished when the police arrived."

"So, what was the cause of death?" Ray asked.

"Natural causes. But the coroner's report listed minute traces of chloroform in the bloodstream. The eyes were bloodshot, the nose appeared pushed in, and the wrists were bruised as if he had been restrained."

"So, it should be classified as a homicide?" Ray replied.

"Not according to the ME's report. This was a death by natural causes. It seems that the ME has been labeling too many reports with the status of 'homicide' or as 'undetermined,' and this is driving the detectives nuts."

"So, are you saying that the detectives assigned aren't doing their jobs?" Ray asked.

"Don't know. There seems to be a lot of pressure on the ME to close cases, and she isn't doing it. Her boss is getting read the riot act by the mayor."

"Are you telling me that there is a problem in the city of Chicago with rampant homicides?" Ray asked.

"I don't know, and I don't care. I am just an attendant here at the morgue. I don't get paid to think about that."

"Ok, thanks for the report."

"Don't mention it. I do mean don't mention where you got it. I will deny it if anyone asks me about it."

"Your secret is safe with me."

"Let me leave first so it doesn't look so obvious," Patrick said.

"I'll leave a few minutes after you. No problem."

Ray waited about five minutes and then left the cafeteria. He could not wait to read the ME's report that was in his breast pocket. He felt like a kid in a candy store.

***

Ray sat in his car with a copy of the ME's report on Paul Cagney. He read and then reread the conclusion section of the report. The victim had died of natural causes. There were minute traces of chloroform in the bloodstream. The eyes were bloodshot. The nose appeared to be pushed in. The wrists were bruised as if the victim had been restrained. It was all consistent with living on the streets of Chicago as a homeless person. The ME concluded that this was an unfortunate death, and no further investigation was warranted. The detectives would not be forwarded this as an open homicide case.

Case closed.

***

Ray drove home and was so full of energy he stayed up to summarize what he had found out about the deceased Paul Cagney. He started to add a fourth column for the article on his corkboard for the latest death. The headline was written on a scrap of paper as "PAUL CAGNEY,

HOMELESS AND DEAD" and then pinned to the fourth column. Under the caption, a piece of paper was pinned in place with a thumbtack and bore the four things he'd found out. There were minute traces of chloroform in the bloodstream. The eyes were bloodshot. The nose appeared pushed in. The wrists were bruised as if the victim had been restrained. Ray thought that the findings could be explained away for a homeless person living on the street. The streets of downtown Chicago were no place to live, and he could picture how all these symptoms could easily have happened to Paul Cagney, who had lived and died on the street.

Chapter 27

Mike was determined to do some snooping on Ray Chambers today to see if he could find out anything on the murders. He'd have to visit Ray's house before the Tuesday afternoon delivery.

Mike ran out the door and yelled toward his mom, who was having lunch, "Mom, I am going to Tommy's house for a little while."

"Ok. Have fun," his mother replied.

"Thanks. I'll go to the newsstand to deliver papers later in the day. So, I'll be home after my paper route."

"I will be gone to work, so check in with your dad later today."

"Will do. Thanks, Mom."

***

Mike left his house and headed toward Tommy's. His plan was to borrow the binoculars from him and go spy on Ray Chambers. As Mike got close to Tommy's house, he saw that Tommy was already out in front of his house with his bike.

"Tommy, what's up today?"

"Not much, Mike. What kind of trouble can we get into today?"

"Can I borrow your binoculars?"

"Sure. Why do you need them?"

"I need to do a little bit of spying on a reporter."

"Are you planning on snooping on Ray Chambers the reporter?" Tommy said as he looked at Mike.

"I sure am. You did it the other day, and you didn't get caught. So, I thought I would try it today."

"Ok. Let me get the binoculars. Can I be your lookout guy?"

"Sure."

***

Mike and Tommy left the bikes at Tommy's house and walked over to Ray Chambers's house on Hoyne Avenue. The binoculars were wrapped around Tommy's neck. The boys walked past Ray's house at first to make sure he was not home.

"Looks like he is not home, Mike."

"Yep. I think you're correct," Mike answered in a nonchalant way.

"Looks like his car is gone from the driveway."

"How do you know that, Tommy?"

"Last time I walked down here, the car was parked on the driveway where there was an oil stain."

"Looks like the oil stain is there and the car is not," Mike agreed with him. "Give me the binoculars."

"Here, take them. Put them around your neck so you don't drop them. I'll get in big trouble if you or I drop them," said Tommy as he handed the binoculars to Mike.

They circled back to Ray's house to get a better look. Tommy stood two doors down as Mike eased onto the property. He wanted to be the lookout man, as Tommy had seen this once in a movie. Mike was happy that Tommy had his back. They'd worked out a loud whistle as the signal to run away if there was trouble. But today the signal was not going to be needed. Ray Chambers had left for work early this morning. Up the tree Mike went with binoculars around his neck. He braced himself against the branch, took off the covers, and stared through the binoculars into the living room. The curtain was open, and the corkboard was exposed to the front window. Mike could see there were now four columns of information, the first being Wally Bass, the second being Kevin Burger, and the third being Joe Dirt. The fourth column was new and was titled "Paul Cagney." There was a scrap of paper pinned just beneath the Paul Cagney title. On the paper were some bullet points pertaining to the deceased.

The victim was homeless.

There were minute traces of chloroform in the bloodstream.

The eyes were bloodshot.

The nose appeared pushed in.

The wrists were bruised as if the victim had been restrained.

Mike had seen all he needed to see. He scurred down the tree in a hurry so as not to get caught by any nosy neighbors. Once he was down the tree, he waved at Tommy to come over so they could leave.

"Tommy, let's go."

"Ok, Mike. What did you see?"

"There is a fourth column on the corkboard for a guy by the name of Paul Cagney."

"Who is that?"

"I don't know, Tommy. That victim's information is new, and I do not recall any information being in the paper."

"Maybe it will be in today's paper."

"Could be."

"We will need to scan the paper later in the afternoon, when we go to deliver the Tuesday afternoon edition."

"We can do that," Tommy agreed.

***

Later that day, Tommy and Mike arrived at the newsstand a few minutes early. Both of the boys rifled through the paper to see if there was any news on the deceased Paul Cagney.

"What are you boys doing here early?" Larry the manager asked.

"We are reading the paper before we deliver it today," Mike answered.

"Is there some news article you're looking for?"

"Yes. Is there any news on a homeless person who may have been found dead recently?"

"I thought there was a small article on a homeless man that was found on North Lower Wacker Drive late last night. It's around page 50-something, way in the back of the paper," Larry replied.

"Here it is. Thanks, Larry. It is on page 51," Mike announced to Tommy.

"Mike, it says that the homeless guy was Paul Cagney, and he was found dead on North Lower Wacker Drive late Tuesday night."

"Tommy, there are no details other than that he died of natural causes."

"What are you boys jabbering about?" Larry interjected.

"We thought there was news of a homeless man being killed. But we're mistaken," Mike answered Larry.

"You boys playing detective again?"

"No. We're just being curious," Mike said as he motioned to Tommy to be quiet.

"You know, you have papers to deliver today. Your customers are waiting for the local news of the day," Larry said as he gently reminded them of their jobs.

"Yes, Larry, we know," Mike answered as he started the rolling and rubber banding process.

Mike waited to say another word to Tommy until they got out of the newsstand office.

Mike and Tommy exited the newsstand with their papers in the bags. They both wrapped the bags around the handles of the bikes that were just outside the building.

"I think Ray hasn't had time to write the report and get it into the paper," Mike said to Tommy.

"I think you're right, Mike. It may not have made today's paper because the death just happened yesterday."

"Maybe he just missed the paper's deadline."

"Maybe," Tommy said in agreement.

Either way, Mike knew he was on to something, and the little detective voice inside him was asking a lot of questions to which he did not know the answers.

Chapter 28

It was late in the afternoon on Tuesday. Ray had already missed the noon deadline for this evening's paper. He was sitting at his desk in the *Chicago Today* office building with two stories to finish. The fluff piece that Lew had assigned to him last Friday was on the tourists who visited the city. The other article was on the murder of Paul Cagney. This was the unauthorized article that Ray was pursuing after his regular hours. Ray proceeded to type some worthless words on the fluff piece. The article headline was "WHO VISITS OUR FAIR CITY?" Ray would go on to write about the out-of-state visitors and some foreigners who were attracted to Chicago because of all the tall buildings. This was his opinion and was based on no facts whatsoever. He would ramble on and on about nothing to fill out at least five hundred words for the article. This way Lew would not yell at him. He could always say he'd made a valiant attempt at reporting this story.

The other article was the one Ray wanted to spend all afternoon typing away on and reporting on in as much detail as possible. This way Lew would be more interested in assigning him the meaty news articles. At least this was what Ray thought.

"Ray, you have that article on who is visiting our city?" Lew barked from his office.

Ray got up from his desk to go to the doorway where Lew was standing.

"I need a few more minutes, Lew."

"Ok, you missed today's deadline at noon."

"Yes, I know, Lew."

"Finish up what you got. I'll see you in thirty minutes in my office. Bring me what you have."

"I need a little more time than thirty minutes."

"Take sixty minutes, and it had better be good," Lew said as he closed the door almost on Ray's nose.

"That ungrateful shit," Ray murmured to himself.

"What did you say, Ray?"

"Nothing, boss."

Ray returned to his desk. He had bought himself another sixty minutes. This was enough time to finish the article on Paul Cagney. The headline of the article would be "PAUL CAGNEY: HOMELESS AND DEAD."

"What the Chicago police are not telling you," he wrote. Ray then listed the four reasons why the death of Paul Cagney was not by natural causes. There was chloroform in the bloodstream. The eyes were bloodshot. The nose was pushed in. The wrists were bruised. All these details were evidence that this person had not died of natural causes but had been killed by one or more individuals. He would add his conclusion that Paul Cagney had been murdered and that the police were misleading the public. Ray went on to say that maybe the police were lazy.

"Maybe the ME is lazy," he wrote. "Maybe there is a killer on the loose in the city of Chicago. You decide." Ray knew that his news article would get Lew's attention, and it could go either way. Good for him or bad for him. He would let it play out.

***

The hour came and went. It was now time for Ray to get up and walk over to Lew's office. He saw that there was someone else in Lew's office and the door was closed, so he stood next to the closed door. Lew signaled to Ray to give him five minutes with his right hand raised and five fingers in the air. Ray gave Lew a thumbs-up.

Ray came back to Lew's office in five minutes. The office was empty, and Ray sat down in one of the chairs. Lew returned in about a minute and proceeded to close the door.

"So, what do you have on the visitors-of-Chicago piece?" Lew asked.

Lew took the article from Ray and started to read it.

"This is crap! What happened to you finding out about who visits our city?" Lew yelled.

"I could not find out much about the visitors except that they are coming to see the tall buildings."

"That's it?"

"Yep. Sorry, Lew."

"This isn't good enough."

"I do have another article."

"What other article?" Lew asked.

"It's about the death of a homeless man who was murdered."

"Murdered?"

"Yes. He was murdered late last night."

"How did you find it?" Lew asked.

"I was listening to my police scanner last night, and I was fortunate to hear of this call that came in over the airwaves."

"Were you having trouble sleeping last night?"

"Yes, I was, Lew."

"How good is this article? Do any of the other newspapers have this story?"

"I don't believe the *Chicago Tribune,* or the *Sun Times* has the story."

"Give me the report. Let me read it."

"Here you are, Lew."

"How do you know he was murdered?" Lew read the article as Ray had written it.

"I had a source confirm it. I will be submitting an expense report for the fifty dollars I paid for the report, so could you approve it once I submit it to you?"

"Sure. I can approve the expense. But what are you implying, that the police department or someone else is covering up crime statistics?

"Yes. I know, Lew."

"Are you sure of this story?"

"Yes. I am, Lew."

"Ok. Let me run this story by our legal department first. If they are ok with it, we will run it in the Wednesday edition."

"Thanks, Lew," said Ray as he exited his office with a smile spread across his face.

Ray sat at his desk pondering what Lew was going to do. He knew that the legal department would be contacted before Lew published the story. That bit of action was up to the editor, and Ray had no control over what would happen. The rest of the afternoon came and went. Lew did not say a word to Ray for the rest of the day. Ray could see that several suits went in and out of Lew's office during the afternoon.

Ray knew he had hit a home run. Then he left for the day.

Chapter 29

Michelle Lynn was sitting in her office at Twenty-Sixth and California Avenue in the Cook County building Tuesday afternoon thinking to herself about the last report she'd finished that morning. *The deceased, Paul Cagney, had minute traces of chloroform in his bloodstream*, she told herself. *Where have I seen this before?* Then it dawned on her. Last week and the week before there had been three other cases with chloroform found in the deceased bodies. She went to the files room to look up all the cases she had rendered reports on. It did not take long to find what she was looking for. Wally Bass had had his throat slit and had minute traces of chloroform in his bloodstream. Kevin Burger had had his wrists slit and had minute traces of chloroform in his bloodstream. Joe Dirt had jumped off a fifth-story building and had minute traces of chloroform in his bloodstream. Michelle Lynn was starting to piece together the puzzle but was not sure of her findings. Since chloroform escaped the bloodstream rather rapidly, she could not be 100 percent certain this was the cause of death for these three victims. *It could be a coincidence, but…but…but why would all three victims have minute traces of the knockout drug in their bloodstreams?* As she pondered these thoughts, she picked up the phone to dial Detective Cato. She answered on the second ring.

"This is Detective Abbey Cato," the detective said as she picked up the receiver.

"Hi, this is Michelle Lynn. Do you and Detective Douglas have a few minutes today to have a conversation about some case files?'

"We could swing by the county building later today."

"What time should I expect you two?" Michelle asked.

"How about four today?"

"Sure. I'll try to make sure I am not cutting anybody up."

"Sounds like a plan. Detective Cato out," Detective Cato said as she hung up the phone with Michelle Lynn.

***

"Hey, lover boy. We have a meeting at 4:00 p.m. today with your girlfriend," Detective Cato said as she looked right into Detective Douglas's eyes and winked.

"What? What are you talking about?" Detective Douglas asked.

"Michelle Lynn wants to share some information on some crime scenes, and she requested we be present at her office later today."

"Ok. Sounds like we have a meeting later today."

"Yep. Let's get our outstanding paperwork done so the watch commander doesn't hunt us down."

"This is going to take the rest of the afternoon, and then we can go see what the ME wants to talk about," Rick replied.

***

Detectives Cato and Douglas drove down to the county building at Twenty-Sixth and California Avenue so as to get there promptly at 4:00

p.m. Michelle Lynn was waiting in her office with her standard-issue white lab coat.

"Hi, Detectives. Thanks for coming down here today. Take a seat. I need to share something with you both," Michelle said as she sat in her seat behind her desk.

"What's going on?" said Detective Cato.

"As you both know, we have four recent deaths that have been labeled as suicide, undetermined, or death by natural causes with a suspicion of homicide: Wally Bass, Kevin Burger, Joe Dirt, and now Paul Cagney."

"Yeah, we have three of these cases."

"The fourth one just happened last night. It was deemed a death by natural causes. But I may revise the conclusion," Michelle explained.

"There seems to be a common thread on all four of these deaths."

"Are you kidding me, Doc?" Detective Cato asked.

"I am going to go out on a limb here," Michelle said. "All four of the deceased had minute traces of chloroform in their bloodstream. They were exceedingly small traces, but all of them had the same knockout drug in their systems."

"Are you telling us that we have a serial murderer loose in the city?"

"I don't want to make that conclusion, Detective Cato."

"How can we prove this theory of yours?"

"We can't. The problem I have is that after one hour the deceased loses just about all traces from the bloodstream. Within twenty-four hours the chloroform is pretty much gone. It is extremely hard to substantiate after the first hour. We need to find a recent victim and perform a blood toxicology report almost immediately."

"Michelle, that's a tall order," Rick said.

"It's a big city, and we are just small potatoes here," Cato said, adding her two cents and pointing out the window.

"Well, we have to do something. If we have a serial killer out there and I don't help you detectives find them, then I am in trouble with my boss and the mayor. I won't have this job for long," Michelle said as she got up from her desk and walked around to the sitting detectives.

The detectives stood from their chairs and started to head out the door.

"We will figure something out and let you know what we come up with, Michelle," Detective Cato said. Cato turned to Rick and patted his shoulder. "Ok, lover boy."

"Stop saying that. Michelle and I are just friends."

Michelle was blushing crimson red as the detectives left her office.

"You know, Rick, if the watch commander finds out you're dating the ME, he may have an issue with the relationship."

"What I do with my love life has no bearing on any of these cases, Cato."

"I know, Rick, but the lieutenant may see it differently."

"I'll deal with that when it comes up."

"Ok, Rick, let's get to work and find out what's going on."

The detectives left the county building with a new sense of urgency. They needed to get some results and fast.

Chapter 30

Mike biked to the newsstand fifteen minutes early on Wednesday afternoon. He needed some time to get there and read the afternoon edition of the *Chicago Today*, maybe have a conversation with Larry the manager about all the news articles being published on the four victims. He needed to discuss this stuff with a grown-up who could help him figure out some of the pieces. Mike could not put it together by himself, but the little voice inside him was saying that something was not as it seemed. The randomness of the conclusion of suicide, murder, or natural causes as the cause of death for each of the four victims on its face was puzzling.

Mike went through the doorway of the newsstand and perched himself at one of the open high benches. This was where all the paperboys rolled and stuffed the papers. There were two benches along the windows that were each ten feet long. They could accommodate up to ten boys rubber banding the papers at the same time at each bench. Mike sat down on one of the stools, and he was the only boy there at this hour.

"You're early today, Mike," said Larry.

"I wanted to get here with enough time to read the paper before I deliver the afternoon edition."

"You're showing some initiative, Mike. I like that from a young boy."

"Maybe I'll take your job when I grow up," said Mike.

"No, you don't want this job, Mike. It doesn't pay enough."

"Then why are you doing it, Larry?"

"I am just doing this as a favor to the paper. I am trying to get a job with the downtown head office and was thinking this would be a doorway in."

"I hope you get what you want, Larry."

"I hope so too. So why are you here early today?" Larry repeated his question.

"I wanted to read the paper before I delivered the news to my customers."

"Well, check out the front-page article; it's about the homeless guy Paul Cagney. You asked me about this the other day."

"Wasn't there an article on this homeless guy on page 51 before?" Mike asked Larry.

"That wasn't front-page news early this week. As it changes and the newspaper reporters update the article, it goes from back page to front page. This sells papers and gets the reporters publicity."

As Mike read the article, he noticed that the reporter was anonymous.

"Larry, what does this mean?" Mike asked.

"This means that the newspaper is trying to keep the reporter out of the public's attention by not publishing the name with the story. There could be a sensitive issue pertaining to the reporter, or possibly it's a ghost reporter."

"What's a ghost reporter?"

"Generally, the paper or the editor does not want to release the reporter's name of record. They are holding it close to the vest so the reporter can continue to report on the story and not get bogged down by unwanted attention at the police department. Or the reporter might have a confidential source that they do not want to divulge. It could compromise the future reports on an article. Kind of like an informant but with immunity."

"What if someone knows of this ghost reporter?"

"What are you talking about, Mike?" Larry asked with a stern voice.

"I think I know who the reporter is," Mike replied.

"How did you figure that out?"

"I kind of stumbled into it."

"Please tell me how you did that," Larry said as he stared deep into Mike's eyes.

This stare made Mike feel really uncomfortable. Like he had done something wrong.

"Mike, I am sorry if I made you feel uncomfortable. I just want to look out for you and make sure you do not get into trouble."

"So, I am in trouble?" Mike replied.

"No, you're not in trouble. What do you know about this? Spill the beans."

"Only if you promise to keep this quiet and tell nobody." Mike waited until Larry promised.

"I promise not to tell anyone."

"I was collecting the paper money last Friday for one of my customers. I noticed a corkboard in the customer's living room had information related to the three victims whose names were printed in the newspaper."

"Go on, Mike."

"I spied on his house the day after another death had occurred. There it was, as plain as day: the information on the fourth victim in a fourth column on the corkboard."

"What was on the corkboard that made you sure it was him?"

"The corkboard in the customer's house had listed in the fourth column the deceased's name and that there was chloroform in the bloodstream, his eyes were bloodshot, his nose was pushed in, and his wrists were bruised. Then below was the conclusion 'murdered.' And none of that information was in the paper."

"Who is the customer, Mike?"

"The customer is Ray Chambers on Hoyne Avenue. He is one of the last customers on my paper route."

"Does he know that you know who he is?"

"I don't think so," Mike said as he turned his head from making eye contact with Larry. "Did I do something wrong, Larry?"

"No, you did not do anything wrong, Mike. You just stumbled into a situation that needs to be unwound somehow."

"Can you help me with this?"

"I can try. Let's not do anything for now about your customer Ray Chambers."

"Ok, I'll leave it alone for now."

"Oh, Mike, who was the fourth victim on the corkboard?"

"The person's name was Paul Cagney."

"The same person who is on page 1 of the *Chicago Today*?"

"I believe it is the same person, Larry." Mike pushed the paper with the story on the front page in front of Larry.

"I am reading between the lines here. I sense that the death of Paul Cagney appears to be a cover-up of crime statistics."

"What do you mean, Larry?"

"It seems that the ME or police appear to be misreporting the facts of the death of this victim."

"What does that mean for me?"

"You may have stumbled into a cover-up situation," Larry replied.

"Again, I'll ask: Am I in trouble?"

"No, Mike, you're not in trouble. You just may have stumbled into a bigger mess than I thought."

"Can you help me on this?"

"I'll try."

The other boys were starting to come into the newsstand to start their paper routes.

Larry turned to Mike. "Let's talk about this some more on Thursday. Can you come in a few minutes early again?"

"Yes, I can. Until then, I'll not say another word about this to anyone."

"That's a good plan," Larry said as he walked away.

Chapter 31

The watch commander of the Jefferson Park precinct did not want to do it. His team, consisting of Detective Abbey Cato and Detective Rick Douglas, now had one more case added to its pile of unsolved murders, the fourth being Paul Cagney, the homeless man who'd supposedly died of natural causes. The ME had added that victim to the list of cases, and Dane Hoy assigned this one to Cato and Douglas. After a full discussion between the ME and the watch commander, they both decided it was clear that the homeless man had been murdered and had not died of natural causes. It was agreed that the Jefferson Park precinct would pick up the case from the Westside precinct because the Westside precinct was shorthanded and could not cover the workload.

***

Mary Wright arrived at the Jefferson Park precinct from the Chicago office and was greeted by the desk sergeant.

"Hi, I am looking for the watch commander. Is he around?"

"Who are you?" the desk sergeant replied.

"I'm Mary Wright with the FBI, here to see Dane Hoy."

"Take a seat, and I'll give him a call."

"Thanks," Mary said as she sat down on the back bench.

The desk sergeant called Dane Hoy on the phone.

"Sir, you have a Mary Wright from the FBI to see you."

Mary could hear the call, and the watch commander said to send her back to his office. Mary Wright anticipated the response and made her way to the desk sergeant.

"You can go down the hall to the third office on the right. The watch commander is expecting you."

"Thanks, sergeant," Mary replied.

Mary walked down the crowded hallway until she saw the sign on the door. "Watch Commander Dane Hoy" was stenciled on the glass. She walked in and was greeted by the watch commander.

"Hi, I am Dane Hoy, the guy in charge of all the detectives here at the Jefferson Park precinct."

"Mary Wright from the FBI," she replied as she shook his hand.

"You are the FBI profiler we requested from the Chicago office?"

"Yes. That's me."

"Glad to have your assistance on these cases we are trying to solve, Agent Wright," replied the watch commander.

"Please call me Mary."

"You can call me Dane."

"I will."

"So how can I be of assistance to you?" Mary said.

"As you know, we now have four deceased individuals who died of mysterious causes, the last one being a homeless man found on North Lower Wacker Drive."

"I am aware of three from the case files you sent me earlier in the week."

"Here is a copy of the fourth one. A Paul Cagney, a homeless man, was found dead on Monday night. The ME originally put down the cause of death as natural causes. She has now changed the status to 'undetermined.'"

"That means the ME is throwing this one back to the detectives as a homicide."

"You are correct, Mary."

"What have your detectives turned up on these cases?" Mary started to scan the Paul Cagney file.

"Nothing concrete. No witnesses. No conclusions. Nothing." Dane threw up his hands in a gesture of frustration.

"Can you give me an hour to review the case file on Paul Cagney?"

"Sure."

"Can I speak with the detectives working the other three cases as well?"

"The detectives are due back in the office in thirty minutes. I'll send them to you as soon as they arrive."

"Thanks. Is there an office I can use for a little bit?"

"Sure, the one next to mine is empty right now. You're welcome to camp out there and get acclimated to the case files. I'll send the detectives to you just as soon as I see them."

"That would be fine," Mary said as she exited his office and walked toward the vacant office next door.

Agent Mary Wright pored over the case file on Paul Cagney. The ME's initial summary listing the cause of death as natural causes caught her eye just a little bit. *How could the ME have made the determination that the homeless man died of natural causes so quickly?* After reading the entire report, Mary got to the revisions and four things that made her uncomfortable. There were four sentences in the report that she read twice. The deceased had minute traces of chloroform in the bloodstream. The eyes were bloodshot. The nose appeared to be pushed in. The wrists were bruised as if the deceased had been restrained. Mary had read the other three case files on Wally Bass, Kevin Burger, and Joe Dirt before arriving at the precinct today. She had a suspicion, but after reading the fourth case file, she was sure of her hunch. The minute traces of chloroform in the bloodstreams of all four victims were leading her to the conclusion that a possible serial murderer was loose in Chicago. She would keep this conclusion to herself until she had a conversation with the detectives. This kind of assumption, which was her opinion, would not go over well with her boss. The detectives would need to add some color to the facts of all four cases.

About an hour had gone by when the detectives were shown into the office where Mary was reviewing the case file.

"Agent Mary Wright, this is Detective Abbey Cato, and this is her partner, Detective Rick Douglas."

"Detectives, nice to meet you," Mary said as she shook both of their hands.

"Likewise," Rick Douglas said as both detectives nodded.

"How can I assist you on these case files?" Mary asked.

"Can you help profile who we are looking for?" Detective Cato asked.

"I can try to point you in the general direction. This is my specialty."

"We were wondering if you could use your specialty and help jump-start our forward progress."

"I sure can give it a whirl. Can you fill me in on the earlier three cases with any details that are not in the reports?"

"There is not much that is new beyond the case files," Detective Cato replied.

"If you read the case files, you're as up to date as we are," replied Detective Douglas.

"Well, I am going to go out on a limb here," said Mary. "You have four cases with one common thread: chloroform in the bloodstreams of all four victims."

"Are you telling us we have a serial killer on the loose?" Detective Cato inferred.

"The case files and the evidence are pointing toward that general direction. I have seen enough of these cases to suspect foul play, and these four cases are screaming at me. But you know that chloroform dissipates in the bloodstream within twenty-four hours."

The detectives both nodded their heads. "The ME, Michelle Lynn, briefed us on this situation earlier this week," replied Cato.

"Then we just have a suspicion and no real conclusion. Only conjecture."

"We will need to brief the watch commander on our discussion and ask him what he would like us to do," Detective Cato said.

***

A brief time later, the watch commander was filled in on the discussion and general conversations between the detectives and the FBI profiler. It was decided that without more evidence linking these four cases together, the department would keep a lid on the possibility of a serial killer. The detectives would proceed under the premise that there was a murderer connected to these four cases but not necessarily a serial killer. There was no need to scare the daylights out of the general public by promoting panic. The watch commander would make a request to add Mary Wright to the detective team. Mary Wright would need to ask her boss if she could be spared to assist the Chicago detectives on these four cases.

Two detectives and one FBI profiler teamed up could make the difference in solving these cases.

Chapter 32

Mike was looking forward to speaking with Larry again. His insight into the news world would help Mike navigate these waters, which he had very little experience in. The plan was to get there about thirty minutes early so the other boys did not hear the conversation. He was conflicted about whom to turn to for help, and he felt good about getting this off his chest and talking with Larry. Mike said his farewell to his mom and got on his bike as on so many other days as he headed for the newsstand. The radio was tuned to WLS 890 AM with Bob Sirott as the afternoon disk jockey spinning records. Mike rode his bike down the center lane of Dickens Avenue as he had done so many times before. Since there were no cars in the street, he owned the road. The song blaring through the radio was "Run Through The Jungle" by Creedence Clearwater Revival. This was one of Mike's favorite bands, and they had just released the album *Cosmos Factory*. Mike thought he would buy the album if his tips were good this week.

***

As Mike traversed the streets of Bucktown on his way to the newsstand, he passed right by Ray Chambers's house on Hoyne Avenue. He wondered if he should peek in on Ray or just keep riding. He chose to keep riding to the newsstand so he could talk some more with Larry. He really wanted some good advice from a grown-up but was not sure Larry would be the right one.

***

Mike arrived at the newsstand about thirty minutes before the other boys would get there. Larry was already in the back office, taking care of some paperwork.

Mike walked back to where Larry was in the office. "Hi, Larry."

"Hi, Mike, how are things going today?"

"Not bad. Do you have a few more minutes today to talk about the Ray Chambers thing?" Mike asked.

"Sure, the rest of the boys aren't around."

"Should I confront Ray Chambers on collection day or just leave him alone?"

"I gave this some thought yesterday, Mike. We are just overreacting."

"Really?" Mike sighed.

"Yes. I have a few contacts down at the head office in Chicago, and I contacted them this morning. It is reasonable for reporters to know a lot more stuff about the articles they are writing than is published. The editor calls this a slow drip of information. They do this so the readers of the paper are hooked into a daily reading of the stories."

"So, this is a plan for the paper guys?" Mike shrugged.

"Yep. It's common for the editors to stretch a story out five to ten days over the weekend to grab readership. This is all very customary in the newspaper business."

"Ok, Larry. I am going to leave this alone for now."

"Sounds good, Mike. Do you remember anything common to any of these victims?"

"I don't believe so, Larry. They were all around twenty-two or twenty-three years old."

"Like four years out of high school," Larry replied.

"I guess so."

"I remember reading about one of them being a recent graduate from Hamilton Tech High School," Larry replied.

"I don't remember that in the story."

"I could have my facts wrong or have misread the story."

"I really don't know anything about that," Mike replied.

"Don't you have an older brother who graduated from Hamilton Tech High School about four years ago?" Larry asked Mike.

"Yes, my older brother, Henry. He was at that school four years ago."

"Maybe you should look in your brother's yearbook for the names of these guys. It could be a wild-ass guess."

"Why do you think the names could be in the yearbook, Larry?"

"Don't know. But all four victims seem really young. Why would four people die at around twenty-two or twenty-three years old within two weeks of each other and in the Chicagoland area?" Larry asked Mike.

"That does seem to be a lot of coincidences."

"Yes, it does."

"I'll try to get my brother's yearbook and take a look for those names."

"I think that would be a clever idea, Mike, but you need to borrow the book from your brother and not let him know what you are doing with it."

"Agreed. I will need to sneak it away from him," Mike replied.

"Do you think you could bring your brother's yearbook here on Friday and we could take a look together?" Larry asked.

"I'll try to borrow it on Friday and bring it down to the newsstand."

***

The boys started to arrive at the newsstand. Larry put his index finger to his lips. Mike understood this meant to be quiet and go wrap his papers. They both broke off the conversation. Larry went into the back office. Mike went to one of the high benches and started to roll his newspapers for the Thursday delivery. With the newspapers rolled, stuffed, and placed in the news pouch, Mike was ready to deliver the Thursday edition of the *Chicago Today*. Mike left the newsstand building with a full load of papers on the handlebars, headed for his route to deliver the fifty papers to his customers.

Mike daydreamed about the yearbook as he delivered the papers. Would he find the four victims in the book? How could he borrow Henry's yearbook? Would Henry miss it for a day? A lot of questions were buzzing in Mike's brain during the paper route delivery on Thursday afternoon.

Chapter 33

How to bring up to Henry, his big brother, that he wanted to borrow his yearbook from Hamilton Tech High School was on Mike's mind early on Friday. What could he say that would make Henry go get the book? He could not be honest and tell his brother that he was being a detective. That would seem silly for a twelve-year-old little brother. He would have to come up with an excuse that would not make Henry curious about what he really wanted the book for. Mike had an idea. He would ask about the high school experience at Hamilton Tech and say he was wondering whether he should go to Hamilton Tech High or Gordon Tech High. He'd compare the two schools and say that Mom wanted him to go to the Catholic high school instead of the public high school. He would pump his brother up and say he wanted to go to Henry's old high school because it was good enough for him. That seemed plausible and could work.

Henry just happened to be home on Friday morning. It was early, and he had not left for work at United Parcel Service. He worked in the downtown area as a driver, delivering packages. His shift started at 9:00 a.m., so he was just getting ready to leave for the day.

"Hey, Henry, I was thinking of going to Hamilton Tech High School instead of Gordon Tech High School in two years. You know Mom wants me to go to Gordon Tech instead of Hamilton Tech," Mike said.

"Yeah, she wants you to go to a Catholic school instead of a public one like I did," Henry replied.

"Why is Mom pushing me to go to Gordon Tech?"

"Mom may have thought the girls were a bad influence on me, and she doesn't want to repeat the same mistake with you."

"There are no girls at Gordon Tech?" Mike said, raising his voice.

"Yep, little brother. No girls at Gordon Tech. Only boys."

"Well, that's not right."

"I don't know what to tell you, Mikey."

"Mom wants me to miss the experience of girls?" Mike looked at Henry with a frown on his face.

"Yep. She thinks they definitely will be a bad influence on you."

"I need to convince Mom that will not be the case."

"I don't know how you're going to do that, Mike. She is convinced you're going to Gordon Tech and not Hamilton Tech. Sorry, little guy."

"Can you talk to Mom and tell her I want to go to Hamilton Tech instead of Gordon Tech?" Mike asked Henry.

"I can try, but if her mind is made up, you're doomed to go to Gordon Tech, Mikey."

"Don't call me Mikey. My name is Mike."

"Just having some fun with you, little brother."

"Can you help me convince her to let me go to Hamilton Tech?"

"How can I do that?"

"Can you show her or tell her all the fun stuff you did at Hamilton Tech and that I would miss if I didn't go there?"

"That's a tall order, Mike. Mom is dead set on having you go to Gordon Tech."

"I need to convince her otherwise."

"I've got nothing to show you other than my yearbook from Hamilton Tech," Henry replied.

"What's a yearbook?" Mike asked.

"It's kind of a summary of all the happenings during the year for the freshman, sophomore, junior, and senior students put into a book."

"Can I look at it, Henry?"

"Sure. It's in the attic in a box of old books. You're welcome to take a look at it."

"Up in the attic."

"Yep. I believe it's in a box under the Ping-Pong table."

"Can I borrow it for a little while?"

"Help yourself, Mike. I still don't think you're going to convince Mom that you're not going to go to Gordon Tech, but it's worth a try."

"Ok. I'll take a look at the book this morning."

"Help yourself. Now I've got to get out of here and get to work," Henry said as he left the house, headed to his day job at United Parcel Service.

Mike went into the attic to look for Henry's yearbook. He started to move some boxes around from under the Ping-Pong table. He moved several boxes, and he could not find any box that looked like it might contain Henry's yearbook. Then he found a box marked "Misc. Books." He opened the box, and there were all kinds of books inside. After emptying the contents of the box onto the floor, he found it. The book was on the bottom of the box. The book did not have much on the cover. It was labeled in big letters "Hamilton Tech," with a caption on the cover reading "Nineteen Hundred Sixty-Six." The book was an eight-by-eleven-inch book and an inch thick. Along the spine of the book was printed "Hamilton Technical High School Vol. XXV." Mike placed all the other books that were on the floor back in the box and pushed the box back under the Ping-Pong table. He grabbed the yearbook and placed it on the Ping-Pong table. Mike was not sure he wanted to open the book, so he left the attic with the yearbook and went downstairs. He decided he would look at it later with Larry at the newsstand.

The book was wrapped in Mike's news pouch where his bike was on the back porch. Henry would not miss his yearbook because he would be at work all day. Henry seldom went into the attic except to play Ping-Pong, and this was not usually until the weekend with his friends. Mike thought to himself that he had a few days until Henry would be missing his yearbook. Henry liked his stuff in neat boxes and did not appreciate anyone moving or borrowing anything. He was a bit of a neat freak. The new plan would be to take the yearbook to Larry at the newsstand, who could help him make sense of the book, and then return it to the box of books by that night. That way Henry would not miss it and no one except Larry and Mike would know the connection, if any, to the four victims.

***

Mike would need to go to the newsstand once again a little bit early on Friday. But Friday was collection day, so all the boys would be in early. He would have to go even earlier than all the other boys or they would know what was going on. Then he would talk with Larry about what he had found.

Chapter 34

Mike said his farewell to his mom once again and got on his bike as on so many other days, headed for the newsstand. The radio was tuned to WLS AM 890 with Bob Sirott as the Friday afternoon disk jockey spinning records. Just before he turned on the radio, Mike thought of what he had been listening to on Thursday. It was a song from the rock band Creedence Clearwater Revival, and he thought it was "Run Through The Jungle." He turned the on-off dial to the on position, and the song "Have You Seen the Rain" by Credence Clearwater Revival was playing over the airwaves. How appropriate for today and what a coincidence—two songs by the same group on two different days. There was a light rain falling on the city. It would be one of those days when the paperboys would have to wrap the papers in the plastic sleeves to keep them dry, a bit of extra work that the boys did not appreciate. But if the paper were not protected from the rain, the customers would complain about a soggy mess of a paper.

Mike rode his bike down the center lane of Dickens Avenue as he had done so many times before. As he passed the house of Mary Crystal on Hoyne Avenue, he could see her on the porch watching him ride his bike.

"Mike, you be careful," Mary yelled at him. "Make sure you get me a dry paper today."

"Will do, Mrs. Crystal," Mike yelled back to her.

"Watch out for those pesky cars."

"I'll do my best to avoid them," Mike said as he rode on past.

***

Mike was traveling to the newsstand with his precious cargo in the front news pouch on the bike. He had thoughts about whether any of the names of the victims, Wally Bass, Kevin Burger, Joe Dirt, and Paul Cagney, would be displayed in the book. He would wait to open up the book until he was with Larry in the newsstand. Since he had never seen a yearbook before, Larry's interpretation of the book would be needed.

Mike arrived at the newsstand early Friday afternoon. None of the regular paperboys were in at this time. So, it was safe to break the book out and show Larry. He had wrapped the yearbook in newspaper so as to disguise it from anyone looking at the contents. Mike brought the wrapped yearbook over to Larry in the back office.

"Hi, Larry, got a couple of minutes?" Mike asked.

"Sure," Larry responded.

"I got the yearbook from my brother, Henry." Mike unwrapped the book from the newspaper.

"Why did you wrap it in old newspapers?"

"I did not want anyone to see what I was carrying."

"Oh. That makes sense. Good move, Mike," Larry replied.

"Can you help me out with what I have here?"

"Sure. The typical yearbook is broken into several sections. One for each class of students: freshmen, sophomores, juniors, and seniors. As the students' progress in their education levels, they will appear in at least four years of the book. So, a student who goes to the same school for four years will appear as a freshman in the first year, a sophomore in the second year, a junior the third year, and a senior the fourth year."

"That kind of makes sense," replied Mike.

"So, let's look in the first section of the book. What were the names of the victims we were looking for?"

"Let me pull out the list I made," said Mike.

"You wrote them down?"

"I did not want to forget the names."

"You're a good boy, Mike. You're going to make a heck of a detective."

"Wally Bass, Kevin Burger, Joe Dirt, and Paul Cagney were the names of the victims from the paper."

"Let's go to the table of contents first." Larry opened the yearbook and said to Mike, "The freshmen start on page 38, the sophomores start on page 80, the juniors start on page 184, and the seniors start on page 226."

Larry thumbed through the pages in front of Mike. He found page 38, where the freshman section started, and all the students were in alphabetical order with their pictures displayed. There was no Wally Bass on page 40. There was no Kevin Burger on page 41. There was no Joe Dirt on page 43. There was no Paul Cagney on page 42.

"Mike, I think we struck out with this group of students," Larry said as he looked at Mike.

"So, these students are not involved with the crimes?"

"Let's move up to the sophomores on page 80," Larry replied.

Larry thumbed through the pages once again in front of Mike. He found the sophomore section of the book starting on page 80. There was no Wally Bass on page 82. There was no Kevin Burger on page 83. There was no Joe Dirt on page 85. There was no Paul Cagney on page 83.

"Mike, I think we struck out once again with the sophomore group of students."

"That's strike number two," Mike replied.

"Let's move up to the juniors, starting on page 184," Larry replied.

Larry thumbed through the pages once again in front of Mike. He found the junior section of the book starting on page 184. There was no Wally Bass on page 186. There was no Kevin Burger on page 187. There was no Joe Dirt on page 189. There was no Paul Cagney on page 187.

"Mike, I think we struck out for a third time with the juniors."

"That's strike number three," Mike replied. "Three strikes and you're out."

"Let's move up to the seniors, starting on page 226. That is the last group of students," Larry replied.

Larry once again thumbed through the pages in front of Mike. He found the senior section of the book starting on page 226. There were Wally Bass's name and picture on page 228. There were Kevin Burger's name and picture on page 230. There were Joe Dirt's name and picture on page 232. There were Paul Cagney's name and picture on page 230.

"Holy shit," Larry shouted. "This is a serious problem."

"I guess I was right," Mike replied to Larry.

"Mike, you're a good detective."

"What do we do about this?"

"Mike, I think you stumbled into a hornets' nest."

"Am I in trouble?"

"No, you're not. I think we need to share this information with the police and keep quiet for a little while."

"Larry, I have the number of the watch commander, Dane Hoy," Mike said as he returned a glance and lowered his head.

"How do you have the watch commander's number?"

"I went down there poking around last week. I was trying to get information on the process of how victims' news gets into the paper. The watch commander gave me his name and number and said if I had any more questions to just give him a call."

"Mike, I have to give you a lot of credit. A twelve-year-old boy with this amount of ambition and balls is impressive." Larry was impressed and proud of one of his paperboys.

"So, what do we do now?" Mike asked.

"We do nothing for now. We don't let anyone know. You don't talk with your friends. Don't talk with the other paperboys either. Don't even tell your parents. I will go down to the Jefferson Park precinct and talk with this Watch Commander Dane Hoy and just have a conversation about general stuff to see if I can figure out some direction forward."

"What do you think you will accomplish by doing that?"

"I may need to protect you, Mike."

"Protect me! What are you taking about?" Mike asked with a concerned look.

"You have stumbled onto something here, and you could be in danger."

"Me, a twelve-year-old boy, in danger from having a little bit of information?" Mike appeared nervous, and his body was shaking a little bit.

"Mike, you could have stumbled onto the killer's trail, and he doesn't know a twelve-year-old boy is on to him."

"You mean Ray Chambers is the killer?"

"No, I do not mean that. But he could be."

"I have to collect the money this week. I will need to knock on his door and get this week's from him."

"Mike, you need to be careful here. Just do the normal delivery and the normal collection routine. Don't ask any questions of Ray Chambers."

"I will not say a word other than 'Give me the money.' Then I'll get the hell out of there."

"Do you want me to go with you to collect from him later today?"

"Could you be down the street watching in case anything goes wrong?"

"I can do that, Mike. You will need to come back here and let me know when you're ready to go to his house. Then I can leave the newsstand for a few minutes."

"He is just down the street on Hoyne Avenue, and he is the second-to-last stop on my route."

"Ok, sounds like a plan, Mike," Larry said and gave Mike a thumbs-up.

Mike returned the gesture.

"Can you hang on to the yearbook until after I get my paper route done today?" Mike asked.

"Sure. I'll keep the book in the back room for now. So, no one finds it."

The boys started to come into the newsstand, and the noise of the boys' conversation abruptly shut down the conversation between Larry and Mike. Larry put a finger up to his lips. Mike left Larry and took one of the chairs next to the high table and started to roll, rubber band, and put the plastic sleeves around his papers.

Chapter 35

The paper route boys were out delivering papers to the customers late in the afternoon on Friday. Larry was thinking that he had an hour before any of the boys would be back with any of the collections from this week's paper deliveries. The office would be quiet, and he could easily slip in a call to Watch Commander Dane Hoy at the Jefferson Park precinct. He would have to be careful as to how he asked the questions so that he did not implicate Mike in the discovery. Larry made the call to the Jefferson Park precinct from the number that Mike had left with him earlier.

"Hello, is this the Jefferson Park precinct police department?" Larry asked.

"This is Art Reed, the desk sergeant. What can I do for you?"

"I am trying to get ahold of Watch Commander Dane Hoy. I have some information related to some crimes, and I would like to talk with him." Larry tried to be as vague as possible to minimize suspicion.

"Let me see if he is available. I'll put you on hold and let the watch commander know you're waiting for him. Can you hold for a few minutes?"

"Sure," Larry replied.

A few minutes later, Officer Dane Hoy answered the phone.

"This is Officer Dane Hoy. How can I help you?"

"My name is Larry West, and I have some information pertaining to Wally Bass, Kevin Burger, Joe Dirt, and Paul Cagney."

"Can you tell me what that information is?" said Officer Hoy.

"I would like to show you what it is," Larry replied.

"Can I send my detectives out to talk with you about these victims?"

"Sure. I run a newsstand for the *Chicago Today* here on Hamilton Avenue, and I can't get away for a couple of hours."

"I can send the detectives assigned to those cases."

"That would be fine. I'll be here a couple more hours until the paperboys return and turn in their collections from this week's paper routes. I run the newsstand at the corner of Webster and Hamilton in the Bucktown area."

"I'll send Detectives Cato and Douglas to talk with you in a little while. Would that be ok, Larry?"

"Sure. That would be fine."

"Thanks for helping on this. We need more citizens to get involved and help us out like you," Officer Hoy said as he hung up the phone.

***

The paperboys started to trickle into the newsstand throughout the afternoon. One by one, the boys would turn in their receipts from the Friday collections to Larry. He hoped that the detectives being sent over from the Jefferson Park precinct would arrive late, after all the boys had finished for the day. Mike would be calling to have Larry shadow him down the street from Ray Chambers's house. But his call to Larry never came. Ray was not home when Mike passed by his house. The car was not in the driveway, so Mike did not run back to the office to give Larry a heads-up. Mike finished his rounds and collections and then headed for the newsstand office.

As Mike walked through the doorway of the newsstand, he was met by Larry at the entrance.

"What happened, Mike? You did not come back to get me so I could keep an eye on you."

"Ray was not home. I delivered his paper and just kept on my route," Mike replied. "I will make the second attempt to collect the weekly bill from him on Saturday morning. Can you make yourself available then?"

"I'll make sure I am around for you."

"Thanks."

"I need to tell you something. I called Watch Commander Dane Hoy, and he is sending over the detectives who are working on the cases of those four individuals we looked at in the yearbook. They will be here a little later in the day. I need to make sure you're not here when they come over. Can you go home ASAP, so they don't see you?"

"Sure thing, Larry. I'll just drop off my collections from today," Mike said as he ran out the door.

"Thanks, Mike," Larry yelled toward Mike.

Larry knew that the detectives would be there soon. He really did not want them to know, but would tell them that a twelve-year-old boy was at the heart of the information he was going to share with them.

***

About fifteen minutes later, two detectives showed up at the newsstand. They announced themselves to Larry West, who was standing in the doorway.

"Hi, I am Detective Cato, and this is my partner, Detective Douglas. We are here to see Larry West."

"That would be me," Larry replied.

"We understand you have some information regarding the investigations of the deaths of Bass, Burger, Dirt, and Cagney."

"Well, kind of."

"What does 'kind of' mean, Larry?"

"One of my paperboys stumbled onto something. I was hoping to keep this away from you and not involve him. The boy is a little bit afraid of being in trouble with the police. He shared it with me, and now I am sharing it with you."

"Why did the boy not talk to us directly?" replied Detective Cato.

"He was afraid of what he uncovered."

"What did he find?" Detective Douglas asked.

"I'll show you both what it is, and then you can do what you want with the information."

"Yes, we'll be the judges of this," Detective Cato replied.

Larry pulled out the yearbook. He thumbed through the pages and then pointed to page 228, with Wally Bass's picture; then to page 230, with Kevin Burger's picture; then to page 232, with Joe Dirt's picture; then back to page 230, with Paul Cagney's picture.

"All four of the victims you're investigating are in the yearbook. This seems to be an unusual coincidence. Don't you think, Detectives?" Larry asked.

"You have a point, " Detective Cato replied as he stared at Detective Douglas. "How did you find this, Larry?"

"We kind of stumbled onto this."

"Can we keep this yearbook for a little while?" Detective Cato asked.

"It is not mine. It belongs to the brother of one of my paperboys."

"We can bring it back after we have made some copies at the precinct."

"I guess this would be fine," Larry replied.

"Thanks. We will bring it back on Monday if that's ok," Detective Cato said as she grabbed the book.

"Do bring it back so I can return it to the paperboy."

"We will need to talk with the paperboy on Monday when we bring the book back. Can you set that up for us?" Detective Cato asked Larry.

"Yes. I'll talk with him and ask him to be here after he delivers his papers on the Monday route."

"We will return on Monday around 5:00 p.m. Will that work?"

"Yes, that will work, Detective Cato. I'll make sure the paperboy is here."

"Thanks," Detective Cato said as she pointed to the door, book in hand.

Larry had not expected the detectives to physically take the book. What would he tell Mike if he asked for the book back? He would have to wait until Monday. Maybe Henry would not miss it until then.

Chapter 36

This was a Friday night like so many other summer nights at the shed. Mike was the first to arrive, as usual. He sneaked into the shed in the backyard of his house on Dickens Avenue through the doorway in the yard, unlocked the hatchway, then exited through the yard, locking the door behind him. He walked out of the yard to the front of the house, then turned right to walk down Dickens Avenue. He made a right turn down the alleyway and then took a short walk through the alley to the hatchway of the shed. Mike climbed through the hatchway and turned the light on in the shed. As he waited for the other boys to arrive, he thought about what he had found in Henry's yearbook. All the recent victims were displayed as seniors in the Hamilton Tech High School yearbook, and he was the one who had figured it out. Mike had not had a chance to catch up with Larry after the detectives talked with him late Friday afternoon.

***

Mike heard one knock followed by two knocks followed by three knocks on the hatchway door.

"Hi, Tommy, what's going on?" he said as he opened the hatchway.

"Not much, Mike, just another Friday night," Tommy replied.

"Who is running for the beer tonight? You and I went last week. So, it's Johnny and Danny's turn."

"Yep. That sounds fair," Tommy replied.

"We will spring it on them when they get here."

"Ok."

Danny and Johnny arrived at the Boys' Clubhouse a few minutes after Tommy.

"Danny and Johnny, it's your turn to get the beer," Mike muttered.

"Yeah, I know," Danny replied. "Johnny will come with me to help carry the beer."

"Sure," said Johnny.

"Everyone cough up two bucks," Mike said.

The four boys put two dollars each in the pot for the night's beer.

"Here you go, Danny, eight bucks for two six-packs of beer. Go get it," Mike said as he passed the money to Danny.

"Ok. Be back in a few minutes. Johnny, are you coming?"

"Sure," Johnny replied.

***

Danny and Johnny exited through the hatchway with the money in hand. They traveled out the alley toward Damen Avenue, where the local liquor store was, a destination that was so familiar to the boys. They hung out at the liquor store's side door next to the alley, staying in the shadows as best they could. They were waiting for a friendly patron to help them get the Friday beer. They asked a young man who looked to be twenty-five years old.

"Hey, mister, can you get us some beer?" Tommy asked the stranger.

"What are you boys doing here?" said the stranger.

"We want you to get us some beer."

"That's illegal. You're minors," said the stranger.

"We will pay eight bucks for two six-packs," Danny replied.

"Well, it's against my better judgment. If I buy you the beer, I get free beer with the extra money. Is that the way it works?" the stranger replied to Danny.

"Yep, you buy us beer and we buy you your beer."

"Ok. Wait in the alley, and I'll get your beer," said the stranger.

Five minutes later, the stranger came out toward the alley. He had two bags of beer. One for the boys and one for himself.

"Nice doing business with you, boys," said the stranger as he passed the bag to Danny.

"Thanks, mister," Danny replied.

"Don't mention it. You never saw me." The stranger walked into the shadows of the alley and disappeared.

Danny and Johnny had a bag containing two cold six-packs of Schlitz beer.

"We got the goods," Danny said to Johnny. "That was easy."

***

The boys walked back to the shed through the back alleys of Damen Avenue and then Dickens Avenue so as not to be seen by anyone. They were successful, and no one noticed two young boys with a bag of cold beer. As the boys arrived back at the shed, they performed the ceremonial knock on the hatchway. Mike unlatched the wooden portal, and the boys climbed through the opening.

"Piece of cake tonight," Danny announced to the boys.

The boys all grabbed beers from the plastic ring of one of the six-packs. No one was talking; they were all just drinking the cold beer. Mike put his beer down for a moment.

"I have to tell you boys what I found out today."

"What's that?" Tommy asked.

"I took my brother's yearbook to Larry, and we found out that the four victims in the paper were displayed in the Hamilton Technical High School yearbook from 1966."

"What are you talking about?" Tommy asked.

"All four victims, Wally Bass, Kevin Burger, Joe Dirt, and Paul Cagney, were in the senior section of the book. All four victims who are dead, as reported in our newspaper over the past two weeks."

"So, what, Mike?" Danny interrupted.

"No, you do not realize what I am saying. I believe that Ray Chambers could be the killer. He could be using the killings for his stories and then reporting on them."

"Mike, you're crazy," Johnny joked.

"No, I am not crazy, just a little bit concerned. Tommy spied on Ray early this week with his binoculars and saw the victims' names on his corkboard in the living room."

"That's right. I did see them. Four victims in four columns of information on the corkboard," Tommy confirmed to the boys.

"Mike, how do you know that Ray is a murderer?" Danny asked.

"He seems to have the story before the police release the information about the crime scene. My little voice inside me is also telling me that my suspicion could be true. It's the detective in me."

"Mike, I agree with Johnny. You're crazy," Danny said, interrupting him.

"I talked with Larry at the newsstand earlier today, and he was going to meet with the watch commander and/or detectives assigned to the cases to discuss what I found. Larry seemed to think I'd stumbled into a hornets' nest. His words, not mine."

"You did not tell us about the Larry-and-the-detectives thing," said Tommy as he almost spilled his beer.

"I just found this out in the last twenty-four hours and discussed it with Larry at the newsstand."

"Maybe you did stumble into a hornets' nest," Tommy said.

"Can we just enjoy our beer and not talk about this anymore?" Johnny asked.

"Sure, let's just enjoy the Friday night at the Boys' Clubhouse," Mike replied.

The boys finished a second beer and then just quietly left the shed. Mike locked the hatchway as the other three boys left. Then he peeked out the doorway to exit through the yard. No one was around to see Mike exit into the yard. He sneaked around to the alley where the other three boys were waiting. All four of them left through the alley back around Dickens Avenue and pretended that nothing was going on. It was just another Friday night in the city, and the boys were feeling a little bit tipsy.

Chapter 37

He got in the blue '66 Chevrolet Chevelle SS and drove to the Northwest Side of Chicago once again. Heading toward the city's Northwest Side was such a familiar trip. Cruising down the Kennedy Expressway would take only twenty-five minutes. He got off at Harlem Avenue, then headed north to Northwest Highway, just across the railroad tracks. There was the company at the corner with a huge parking lot named Northwest Machinery Inc. Here he knew Mike Conners would be drinking with the second shift of machine shop operators in the parking lot. They were always drinking after the workweek had ended. He knew the pattern so well and had seen it repeated over and over the past few weeks. Mike was the one who always stayed the longest time drinking in the parking lot. He waited till Mike was all by himself before he approached.

"Hey, can anyone get a drink here?" the killer asked Mike.

"We always have a drink after work. Who are you?" Mike asked.

"I work down the street at the canning company."

"Ok. Don't they drink down there?" Mike replied.

"Nope. They all go home after the second shift," he replied.

"Well, sit down and have a beer."

"I have some cold ones in the car. Let me get my cooler."

He had one beer already opened sitting in the cooler, and it was laced with knockout drops. He retrieved the cooler and popped the top of the beer but switched the can to the opened one with the knockout drops in it. He handed the tainted beer to Mike.

"Hey, this is good beer," Mike said as he took a swig from the can.

"Yep, I like it cold."

"It sure is cold."

Mike consumed the full can of beer and began to feel its effects immediately. He felt sleepy and began to nod off. His body went limp and would be easy to manipulate. The knockout drops worked very well.

He had to work fast just in case anyone saw him in the parking lot. He placed Mike in the passenger seat of his car. He applied a second dose of knockout drops to a rag and placed it over Mike's nose. He put the handcuffs on Mike's hands behind the front seat. He placed a hat on Mike's head in case anyone driving by noticed anything was funny. Now it was time to drive to a secluded spot and finish him off.

***

He drove to Caldwell Woods, a park off Nagle Avenue, and found a secluded spot in the parking lot. He pulled a roll of plastic wrap from behind the seat. He wrapped the plastic material around Mike's head, nose, and mouth so as to suffocate the victim. After ten wraps around the victim's head, he stopped. This did not take long, and Mike stopped breathing in just five minutes. He checked the pulse on Mike's right arm, and the heart had stopped beating. He removed the plastic wrap from around the head of his victim.

***

The drive back to the Northwest Machinery Inc. parking lot would take only a few minutes. He arrived back in the lot, and there appeared to be no one working late that night. There was only one car in the lot, and that was the car of the deceased Mike Conners. He drove his car close to the only one in the parking lot. He removed the cuffs from the victim. He pulled the keys out of the pocket of one dead Mike Conners's pants pocket. He opened the door and placed Mike's body in the driver's seat. For good measure, he poured a few cans of beer onto the floorboards of the car and on the ground. He discarded the empties on the passenger side floorboards. This way it would appear that Mike had drunk himself to death. He carefully removed the empty can of beer that he had offered to Mike from the scene. He did not want any evidence to tie him back to the victim. He placed the car keys back in the dead man's pants pocket. He closed the driver's side door and wiped the door handle clean. Then he fled from the scene in his prized Chevy.

***

Later that night a security guard happened to be making the rounds of the Northwest Machinery Inc. grounds. He noticed a single car in the employee parking lot. The second shift had ended at 11:00 p.m., and it was almost midnight. *Why would any cars be in the parking lot at this time?* The guard was asking himself. The security guard approached the car and tapped on the glass of the driver's side window.

"Hey, buddy, you can't stay here."

No answer from the occupant of the car.

"Hey, buddy, did you hear me?" said the security guard.

The security guard opened the driver's side door, and the body of

Mike Conners fell into the parking lot. At this point, the guard thought he was drunk from all the beer he had consumed. From the smell of beer in the car, it was very evident that the occupant had been drinking. The smell of spilled beer was coming from the floorboards of the car. He felt for Mike's pulse, and there was none. He immediately went to the guard shack and called 911 and reported what had happened to the police.

"I want to report a dead body at the Northwest Machinery Inc. parking lot," said the guard to the dispatcher on the other end.

The operator said they would send the police out as fast as possible and not to touch anything.

"I already checked his pulse, and I could not find any," said the guard to the operator.

The operator asked that he stay at the scene until the police arrived. The guard said he would comply.

"No problem. I'll stay here until the police arrive and not let anyone get near this guy."

The security guard hung up and waited for the police.

***

The police arrived within five minutes.

"Are you the one who found the body?" the police officer asked the security guard.

"Yes. I found him when I opened the door. He had no pulse, and then I called it in to 911."

"Thanks, we will take it from here," said the officer. "Can you stick around so we can get a statement from you?"

"Sure. I work the night shift from 11:00 p.m. to 7:00 a.m. here at the company."

"What did you say your name was?"

"Bill Jacobs. I am the nighttime security guard here."

"Ok. Bill, can you hang out a little while?"

"Sure thing."

The officer went over to where Mike Conners was slumped over on the ground. He felt for his pulse. He called into dispatch on his car radio that the ME and the coroner would be needed for this crime scene. The dispatcher confirmed and advised the officer not to touch a thing at the crime scene and told him the ME would be there in fifteen minutes.

***

On the other end of town, Ray was listening to this exchange on his police scanner. He heard everything that was said between the officer on the scene and the dispatcher on the radio. He was wondering if it was worth racing out to the Northwest Side to poke around for another story. Ray decided to get out of his pj's and get dressed and get in the car to go over to the crime scene at Northwest Machinery, Inc.

***

A short drive later, Ray was at the parking lot of the Northwest Machinery Inc. building at Harlem Avenue and Northwest Highway. The area was roped off, so he could not get near the crime scene. But his police scanner was a valuable eavesdropping tool. He sat in his car and heard that the deceased was Mike Conners and that he may have died from drinking too much alcohol. But the police were not sure. There were some suspicious things at the crime scene that did not add up. The officer requested that the ME make the final call on the cause of death. Ray knew he had another story and tried several times to talk with the police on-site. They all pushed him back away from the crime scene. After forty-five minutes, the crime scene emptied out, and all the police presence was gone. Ray left for home to get some sleep.

It was another story for the *Chicago Today*, and Ray Chambers had appeared to beat all the other reporters to the punch. Ray was proud of himself for racing out to this crime scene on a Friday night, which now turned out to be early Saturday morning.

Chapter 38

Ray slept in on Saturday morning since he had still been at the crime scene late the previous night. He did not even hear the paperboy knock on the door as the early edition of the *Chicago Today* was being delivered to his doorstep. A cup of coffee sounded good, so Ray made one. He stared at the corkboard with his coffee in hand and updated the fifth victim's name on the board. "Mike Conners" was the title. Died of alcohol-related symptoms. The location was the Northwest Machinery Inc. parking lot. The time was late Friday night or early Saturday morning. The police had slipped and let out over the airwaves that there were a lot of suspicious circumstances surrounding the deceased. The ME and/or coroner would need to have the final word on the cause of death. Ray thought about calling his inside guy at the Cook County morgue but knew that Patrick Duffy would not be in to work until Monday. The story could not wait, so Ray decided to bend the facts just a little bit.

As he banged away on the typewriter, he decided the story would be headlined "WHO MURDERED MIKE CONNERS?" The listed facts would that he'd died in the parking lot, drinking alone, that the police were suspicious, and that the ME would need to come up with the cause of death. In the details of the story, he would mention knockout drops as a teaser to hook the reader. This was a bit of a stretch. But since his stories were all reported as anonymous, he could bend the truth a little and get away with it. Lew would most likely allow the transgression to a point. He finished the report on Mike Conners and put it down. He would need a second cup of coffee to continue to wake him up. He added more notes to column five on the corkboard for this new victim, Mike Conners.

***

Mike arrived at the newsstand early on Saturday morning, as usual. He rolled, rubber banded, and stuffed the fifty papers into his news pouch and then strapped the bag onto the bike. He proceeded on his paper route as on so many other Saturdays. It was very uneventful, and he dreaded the second-to-last stop on the paper route. Mike approached the house and began to get extremely nervous. He rang the doorbell, and there was no answer. After a few seconds, Mike placed the paper in front of the door and got back on his bike. No one had answered the door at Ray Chambers's house. Mike finished his route and then returned to the newsstand.

Larry was hanging out in the doorway and saw Mike as he came into the newsstand.

"How is it going today, Mike?"

"Not bad for a Saturday," Mike replied.

"Did you see Ray Chambers on your deliveries this morning?"

"No one answered the door. I don't think he was home early this morning. Maybe he was sleeping."

"Are you going to try one more time later today to collect from him?"

"Unfortunately, yes. I'll make another attempt to collect this week's paper bill," Mike replied.

"Do you still need me to shadow you when you go to collect?"

"No. I think I'll be ok. It is during the day, and there are lots of people around the neighborhood."

"Well, just let me know when you go so I can kind of keep a timeline on you."

"Will do. Thanks, Larry," Mike said as he left the newsstand office.

***

Mike waited till late in the afternoon to go collect this week's bills from the customers. This was the second attempt to collect, and most of the patrons had already paid. He had five customers to collect from, and Ray was the last one on the list. As he progressed through the neighborhood, all the remaining customers paid up. Mike was now headed to Ray's house. Again, as he got close, his nerves started to get the best of him. He started to shake just a little. The little voice inside was saying to be calm. *You can do this*, it said. *Don't let him get to you.* Mike got off his bike and rang the doorbell of Ray's house on Hoyne Avenue as he had done so many times before. Ray was home this time.

"Hi, Mike. Are you here to collect this week's bill?" Ray asked.

"Yes, I am," Mike replied.

"How much do I owe you?"

"It's $1.40 for the week."

"Step into the house and I'll get my wallet." Ray stepped back into the kitchen and disappeared for about thirty seconds. To Mike it seemed like an hour. Mike eased into the foyer of Ray's house to wait. He was a little nervous. Mike's wandering eyes searched for the corkboard. There he saw a fifth entry on the board. A column of information on Mike Conners was listed. He could see only one more sentence on the board. "He died of alcohol consumption." The rest of the board was blocked by a chair that was in his line of sight. Mike froze and thought to himself that another death might have just happened at the hands of this reporter and only the two of them knew about it.

"Here you go, Mike," Ray said as he handed him two dollars. "Keep the change."

"Thanks, Mr. Chambers."

"Did you buy your catcher's mitt yet?" Ray replied, catching Mike off guard.

"No, not yet. My mom did not take me down to the store." That was fast thinking and a good comeback from Mike.

"Well, let me know if I gave you enough for the mitt."

"Thanks again, Mr. Chambers."

"Just call me Ray from now on."

"Ok. Ray."

Mike left Ray's house and went straight to the newsstand. He had to tell Larry what he'd just seen at the reporter's house. He pedaled just as fast as his two legs could on his bike to get to the newsstand.

***

As Mike walked into the newsstand, he found Larry in the back office all alone, doing some paperwork.

"Larry. There is another victim on the corkboard in Ray Chambers's house."

"What, Mike?"

"There is another name on the board. Mike Conners." Mike started to shake. "Something about dying of alcohol consumption."

"Calm down, Mike."

"Where is the book? We need to check to see if the name is in there like the other four."

"The detectives took the book late Friday afternoon. I did not get a chance to let you know."

"They have Henry's yearbook? What do I tell Henry if he is looking for it?"

"Just tell him I have it."

"I think that would be ok. Henry really doesn't look at it on a daily basis," Mike replied.

"By the way. The detectives want to talk with you and me on Monday in the afternoon. Can you be here for the meeting?"

"Why do they want to talk to me?"

"Just routine questions."

"I guess so," Mike replied with a nervous voice.

"Mike, it will be ok. I'll be here with you. Just routine questions."

"What do we do about the fifth name?"

"I hope that name is not in the book," Larry replied.

"I hope so too."

"Mike, just go home and try not to worry about this. Whatever you do, don't go by Ray Chambers's house. Ok?" Larry was looking for a nod from Mike.

Mike nodded his head and left the newsstand in an incredibly quiet way.

Larry was thinking that he hoped the boy was ok. The thought occurred to him that his parents might need to be informed of this situation. But Larry was thinking it was still too early to get them into the mix of this discovery.

What had this little boy stumbled into?

Chapter 39

It was Monday morning at the Jefferson Park precinct, and the detectives would need to have an update meeting with Watch Commander Dane Hoy. The discussion would be on the progress of all their active case files and who was being pursued as possible suspects. Officer Hoy wanted results from his detectives, or he would read them the riot act. He was a bit of a bull in a china shop, but his closing record was above 85 percent on murder cases.

"Where are Detectives Cato and Douglas?" the watch commander shouted in the precinct office.

"They have not checked in yet this morning," Art Reed, the desk sergeant, offered up in answer.

"When you see them, send them to my office first thing this morning," Officer Dane Hoy barked back at the desk sergeant.

"Will do. As soon as I see them."

About fifteen minutes later, Detectives Cato and Douglas strolled through the front door of the precinct. They both proceeded to go to their desks to settle in. The desk sergeant came over to them and pointed to the watch commander's office with his finger.

"You have been summoned to the watch commander's office. Don't bother to sit down."

"Thanks, Art, for the message."

"It was not a message, Cato. It was an order. Get into the watch commander's office. Now!"

"Are we in hot water?" Rick said as he looked at Abbey.

"Just the watch commander pushing his weight around."

The two detectives proceeded to the watch commander's office. Officer Hoy was on the phone, talking with the chief of police. He pointed to his two detectives and to the two seats in his office. Cato and Douglas understood what that meant and sat down while Officer Hoy was still on the phone. The door was closed, and Officer Hoy was pacing back and forth with the phone still next to his ear. It appeared that the chief was not happy and that he was getting yelled at repeatedly. Officer Hoy hung up the phone and just stared at the two detectives sitting in his office.

"That was the chief on the phone, as you could tell. He is not happy with me because we don't have any results on the four victims: Bass, Burger, Dirt, and Cagney. Please tell me you two have something solid on these open cases." Officer Hoy sat down behind his desk and waited for his detectives to say something.

Detective Cato said, "We have followed up on a lead we got on Friday from a newsstand manager named Larry West. It seems that a paperboy stumbled onto the fact that all four victims' names and pictures are in a yearbook."

"A yearbook. Are you two making this shit up?" Officer Hoy said with bewilderment.

"No, we are not making this shit up. Let me expand on what I said."

"Go on, Detective Cato," Officer Hoy replied.

"It seems that this newspaper boy stumbled onto a possible

connection to all four of our victims. All four victims appear in the Hamilton Technical High School yearbook dated 1966. They were all seniors."

"Is there more of a connection?" Officer Hoy asked.

"We don't know," Detective Cato replied. "That's what we are trying to figure out."

"Well, you'd better figure it out fast. The chief is chewing my ear off about these cases, and I don't have much left on one side. Oh, by the way, the request for the FBI profiler was declined. She will not be added to our team. She has been assigned to a 'high-profile' murder case in St. Louis."

"We understand that the chief is placing you under a lot of pressure. But we need a little time to investigate and turn something up. Now, with no FBI assistance, we will need even more time," Detective Cato replied.

"Get me some results," Officer Hoy replied.

"We will be interviewing the paperboy later this afternoon."

"That's a good start. Why don't you two go and interview the principal at Hamilton Technical High School? That seems like a logical place to continue this investigation," Officer Hoy said as he was thumbing through the yearbook.

"That's why you're the watch commander," said Detective Douglas. "You make the big bucks, and we make the small bucks."

"Get out of my office. Take the yearbook with you. Get me some results," Officer Hoy said, starting to raise his voice.

The two detectives left his office and went to their desks.

"Boy is he hot today," Rick said to Cato.

"Yep, Officer Hoy must have had a good chewing out from the chief."

"Let's go interview the principal at Hamilton Tech and see where this thing takes us," Rick said, giving Cato a look.

"That's a good idea," Cato said as she returned the look to Rick.

"Grab the yearbook and let's get out of here."

***

The drive over to Hamilton Technical High School took longer than expected. A wreck at the Montrose Avenue exit was blocking two of the three lanes. The traffic was squeaking by in the one left lane. What a nightmare for the two detectives. Detective Cato thought about putting on the siren, but that would have been an abuse of police authority. So, they sat in traffic until it was their turn to pass the wreck on the right side. It was a semi and two mangled cars, and the emergency crews were on-site taking care of the situation. The two detectives waved to the emergency personnel as they passed them by. A tip of the hat and a salute were all that was needed. A few minutes later, the detectives exited onto Addison Street, heading east to North Western Avenue. They took a left on North Western Avenue headed north, and they found the parking lot for all students and faculty.

The detectives parked their car and headed for the principal's office. There were signs that read "Administration Building," and that was where they would start. They stumbled around the campus, and a few minutes later they found the principal's office. The office had a sign that read "Principal Lauren Powers." The two detectives opened the door and were greeted by the secretary.

"Can I help you, Detectives?" Lacy Jones, the secretary, asked.

"I am Detective Abbey Cato, and this is Detective Rick Douglas from the Chicago Police Department, Jefferson Park precinct. We need to talk with the principal of your school."

"Can I ask what this pertains to, and do you have an appointment?"

"No, we do not have an appointment," Detective Cato replied. "This is a serious matter, and we need to discuss it with your principal. This matter involves the deaths of some of your students."

"Let me see if she is available."

The secretary left her desk and entered the principal's office. A few minutes later, Lacy Jones returned to her desk.

"The principal will see you now. You can go into her office," Lacy Jones said as she pointed to the doorway.

"Thanks, Miss Jones," Cato replied.

The detectives proceeded to the principal's office where she was waiting.

"Hi, I am Principal Lauren Powers. I understand you needed to see me about something you're working on?"

"Thanks for seeing us on such short notice. I am Detective Abbey Cato, and this is my partner, Detective Rick Douglas," Detective Cato said as both detectives shook the principal's hand.

"Nice to meet you both. Please sit down." Lauren Powers motioned to the chairs in front of her desk.

"We would like to show you this yearbook that was given to us," Detective Cato said. "It is a Hamilton Technical yearbook from the year 1966."

"Yes, that is one of our yearbooks. How can I help you on this?"

"We are working on the cases of four victims: Wally Bass, Kevin Burger, Joe Dirt, and Paul Cagney. They all died of mysterious causes, and they are all listed as seniors in the Hamilton Tech High School yearbook."

"Oh my gosh. This is not good news for our school," Lauren Powers replied.

"We were wondering if there is anything you can tell us about any of these students that would help our investigations," Detective Cato said.

"I would be shocked if these students in any way could have been involved in any criminal activities that were going on around this high school. I cannot think of any reason for these four students to be harmed in any way," replied Principal Powers. "Is it public knowledge that Hamilton Technical High School is involved?"

"Not yet. We are trying to keep your school out of it," Detective Cato replied. "Could you tell us if there were any clubs or committees that these students attended?"

"I cannot think of any clubs at this time. I will ask my secretary and some of the faculty to review their attendance records to see if we can come up with any details," replied Principal Powers.

"It would be very helpful if you could do that for us," Detective Cato replied.

"Please try to keep our school out of your investigation. This is not good for our students, parents, or teaching staff. This kind of news could affect us in a very disastrous way."

"We will do the best we can," replied Detective Cato. "If you think of anything about these four deceased students that could help us out, please reach out to us. Here is my card with my number at the office." Detective Cato handed her card to Principal Lauren Powers.

"If I think of anything that could be relevant, I'll give you a call. Can I ask what these four students died of?"

"They all died of different causes but under very suspicious circumstances. That is all we are allowed to tell you for now. These are active investigations, and we do not want to release too much information."

"I will need to inform our board of directors of your active investigations of these four students," Principal Powers said.

"You can inform them, but please be careful. We do not want to scare anyone with these cases or cause a panic until we have more information," Detective Cato replied.

"Thank you for coming out to see me under these circumstances," Principal Powers said as she showed the detectives to the door.

"Thank you for your time. I wish it were under better conditions," Detective Cato said as she shook her hand and left the principal's office.

The detectives also thanked the secretary, Lacy Jones, as they exited the principal's office of Hamilton Technical High School.

Lacy Jones volunteered to review all student records with the teachers during the next couple of days and look for anything to do with the four students. Both detectives were very appreciative of the effort and thanked her in advance for all the assistance.

Both detectives were wondering whether they'd hit a dead end.

"Hey, can we get sub sandwiches for lunch?" Rick asked.

"Sure. Didn't we see a sub shop at the corner of Addison and Western? The place was called Hero's Sub Shop or something like that."

"Yes, I believe you are correct."

"Then let's get some lunch before we head back to the precinct."

"Sounds good," Rick replied. "Why don't we stop in that sub shop and maybe talk with some of the local students. You never know what kind of information you're going to get from the locals."

Chapter 40

The Cook County coroner's office was extremely low on personnel and was scraping the bottom of the barrel to stay afloat with the quality of people they could keep. No one wanted to work for the coroner's office dealing with dead bodies all day long. There were so many people who didn't care to do any of these jobs, and nobody was applying for the positions in the department. The weekend ME called in sick, so that meant any bodies found in the city over the weekend would be kept in the refrigerated morgue until processed on Monday.

***

The ME on duty for Monday was Michelle Lynn. She actually enjoyed her job but was overwhelmed with the number of bodies coming in and out of the Cook County morgue on a daily basis. She was informed that the weekend ME had called in sick, so this meant a large number of autopsies that would need to be done on Monday. This would be an exceptionally long day to catch up with the twenty bodies that needed to be processed.

Mike Conners's body was number fifteen on the list. It was late in the afternoon, and Michelle Lynn was one tired woman. She went through the normal autopsy for a person who had drunk himself to death. A blood toxicology screen would need to be performed since alcohol was involved. A rush on this would be added so that she could finish the autopsy at the same time she received the blood toxicology results. After Michelle Lynn had done the typical thirty-minute autopsy, she wrote up the report summary details. There was nothing out of the ordinary while the procedure was completed. The autopsy results would be summarized and put into the report. The deceased Mike Conners had died of blood poisoning due to alcohol consumption. His blood alcohol concentration (BAC) was .30. The state's BAC limit at this time was .10. He was at three times the legal limit. This consumption of excessive amounts of alcohol had caused his heart to go into cardiac arrest, and his heart had failed. The eyes appeared to be bloodshot. The nose was pushed in slightly. There were abrasions on both wrists. The cause of death circled on the form was death by natural causes. Case closed. Michelle Lynn signed her name to the bottom of the report. She dated the report and placed it in the tray of other autopsies that were completed today. This reported death by natural causes would not go to the desk of the watch commander at the Jefferson Park precinct. Detectives Cato and Douglas would not see this report either unless they requested it from the ME's office. For all involved, this was an ordinary death, and no investigations were to be made into the deceased Mike Conners.

Chapter 41

Monday night Ray got a call from Patrick Duffy. The phone rang at Ray's house, and he just happened to be home.

"Hello."

"Is this Ray Chambers?"

"Who is this?"

"Patrick Duffy from the coroner's office." He spoke in a hushed voice.

"What's up?" Ray replied.

"Hey, we had twenty autopsies today. Are you interested in any of them?"

"If you got one there on Mike Conners, I'm interested," Ray replied.

"Let me look at the list." A moment later Patrick responded, "Mike Conners was number 15 on the list of completed autopsies."

"I could use the report on him if you can get it."

"Sure thing. Same deal as before: fifty bucks. Meet me in the cafeteria in one hour."

"See you then. Thanks, Patrick," Ray said as he hung up the phone.

***

Ray arrived one hour later at the usual place, which was the cafeteria on the main floor of the Cook County building at Twenty-Sixth and California. Ray grabbed a cup of coffee and sat down at one of the many tables, in a corner of the room. Patrick arrived a few minutes after Ray sat down. Ray palmed the fifty dollars and saw that Patrick had an envelope in his hand. The two passed the dollars and the envelope simultaneously to each other, and not a word was spoken between the two. Ray stuffed the envelope into his coat and then slowly finished his coffee. A few minutes later, Ray got up and left the building. He headed for home so he could carefully review the report he had received from Patrick.

***

Ray got home a half hour later from the meeting with the mole on Monday night. He had already turned the article on Mike Conners in to Lew Monday afternoon. The story had run in the Monday edition. "WHO MURDERED MIKE CONNERS?" was on page 1 of the newspaper. The article went on to say that Mike Conners had died of alcohol-related symptoms and that the circumstances were very suspicious. Ray had also put the teaser of knockout drops in the article to keep the readers interested. The first item was a fact, and the second item was an embellishment. Now he had the summary report from the ME's office, and he needed to see if his transgression was in fact going to get him in trouble with Lew.

Ray opened the envelope that contained the ME's report on Mike Conners, compliments of one Patrick Duffy and fifty dollars.

The report read as follows: "The deceased Mike Conners died of blood poisoning due to alcohol consumption. His blood alcohol concentration was .30. The state's BAC limit at this time is .10. He was at three times the legal limit. This consumption of alcohol caused his heart to go into cardiac arrest, and his heart failed. There were minute traces of knockout drops found in the bloodstream. The eyes appeared to be bloodshot. The nose was pushed in slightly. There were abrasions on both wrists."

The cause of death circled on the form was "death by natural causes."

Ray knew he was off the hook with Lew. The summary report corroborated his embellished reporting on Mike Conners.

Chapter 42

Mike said his farewell to his mom once again and got on his bike as on so many other days, headed for the newsstand. The radio was tuned to WLS 890 AM with Larry Lujack as the Monday afternoon disk jockey spinning records. Larry was spinning records because Bob Sirott was sick today. The music coming out of Mike's radio was a song from Creedence Clearwater Revival, "Fortunate Son." Mike was a little shocked that three times in three days a Creedence Clearwater Revival song would be on at the exact time he was headed to the newsstand. He was beginning to think that the payola scandal might have had something to do with it. Mike drove down the center line on Dickens and then down Hoyne on his way to the newsstand. There was Mary Crystal sitting on the porch, watching him ride his bike.

"Make sure I get my paper today," Mary Crystal yelled toward Mike.

"Will do, Mrs. Crystal," Mike yelled back to her.

"Don't forget to watch out for those pesky cars."

Mike just waved at Mrs. Crystal as he passed her by.

Mike arrived at the newsstand and went to one of the high tables where there was a stack of papers waiting for the paperboys. He started to roll, rubber band, and stuff the papers into the news pouch. Larry was in the back office and saw that Mike had arrived. He went to Mike to talk with him.

"Hey, Mike, I got a call this morning. The guys need to reschedule that meeting to Tuesday afternoon."

"Ok. So come back after my deliveries on Tuesday?" Mike asked Larry. "What about the yearbook?"

"Yes, please come back after your Tuesday ride. Sorry about the delay. Those guys did not say why, just that something came up on their end. Don't know about the yearbook. But I am sure they will bring it back."

"I will come back later on Tuesday afternoon, around 4:30 p.m."

"Sounds good, Mike. Now get those papers delivered today."

"Will do," Mike said as he left the newsstand to deliver his papers.

Mike was thinking to himself that he would have to wait another day before he would get Henry's yearbook back. If Henry wanted the book, he would have to make something up. The little voice inside him was saying all kinds of things to him. He settled on an answer of "I left it back at the newsstand." He hoped Henry would not need it or want it back for at least another day. That was going to be the stock answer if his big brother asked. But only if he asked.

The newspaper deliveries for a Monday afternoon were fairly routine: a nice ride during a sunny, dry, and warm day in June. When Mike passed by the house of Ray Chambers, he threw the paper toward the door and sped away as fast as his legs could carry him. About forty-five minutes later, Mike was done for the day. He did not have to go back to the newsstand to talk with the detectives. That was a relief for now. He knew the meeting had been pushed to Tuesday afternoon, and then the book could be looked at. Would the name of the fifth victim, Mike Conners, appear on the pages? This was the question Mike did not want to get an answer to.

Mike put his bike away on the back porch of the house and then went out to play ball with Tommy in front of the house on Dickens. It was just Tommy and Mike playing street ball against each other. Mike knew he had a little bit of time until dinner or until his mom yelled to get in the house. Tommy was winning the game today.

"Hey, Mike, you're not concentrating on the game. What's up?" Tommy asked.

"I am worried about talking with the detectives on Tuesday afternoon."

"What are you talking about, Mike?" Tommy asked.

"The Chicago police detectives asked to talk with Larry and me on Monday. But they pushed the meeting to Tuesday afternoon. Something came up on their end to delay the meeting."

"Why do they need you there at the newsstand, Mike?" Tommy replied.

"Because I found a yearbook with the four victims' names."

"Oh boy. Do your mom and dad know about this?"

"No. I have not mentioned it to either of them."

"You are going to get in trouble."

"Larry told me to say nothing until we talk with the detectives."

"You're in a pickle, Mike."

"Yes. I am. Can we just play ball?"

"You're up, Mike," Tommy replied.

The boys finished the game of street ball on a warm Monday afternoon. Mike lost badly to Tommy. The score ended up Tommy 10 and Mike 5. Tommy knew that Mike was not into playing the game today. He was worried about the meeting on Tuesday with Larry and the detectives.

"Hey, Mike, your mom is calling," Tommy shouted to Mike.

"Yes, she's calling me to dinner."

"Ok. Mike, we can have a rematch after dinner."

"Sounds good. I'll win that one," replied Mike.

"See you later."

Mike went home for dinner. As Mike crossed the street to go home, he was hoping that Henry would not ask him where his yearbook was. Mike dodged this bullet today. Henry was out for the evening.

Chapter 43

Detective Cato called Larry to confirm the meeting for 4:30 p.m. Tuesday at the newsstand. The request was to have Mike there so that the detectives could ask him a few questions. Larry agreed with the detectives and requested that the yearbook be returned. The detectives would bring the yearbook to the meeting later that day. The pages that displayed the photos of the four victims had been xeroxed and placed in the crime scene files.

***

Mike had finished his paper route a little early on Tuesday afternoon. It could have been in anticipation of the meeting with the police or that he wanted Henry's property back. Either way, Mike wanted to get this over with and get the book back into the box of books in the attic.

He drove his bike down the middle of the streets as he had done so many times before. This time in the late afternoon, there were more cars on the road, and a game of dodge-the-traffic was being played by Mike and the drivers. Mike finally arrived at the newsstand, and Larry was there in the doorway as usual.

"You made it," Larry said to Mike.

"I am a bit nervous. What do these detectives want from me?" Mike asked Larry.

"They just want to ask a couple of questions. Then you will be out of here."

"I have to get home for dinner in a few minutes."

"I'll make sure you get home in time for dinner."

Just at that moment, a car pulled up and parked next to the newsstand building. Two detectives got out of the car and walked toward the newsstand.

"Hi, Mike? I am Detective Cato, and this is my partner, Detective Douglas."

"Nice to see you both," Mike said nervously. "I'm Michael John Peters."

"Hi, Larry."

"Detectives, welcome. Come right in," Larry said as he motioned them into the newsstand office.

The other paperboys were all out delivering the Tuesday edition of the *Chicago Today*. The office was empty except for Detective Cato, Detective Douglas, Larry, and Mike.

"Mike has to get home for dinner, so can we hurry this up?" Larry asked the detectives.

"Sure, no problem," answered Detective Cato. "So, Mike, how did you find this yearbook and realize that the four names were in the senior section of the book?" Cato asked.

"I was talking with Larry over a few days about the murders or suicides of these four individuals. I told Larry I was going to solve them. Larry thought I was crazy. You know, I want to be a detective when I grow up. Just like you two."

"That is an admirable goal, Mike," Detective Cato said. "Go on, Mike—finish your thoughts."

"Well, when I kept reading about the stories and the victims, I noticed that they were all around twenty-two or twenty-three years of age. I thought it was a funny coincidence that they were all young. They had their whole lives ahead of them. Then, when I started to talk to Larry, a light bulb went off in my head. What if they were all related to a high school club or something? That's when Larry asked me to check my older brother's yearbook. And that's where we found the four names: in the senior section of the Hamilton Technical High School yearbook. Then Larry said he was going to contact the watch commander, Dane Hoy."

"How did you have his number?" Detective Cato asked.

"I went down to the Jefferson Park precinct last week to ask some questions about how the police information gets into the newspapers. That's where I got his name and number. The desk sergeant was nice enough to get me a few minutes with your watch commander."

"You're a resourceful kid," Detective Douglas replied.

"Go on, finish your story," Detective Cato interjected.

"There is more, but I am afraid to tell you," Mike said as he pulled away.

"Tell them about Ray," Larry told Mike.

"There is a news reporter on my paper route. His name is Ray Chambers. He is the second-to-last delivery on my route. He has a corkboard in his living room, and I saw it when I was collecting the weekly money two weeks ago on a Friday, and then again on the Saturday just past, with information on the murdered victims."

"How do you know they were murdered, Mike?" Cato asked.

"I did not know. The corkboard just had names and information, with a bottom line that said 'murdered.' After I talked with Larry, it seemed that Ray Chambers always seemed to have the information ahead of everyone else, including the police."

"What makes you think that, Mike?" Detective Cato asked.

"The little voice inside me said that."

"Where can we find this Ray Chambers the reporter?" Detective Cato asked.

"He lives on Hoyne Avenue, just down the street."

"I can look up his address for you two," Larry said.

"Thanks, Larry. That would be appreciated," Detective Cato replied.

"Please don't tell him I sent you. I'll be in trouble," Mike said to the detectives.

Detective Cato said, "We will be sensitive to the relationship you have with him, Mike. We will just ask him a couple of questions and see where it goes. Thanks for your time."

"Can I have my brother's yearbook back?" Mike asked.

"Rick, can you get it? We left it in the car."

"Sure, thing, Cato. Give me a minute."

Rick went to the patrol car to get the yearbook. As he strolled back into the newsstand office, Mike grabbed the book. He thumbed through the book and stopped on page 231.

"Larry, his name is in the book!" Mike yelled.

"Shit," Larry yelled aloud.

The two detectives both looked at Larry and Mike and wondered what they were getting so agitated about.

"Mike Conners was on the front page of the *Chicago Today* on Monday," Larry replied.

"We are not investigating a case on Mike Conners," Detective Cato answered.

"Well, maybe you two should be. You may want to add him to your list of victims," Mike mumbled.

"How did you know he might be in the book, Mike?" Detective Cato asked.

"I saw his name in column five on the corkboard in Ray Chambers's house on Saturday."

"Detectives, Mike has to get back home for dinner. Do we need to continue this with him?" Larry said.

"We have enough of information from Mike. Please don't say anything to anyone about what we talked about here. Give us a day or two to try to find the underlying cause of this," Cato requested.

"Ok. I will not say anything until you tell Larry." Mike nodded his head in agreement.

"Mike, you go home and have dinner with your family," Larry said as he walked him out the door.

"Can we get the exact address of Ray Chambers?" Detective Cato asked Larry.

"Sure, give me a minute to look it up."

"Douglas, what do you think?"

"That kid is pretty sharp. He is going to make a good detective."

"Agreed. If we don't watch out, he could eat our lunch." Detective Cato nodded.

Larry wrote down the exact address of Ray Chambers on Hoyne Avenue on a piece of paper and handed it to the detectives.

"Thanks for your help on this, Larry."

"Anytime. Let me know what happens. I'll keep an eye on Mike. He is one of best and brightest paperboys. Please keep the newsstand and Mike out of your conversations with Ray."

"Will do."

Detectives Cato and Douglas left the newsstand in the direction of one *Chicago Today* news reporter Ray Chambers on Hoyne Avenue.

Chapter 44

It was Wednesday morning at the Jefferson Park precinct. Detectives Cato and Douglas were at their assigned desks, reviewing the information from yesterday's meeting with Larry and Mike. It was interesting that the paperboy had stumbled onto the yearbook and that all the victims were in the senior section of Hamilton Technical High School for the year 1966. This was an angle that neither of the detectives had had as of last night.

"Hey, Rick, could this be a cult thing or maybe a fraternity thing that all the students were part of?" Detective Cato said.

"I don't know, Cato. It seems very strange that four victims and now the fifth, Mike Conners, appeared in the book. We don't even have a case file on the fifth victim. I wonder why we were not informed on this one."

"You may have to ask your girlfriend about that," Cato replied.

"That's not a bad idea. She is not my girlfriend. We just went out on one date. That's it." Detective Douglas blushed.

"We should go down and have a conversation with her on the Mike Conners case later today. Can you call her and see when she is free to discuss the Conners situation?"

"I can do that in just a few minutes," Douglas replied.

"Cato, Douglas, get in here," the watch commander shouted across the precinct office from his doorway.

The whole precinct could hear this, and everyone knew that Cato and Douglas were in a heap of trouble. The officers in the bullpen were all shrinking and pretending that they did not hear the shouting. But they all knew shit was going to fly this morning. Cato and Douglas were going to be the proud recipients of the flying crap. Cato and Douglas walked over to the watch commander's office. As they did, Officer Hoy closed the door behind them and pointed to the two chairs in front of his desk. They were going to get reamed out on their cases if they didn't have any updates.

"So, what is the latest on your case files for Bass, Burger, Dirt, and Cagney?" Officer Hoy barked.

Cato said, "We interviewed a Larry West. who is a *Chicago Today* newsstand manager, and a Mike Peters, a twelve-year-old paperboy. It seems that the paperboy, Mike, put two and two together and figured out that our four victims are in a yearbook.

"A what?" Officer Hoy asked.

"All four of our victims are listed as seniors in the Hamilton Technical High School yearbook, in the class of '66."

"Go on."

"There is also a reporter for the *Chicago Today* who seems to be well informed about the victims. Almost too well informed. Like he may have something to do with the crime scenes."

"Have you spoken with this reporter?" Office Hoy asked.

Douglas said, "Not yet. He was not home last night."

"What makes you think that this reporter knows something about the cases you're investigating?" Officer Hoy replied.

"The paperboy Mike seems to think the reporter Ray Chambers

knows about the crime scenes before everyone else does," Cato said. "Then he reports on it to his editor. I won't know if he is involved until we talk with him."

"Well, get out of here and talk to him," Officer Hoy yelled at the two detectives. "Get out of my office and do your jobs."

Detectives Cato and Douglas left the office of the watch commander feeling a little bit smaller than when they went in.

"Let's go see if we can find the reporter Ray Chambers." Detective Cato motioned to Detective Douglas.

"He works for the *Chicago Today*, so let's start with his editor."

"Let's take a ride down to the *Chicago Today* building downtown. This way we can find out where Ray Chambers is, and we can talk with the editor of the paper."

"Sounds good, Cato."

***

The detectives jumped into the patrol car and traveled downtown to the *Chicago Today* building. Cato was familiar with where the building was downtown, as she had been there many times before. This time, traveling down the Kennedy Expressway, they didn't encounter any accidents.

The detectives parked in the employee parking lot of the *Chicago Today* building. The directory of the building showed that the editor in charge was Lew Kelly, and he was located on the thirteenth floor. The detectives rode the elevator up to the thirteenth floor. As the elevator opened, they noticed that this floor was one big bullpen with lots of desks and reporters. They both looked toward the windows, and there was the office of Lew Kelly with the title of "Editor" stenciled on his window. They walked through the maze of people and desks and approached the office of Lew Kelly.

"Are you Lew Kelly?" Detective Cato asked as she knocked on the open glass door.

"Who wants to know?" Lew Kelly responded.

Cato said, "I am Detective Abbey Cato, and this is my partner, Detective Rick Douglas, from the Chicago police department."

"What do you two want with me?" Kelly fired back.

"We would like to talk to you about some cases we are working on and one of your reporters, a Ray Chambers."

"Ray is one of our reporters," Lew replied. "What do you want with him?"

"We would like to talk with him if that is possible."

"He is on assignment, and I don't see him at his desk," Lew responded.

"When do you expect him back?" asked Cato.

"Don't know. I can give him a message that you two want to talk with him."

"That would be fine." Cato left him a card with the name and number of the Jefferson Park precinct's phone number.

"Have him call us as soon as possible. Ask for Detective Cato or Detective Douglas."

"I will," replied Lew. "Can I tell him what this pertains to?"

"We are investigating the deaths of Wally Bass, Kevin Burger, Joe Dirt, and Paul Cagney," Cato said. "We believe Ray Chambers may have information to help us solve these crimes."

"You know our reporters are protected by the First Amendment," Lew replied. "The police have burned our reporters in the past, and some are a little gun shy of your tactics."

"Yes, we know that. We just want Ray Chambers to help us with our investigations. We would like his cooperation to understand if we are missing any critical information that we can use to help solve the crimes."

"I will give him the message." Detective Cato gave Lew the card containing the number of the Jefferson Park police precinct.

"By the way, who is the reporter of record who has been authoring the reports on the four victims?" Cato asked.

"I can't tell you that, Detective Cato. We cannot reveal our sources of information. Sorry," Lew replied.

"We really would like your cooperation here, Lew."

"I'll give Ray Chambers the message and your number. Thanks. Now can you two get out of my office? I have a paper to run," he said as he pointed to the door. This was the second time today that the two detectives had been told to get out of an office.

"This is not over, Mr. Editor," Detective Douglas said as he passed by Lew and left the office in front of Detective Cato.

"Can you please make sure that Ray Chambers gets this message?" Detective Cato asked once more.

"I'll give him the message," Lew replied.

The detectives left the office of the editor Lew Kelly and were pissed off that this line of questioning had produced zero results. They knew that they would have to find Ray Chambers and press him hard to get any information out of him. They had his home address but did not know where he was today. The editor said he was on assignment. He could be anywhere in the city.

"Maybe we should just stake his house out," Cato replied to Douglas.

"That is a great idea. He has to come home eventually."

"How about 6:00 p.m., during dinner?" Cato replied.

"Sounds good to me."

Chapter 45

Driving from the *Chicago Today* building back to the precinct, Detective Rick Douglas had a thought.

"Hey, Cato, I forgot to make that call to Michelle Lynn."

"Yes, you did. That was before the watch commander yelled at us."

"Let's stop by and see the ME and find out why the Mike Conners case file never came across our desk," Detective Douglas said.

"That's an excellent idea. The county building is right on the way back to the precinct. Then you can see your girlfriend once again."

"I told you she is not my girlfriend. We just went on one date."

"You went to Luigi's on Harlem Avenue?"

"Yes, we did."

"That's a pretty nice date, Rick."

"Well, let's just say I am interested in her."

"Is she interested in you?"

"Maybe."

"Lover boy."

"Can we just keep this civil? I mean when we see her?"

"Sure."

***

A short drive later, the two detectives were at the county building. Cato and Douglas flashed their badges, and this gave them immediate access to the Cook County buildings. They proceeded to the county morgue, where they thought Michelle Lynn would be. They were in luck. She had just finished an autopsy and was having a coffee break.

"Hi, Rick, what brings you down here?"

"Detective Cato and I were in the neighborhood and wanted to ask you something."

"What do you need?" Michelle Lynn said as she sipped her coffee.

"Did you do an autopsy on a Mike Conners this past week?"

"Let me think. I have done about thirty autopsies this week so far. They are all blended together. Yes, I did a Mike Conners on Monday. It was an alcohol-related death. It was a natural causes situation. A case file was never generated and sent to your watch commander."

"Can we see the summary report on Mike Conners?" Cato asked.

"Sure. Give me a minute, and I'll go into the records room. Wait here; I'll be right back."

A few minutes later, Michelle Lynn came back with the file on Mike Conners.

"He was admitted to the morgue on Sunday morning in the early-morning hours. The weekend ME was sick. So, I got the short straw to perform the autopsy on Monday."

"What was the cause of death?" Detective Cato asked.

"Let me see. Here is the summary. His blood alcohol level was three times the allowable limit. So, he poisoned himself by drinking too much," Michelle replied.

"Is it possible he was murdered?" Cato asked.

"Not likely. With three times the blood alcohol limit in his system, it is not conceivable that this guy could even stand up. The consumption of this much alcohol must have caused the heart to go into cardiac arrest, and the heart failed."

"Was there anything else in the report that may have been a little bit suspicious?" Detective Douglas interjected.

"There were a few details in the summary. There were minute traces of knockout drops in the bloodstream. The nose was pushed in slightly. There were abrasions on both wrists," Michelle stated.

"Do the knockout drops, nose, or abrasions seem a little bit odd?" Detective Cato asked.

"Not really. The victim could have received the abrasions from the machine shop where he worked. The nose injury could have been from the fall out of the car onto the pavement. The security guard said that the body fell out of the car when he opened the door."

"What about the minute traces of knockout drops in the blood?" Detective Cato asked once again.

"If there are knockout drops in the bloodstream, they dissipate after an hour of being administered. The security guard said the victim, Mike Conners, was alone drinking in the parking lot after his shift. Minute traces of knockout drops are in lots of places."

"What if someone has been using knockout drops to subdue the victims and then killing them to make the deaths look like accidents?" Detective Cato asked Michelle. "Sort of like practicing the art of subduing and then killing people for pleasure."

"Detective Cato, it is possible. This is extremely hard to evaluate for and find in the bloodstream. I could have missed it because of all of the bodies I processed that day due to being tired and off my game."

"But it is possible?"

"Yes, it is possible. Testing for knockout drops is a tricky process. You need to do this within the first hour of when a person becomes deceased."

"All I am saying is that this is possible."

"I'll agree with you on that point. My break is over. I need to get back to work."

"Are we still on for Saturday night?" Rick said as his eyes wandered toward Michelle.

"Yep. Pick me up at 7:00 p.m."

Rick had a goofy smile on his face.

"Come on, lover boy; we need to stake out a house," Cato said as she pointed to the door.

Chapter 46

The detectives decided to swing by the house of Ray Chambers on Hoyne Avenue. This was on the way from the Cook County building, headed back to the Jefferson Park precinct. An unannounced visit to this house was the plan, since they knew that Lew the editor had said Ray was on assignment somewhere in the city. The detectives were feeling a bit lucky, so they thought they would take a chance.

***

The detectives pulled up in front of Ray Chambers's house and parked right in the front spot on Hoyne Avenue. The house was a two-story bungalow and looked to have two entrances on the Hoyne Avenue side of the street. The detective observed a basement apartment with a walkway down and a main second floor with a set of stairs up. This was a typical bungalow style of house built back in the 1950s when the war vets came home. The detectives walked up the flight of stairs and rang the doorbell. The mail slot had a piece of paper at the bottom of the box that said "Ray Chambers" in small print. No one answered the door after they rang the bell two more times. The reporter must have been out on assignment, just as Lew the editor had told them that morning. Again, the thought was to come back around dinnertime, or

6:00 p.m., to try to catch Ray at home. Just as the detectives were walking down the stairs to leave, a man came out of the downstairs apartment.

"Are you Ray Chambers?" Detective Cato asked.

"No. Ray is my brother. He lives upstairs. Who wants to know?"

"I am Detective Cato, and this is my partner, Detective Douglas. We are trying to get in touch with Ray Chambers."

"Why do you want to see him?"

"Just some routine questions regarding some cases we are working on. What did you say your name was?"

"My name is Ricky Chambers. I am his younger brother. I was headed to the corner store for some groceries."

"We rang his doorbell, and Ray does not seem to be home today."

"He is probably at the office or around town looking for a story," Ricky replied.

"Do you know when he will be home?" Cato asked.

"Don't know. He's a reporter, and he doesn't keep any regular hours."

"We understand that" Cato replied.

"I can tell him you're looking for him and to call you when he gets home."

"That would be great. Here is my card with my number," Cato said as she handed Ricky a business card.

"I'll give it to him later tonight, if I see him."

"Thanks. We appreciate it."

Detective Cato and Detective Douglas left Ricky and headed for the patrol car. They saw Ricky walk up the flight of stairs and stuff the business card in the mail slot. Then Ricky walked away from the house and headed toward the corner grocery store.

"I think we need to come back later today," Cato said to Douglas as they headed for the car.

"You're right, Cato. We need to come back and catch this guy. To me something feels really wrong here."

"What makes you think that, Rick?"

"I just have a funny feeling. The hairs on my back are standing up. You know that when that happens, when I get a bad feeling, I'm usually right."

"I have worked enough years with you, Rick, to know you're seldom wrong," Cato replied.

"Let's get some dinner and come back later tonight."

"Roger that, Rick."

Chapter 47

The detectives stopped to get a bite to eat at a local hot dog vendor a mile away from Ray Chambers's house. The detectives wanted to hang around and cruise by the house a couple of times to scope out the neighborhood. Rick's antenna was going off, and Cato knew he was seldom wrong when it came to sniffing out crime details.

***

The first time the detectives traveled down Dickens Avenue in the patrol car, they saw Mike playing ball against a building.

"Hey, Rick, that boy there playing ball with the other kid is Mike, the paperboy we interviewed on Tuesday."

"Yep, that's the paperboy all right," replied Cato.

"Let's make another pass around Hoyne Avenue to see if Ray is home."

They drove around the block.

"Don't let the kid see us."

"The kid's playing ball with that other boy," replied Douglas.

After circling the block several times, they stopped in front of Ray's house on Hoyne Avenue. A light was on in the front room, so maybe they were going to get lucky and catch him at home. The detectives decided to park the car in front of the house and knock on the door once again. They both got out and walked up the flight of stairs. Detective Cato pushed the doorbell, and a few seconds later, the front door opened.

"Are you Ray Chambers?"

"Yes. I am Ray Chambers. What can I do for you two?"

"I am Detective Cato, and this is my partner, Detective Douglas." Both detectives flashed their badges, and Ray took a good look at them.

"What can I do for you, Detectives?" Ray asked.

"We are investigating a few cases regarding the recently deceased men Bass, Burger, Dirt, and Cagney. Are you aware of these men?" Detective Cato asked.

"I have been following these cases, and I have reported the news on these stories over the past two weeks. It's my job for the newspaper."

"Are you aware of any information above and beyond what is being released from the watch commander?" Detective Cato asked.

"What are you implying, Officer?" Ray replied.

"We are not implying anything. We just want to know what you know and if you can help provide information to help us solve the cases."

"I only know what I have reported in the *Chicago Today*."

"Are you sure, Ray?" Detective Cato asked once again.

"Guys. I go to the crime scenes and report on the news as it happens. I am just a reporter trying to make a living."

"We understand that you have knowledge of the crime scenes that most reporters don't have."

"I don't know what you guys are taking about," Ray fired back at Cato.

"We think you know more than you're letting on here, Ray."

"Detectives, I don't know what you're talking about," Ray fired back at Cato, with daggers in his eyes.

"We can do this the easy way or the hard way, Ray," Detective Cato said. "Just help us out. If you know something, please tell us so we can figure out who is doing this."

"As I said before, I don't know anything more than what I report on in the newspaper."

"Ray, are you leveling with us?" Detective Cato asked again.

"Yes, I just report on the news. I send my stories to my editor, and he puts them in the paper. That's it. No mystery and no magic."

"If you're lying, Ray, we will arrest you and throw you in jail," Detective Cato replied.

"I'm telling you—I don't know anything more than I already told you guys."

"Ok, Ray. But if we come back and find out you're holding out, we will bust you," Detective Douglas yelled.

"I understand, Detectives."

"Ray, we're going to go now, but we would like your cooperation. If you know something that might help us solve these crimes, we would greatly appreciative it if you shared the information."

"So, you're the good cop, Detective Cato, and you're the bad cop, Detective Douglas?"

"Ray, that is not necessary," Detective Cato replied.

"Ok. I'll try to help you out. If I find something out, I'll call you. Is that acceptable?"

"That would be fine, Ray. We need to work together here," Detective Cato said. "We left a card in your mailbox."

"Yes, I got it. Can I go have my dinner now?" Ray asked the detectives.

"We are done here, Ray. But we will be back."

"I am sure you two will be."

The detectives left the doorway of Ray Chambers's house and walked to their patrol car. As they got into the car, Rick and Cato looked at each other funny.

"He is dirty, Rick," Cato said.

"I agree, Cato. He is very dirty. We will need to do some investigative work on Ray Chambers."

The detectives drove out of the Bucktown neighborhood that night knowing that they would need to dig very deep into the background material on the reporter Ray Chambers. Something smelled foul here, and the reporter was hiding something.

Chapter 48

The detectives decided to take a ride by Ray Chambers's house that Thursday morning. Before they got involved in trying to investigate him, a drive by the neighborhood was warranted. They would have liked to catch Ray doing something illegal, but he was a reporter and could stand behind the First Amendment. The reporters liked the right-to-free-speech angle. Many reporters had used this same argument as a false front to avoid the detectives. Some had even gone as far as using this reasoning as a tool to bend the law. Both of the detectives had known this logic too well as an excuse not to help them find criminals. To the detectives this was a major pain in the ass. Some detectives liked to bend the law a little to get crimes solved. Cato and Douglas were not the type to bend the law. They did everything by the book. No exceptions. Their watch commander knew this was the case with these detectives and had full faith and confidence in them. If anyone could solve the cases of Bass, Burger, Dirt, and Cagney, Cato and Douglas were the team.

***

The detectives cruised down Dickens Avenue on their way to Hoyne Avenue to see Ray Chambers. They had to slow down in the middle of the street because two boys were bouncing a rubber baseball off the ledge of a building. They were blocking the street, so cars had to slow down so the boys could get out of the way. As the patrol car crossed by where the boys were playing, Cato noticed who the kids were.

"Hey, Rick, the kid with the glove is Mike, the kid we interviewed earlier this week."

"Yeah, he lives on this block," Rick replied.

Cato decided to stop across from the boys and interrupt their game.

"Hi, Mike. Remember us?" Cato shouted out the window.

"Yeah, I remember you two," Mike said as he and Tommy approached the patrol car.

"Who is winning today?" Cato asked.

"We just started this morning. This is my friend Tommy."

"Nice to meet you, Tommy. I am Detective Cato, and this is my partner, Detective Douglas."

"Hi," Tommy replied.

"What are you two detectives doing here this morning?" Mike asked.

"Oh, we are just here to see someone and do some follow-up on our investigations," Cato said in a quiet voice.

"Are you here to see Ray Chambers? He is gone."

"What do you mean, Mike?" Cato was puzzled.

"He left the neighborhood a few minutes ago. He almost ran us over."

"Do you know where he was going?" Cato asked.

"No. He was listening to a radio, and it was not playing music."

"What kind of radio?" Cato asked.

"It looked like one of those police scanners that everyone is talking about. Like the ones the truckers have. You know, with a microphone attached."

"Why do you think it was a police scanner?" Detective Cato asked.

"It looks like what you have in your car," Mike replied. "Right, Tommy?"

"Yep, looks like that one." Tommy pointed into the patrol car.

"You boys are very observant. Thanks for this bit of information."

"Can we get back to the game?" Tommy asked as he bounced the rubber ball on the street.

"Go ahead and play, Mike. Enjoy your game, and thanks for the conversation," Cato replied.

"Let's get going," Cato said to Rick.

"So that is how Ray is getting to the crime scenes and finding out about the victims. He is using a police scanner."

"Exactly."

***

The detectives decided to drive by the house of Ray Chambers for the heck of it. They knew based on what the boys said that he would not be home. This would be a wasted drive-by this morning.

"We need to get to the precinct and do some background work on Ray Chambers," Cato remarked.

"Yep. Can we get some breakfast on the way, or at least a coffee?"

"You're always hungry, aren't you?"

"Yep. Finding suspects always works up an appetite," Rick responded.

"We can get a coffee back at the precinct."

Chapter 49

The detectives were back at the Jefferson Park precinct at their desks later in the morning on Thursday. The drive-by at Ray's house had been a bust. But the stop to talk with the kids had been a gold mine. Cato and Douglas were at their desks, and they were digging through the case files. They were anticipating a summary report that needed to be prepared and submitted to the watch commander. A review of the facts on the cases was warranted, and a verbalization between the two detectives might pull a thread that had been overlooked. Sometimes the detectives were known to rehash the details over and over again to search for an overlooked fact.

The case file on Wally Bass had the following points of interest: male, twenty-two years of age, knife wound from ear to ear, six-inch blade, possibly drugged, body found on a chair, class of 1966 at Hamilton Technical High School. This file described an unidentified bloody fingerprint found on the light switch.

The case file on Kevin Burger had the following points of interest: male, twenty-two years of age, wrists slit, four-inch blade, scissors, found in the bedroom, class of 1966 at Hamilton Technical High School. This file also described an unidentified fingerprint on a pair of scissors.

The case file on Joe Dirt had the following points of interest: male, twenty-two years old, jumped off a building, minute traces of chloroform, suicide note, class of 1966 at Hamilton Technical High School. This file also described an unidentified fingerprint on the stairwell door.

The case file on Paul Cagney had the following points of interest: male, twenty-two years old, homeless, died of natural causes, minute traces of chloroform, eyes bloodshot, nose appeared pushed in, wrists had abrasions, class of 1966 at Hamilton Technical High School. This file also described a witness who had seen a blue '66 Chevy just before the body was found.

The file from the ME's office on Mike Conners had the following points of interest: male, twenty-two years of age, alcohol poisoning, natural causes, cardiac arrest, BAC was .30, three times the legal limit, possible suicide, eyes bloodshot, nose pushed in, minute traces of knockout drops, wrist abrasions, found in the parking lot, class of 1966 at Hamilton Technical High School. This file had been closed and never turned over to the watch commander. There had been an unidentified fingerprint on one of the many beer cans.

As the detectives read through the files over and over, nothing jumped off the page at them.

"So, what do we know about Ray Chambers?" Cato asked Douglas.

"Nothing. He is a reporter for the *Chicago Today*. He has no record, and there is absolutely nothing in his jacket." Douglas let out a sigh of hopelessness. "There is one thing here. Ray is a graduate of Hamilton Technical High School, but class of '65."

"So, Ray is one year older than all the victims."

"That is correct," Douglas replied.

"So, what is the connection, Rick? There has to be a connection among all these victims."

"Let's compare all the fingerprints we have from the crime scenes," Rick proposed to Cato.

The unidentified fingerprints were pulled from the cases of Bass, Burger, Dirt, and Conners. There were no prints on the Cagney file. The detectives made copies of all four. Then the photocopies of all four prints were transferred onto a blank plastic overhead sheet. They were stacked on top of each other on the overhead projector with the lamp on.

"Holy shit," said Cato.

"It was staring us right in the face," Rick replied.

"All four victims were murdered by the same person."

"Cato, how the heck did we miss this?"

"At least we can tell the watch commander we have some results."

"Now we have to find the person who matches this fingerprint," replied Rick.

"Let's try to run the fingerprint through our database of known criminals," Cato agreed.

***

The detectives walked down to the fingerprint department with the print. They needed to see who owned this fingerprint. The detectives filled out a request for the clerk at the fingerprint desk to search the database of recorded fingerprints. The attendant said it would take a little while because of other requests with higher priorities. The request would be turned around in about twenty-four hours, which was the normal time for a search through the paper file database. Detectives Cato and Douglas would now be able to tell their watch commander that they had some results, and they just needed a little bit of time to continue to work the case files.

"Hey, Rick, what do you think if we go and get Ray Chambers's fingerprints and see if they match our unidentified print?"

"Cato, I think that is an excellent idea."

"Let's put in another request to the fingerprint department for Ray Chambers," replied Cato.

"What if we strike out there?" Rick had an idea. "Let's go get his prints from Ray Chambers direct."

"How are we going to do that, Rick?"

"We could use the kid to get his prints."

"That is a fantastic idea," Cato replied.

"Or maybe we don't use the kid. How about going through his trash on garbage day?"

"That's an even better idea. If he drinks beer or pop in cans or bottles, his prints would be all over the empties," Cato said as he smiled like the Cheshire cat.

"Let's take a run out there today. He's probably still at work, and if we go into the alley, no one will even know we were there." Rick was smiling.

"Let's go back to Ray's house."

**

The detectives drove back to Ray's house. But this time they needed to be sneaky. They circled the block to look for Ray. There was no light on in the front room. So, they knew he still was not home from work. The detectives cruised the alley in the back of Hoyne Avenue. They located the trash cans, two of which had Ray's apartment number on them. The detectives parked the car next to the cans and left the engine running. They sprang to action, pulled the top off, and pulled out several glass jars and a few cans. Carefully, they put them into an evidence bag, closed the trash cans, and exited the alley just as fast as they came in. The detectives were sure they had their prize, and now they just needed to get the containers processed by the fingerprint department.

The fingerprint department would be closed by the time they got back to the precinct, so this would have to wait till Friday. They would turn in the evidence, get it printed, and keep their fingers crossed.

Chapter 50

It was Friday late in the afternoon, and Watch Commander Dane Hoy was looking for Detectives Cato and Douglas.

"Where are Cato and Douglas?" Officer Hoy yelled through the bullpen of the Jefferson Park precinct. All the officers in the room knew that these two were in serious trouble when the watch commander started yelling.

The desk sergeant, Art Reed, walked over to Hoy's office door to reply.

"I saw them both going down to the fingerprint department to get some test results on what they submitted earlier this morning."

"When you see them, please instruct them to get their butts into my office," Officer Hoy requested.

"Will do."

The desk sergeant did not want to be in the shoes of those detectives. The watch commander was hot under the collar, and he was going to get a pound of flesh out of them.

The two detectives returned from the fingerprint department with unhappy looks on their faces. The print submitted from the crime scene did not match anyone in the fingerprint database. What was also discouraging was that the prints for Ray Chambers from the dumpster dive event did not match the print from the crime scene either. Two strikes on this assumption they'd made. Another dead end.

"Hey, the watch commander wants to see you," Art Reed, the desk sergeant, said as he stood in front of their desks.

"Douglas, come on; the Watch Commander wants us," Cato said as she motioned with her finger.

"I'll be right there."

The two detectives walked into the office. Officer Hoy closed the door and did his pointing routine, telling them to park their butts in his two chairs.

"So, what progress have you two made this week?" Officer Hoy asked. "The chief is chewing out my ass on these cases. Please tell me you two have something."

Cato said, "We were running down a theory on the fingerprints. We compared them across multiple crime scenes. We have a fingerprint that matches the Bass, Burger, Dirt, and Conners crime files."

"Hold on. Did you say Conners? What happened to Cagney?" Officer Hoy asked.

"The Conners case was never submitted to us by the ME. But there was a partial fingerprint found at the scene on a beer can. The Cagney case had no fingerprints in the case file."

"Well, this is good news. I can tell the chief we are making progress," replied Officer Hoy.

"The bad news is we do not have any suspects," Cato said, responding to the watch commander's next thought.

"No suspects, Detective Cato?"

"That is correct. We do not have any suspects. The unidentified fingerprints do not match anyone in the database," Cato responded.

"Well, you two need to find one."

"Yes, we do."

"Get out of my office and get me some results." Officer Hoy barked out the order and pointed to the bullpen.

The two detectives left the office with their tails between their legs. They now knew that a killer was on the loose in the city, and the cases just went cold. What was also troubling was that the watch commander knew, and that the chief would be informed of this development soon. The whole city would figure it out, or it would leak somehow to the general public. Either way, the weekend press was going to be extremely hard on the police department of Chicago for not informing its readers that a killer was loose in the city.

Chapter 51

Friday was here again, and that meant it was time to collect from the paper route customers. Mike already had his GE radio fastened to the handlebars of his Sting-Ray bike and was ready to roll. As he left the house on Dickens, he turned it on to hear WLS 890 AM radio. Larry Lujack was on the radio today. The tune playing was "The End" by the Doors, and Mike was getting into the song. It seemed a little psychedelic, since the song was from the late '60s. Mike was guessing 1967 was when the album was released. This was the one thing Mike really enjoyed. Playing music and being outdoors delivering newspapers to the neighborhood. It was an early afternoon, and the ride to the newsstand would be down the middle of Hoyne Avenue. Mike wondered if Mary Crystal would be looking out for him as she had done so many times before. There was Mary Crystal sitting on her porch, watching him ride his bike.

"Make sure I get my paper today," Mary Crystal yelled toward Mike.

"Will do, Mrs. Crystal," Mike yelled back to her.

"Don't forget to watch out for those pesky cars."

Mike had heard this response from Mary Crystal so many times before. Mike waved at Mrs. Crystal as he passed her by.

***

THE GRUDGE LIST

Mike arrived at the newsstand and went to one of the high tables where there was a stack of papers waiting for the paperboys. He picked a corner spot in the room and started to roll, rubber band, and stuff the news pouch with papers. Mike had arrived a little early and was the only paperboy at the high table. Larry was in the back office and saw Mike by himself. Larry went over to Mike to see how he was doing.

"How is it going today, Mike?" Larry asked.

"Ok. I guess," Mike replied.

"I have not heard anything from the detectives since we had that meeting on Tuesday."

"So, no news is good news." Mike was kind of funny.

"That was a good one, Mike," Larry replied.

"It's Friday, and that means payday."

"You're correct, Mike."

"What do I do if I see Ray Chambers on my paper route?" Mike asked Larry.

"Just try to avoid him. I can make myself available when you go by his house."

"I have to knock on his door and collect for this week."

"Yes. That's right. Just don't say anything else to him," Larry responded.

"I'll try."

"Good boy. Now get out of here and deliver those papers."

***

Mike left the newsstand with fifty papers in his news pouch. His paper route would take him down Webster, Shakespeare, Dickens, and Mclean and then finish on Hoyne Avenue, where one Ray Chambers, newspaper reporter, would be sitting in waiting to ambush a little boy.

At least that was what Mike thought today. As Mike delivered papers and collected the money for this week, nothing out of the ordinary was happening. It was just a run-of-the-mill Friday afternoon in the summertime. The temperature was in the seventies, and the sun was still out. All in all, it was a really enjoyable day to be alive.

As Mike rounded the corner, he was headed to Ray Chambers's house on Hoyne Avenue. This was the second-to-last stop on his paper route. He stopped in front of Ray Chambers's house. He got off the bike and proceeded up the flight of stairs to ring the doorbell, deliver the paper, and collect this week's bill. No answer. Mike was relieved that Ray was not at home or not answering the doorbell. He started to go down the flight of stairs and was just on his bike ready to take off when a voice from below spoke.

"Are you Mike the paperboy?" said the stranger.

"Yes, I am Mike the paperboy."

"I'm Ricky, Ray's younger brother."

"Hi. I didn't know Ray had a younger brother."

"I'm his younger brother by just one year."

"Oh."

"I live in the garden apartment below Ray," Ricky replied.

"Ok. Nice to meet you. I have to finish my route. See you later."

"Hold on," said Ricky. "Ray said to pay you for the weekly papers if I saw the paperboy. Ray went to Lake Geneva for the weekend. He left on Thursday and will not be back until late Sunday night."

"I can wait till Monday then," Mike replied.

"Nonsense. Let me take care of the bill. Step inside so I can get my wallet and pay you."

Mike moved his bike to the lower landing of the garden apartment.

"You can step inside the foyer while I go get my wallet," Ricky said as he opened the door.

Mike eased into the foyer of Ricky's garden apartment. The door was open, and Ricky was looking for his wallet.

"It's here somewhere."

"I can come back on Monday when Ray is back," Mike replied.

"Just give me a second to find my wallet," Ricky repeated. "Oh, I left it in my car in the garage. Can you hang on just a little bit longer while I go get it?"

"Sure," Mike responded.

Ricky went to the garage to go and retrieve his wallet. At least that was where he thought he'd left it.

Out of the corner of his eye, Mike spotted a book on the coffee table just inside the front room. It looked like a Hamilton Technical High School yearbook. Mike moved a few steps inside the front room and was shocked by the book. It was the Hamilton Technical High School yearbook, 1966 edition. It was sitting there in plain sight. Mike knew he had only a few seconds before Ricky came back from the garage. *Should I open it or not?* Mike's little voice said to open it to page 228 and look. Mike decided he was going to peek in the book but make sure he did not get caught by Ricky. He turned to page 228, where Wally Bass was pictured. There he saw it. Wally Bass's picture had a circle and an *x* marked on the picture. The word "dead" was written under his face. Page 230 had Kevin Burger's picture with an *x* and the word "dead" on the bottom. There were an *x* and the word "dead" on Joe Dirt's picture, Paul Cagney's picture, and Mike Conners's picture. Mike had seen enough. As he started to close the book, a photo was sticking out between pages 240 and 241. It was a picture of Karen Mille.

On page 240 of the yearbook, a circle had been made around Karen's picture, but no words were written below her name. Mike could hear Ricky coming back from the garage. He closed the yearbook, pushed the picture back between the pages, and returned the yearbook to its exact spot on the coffee table, then moved to the foyer where Ricky told him to wait.

"I did leave my wallet in my car. Sorry about that, Mike," Ricky said as he looked at Mike.

Mike was in shock and did not know what to say.

"How much does Ray owe you?" Rick asked.

"Uh, uh, $1.40 for last week," Mike nervously answered.

"Here is two dollars. Is that enough?" Ricky asked Mike.

"Yep. That's fine. Thanks for the tip."

"Anytime. Thanks for the paper deliveries this week. I read the papers when Ray is done with them."

"Thanks." Mike quickly left the foyer of Ricky's house.

Mike got on his bike and headed for the last stop. Mary Crystal was the only one left for the delivery today; then Mike would be done until the second round of collections on Friday night. Mike was not sure of what he had just seen in the yearbook that Ricky had. He was not sure what to do. But he was extremely nervous about what he had just uncovered.

Chapter 52

This was another Friday night at the Boys' Clubhouse. Mike would enter through the yard, unlock the hatchway, then relock the door facing the yard and slip around to the alley along Dickens Avenue. Mike would wait for the other boys until he heard the signal. One knock followed by two knocks followed by three was the standard, but Mike had changed the signal this week due to a nosy neighbor poking around last week. The new signal was three knocks, then two knocks, and then one knock. The boys needed to be careful, so their parents did not find out what they were up to on a Friday night. The boys did not want to lose the clubhouse.

Mike heard three knocks, then two knocks, followed by one knock. He opened the hatchway. The three boys were together. Tommy, Johnny, and Danny all climbed into the Boys' Clubhouse.

"Boys. How's it hanging?" Mike asked.

Tommy said, "Fine."

Danny said, "Ok."

Johnny said, "It's your turn, Mike and Tommy, to buy the beer tonight."

"Everybody cough up two bucks," Mike replied and collected the two dollars from each of the boys.

"Let's go get the beer." Mike looked at Tommy and pointed to the hatchway. "We will be back in a couple of minutes."

***

Tommy and Mike left through the hatchway with the beer money. They were headed to the liquor store on Damen Avenue. They hung out in the alley next to the store until the right person came along.

"Mike, that guy bought us beer last time." Tommy pointed the person out to Mike.

"You're right."

"Mister, can you buy us some beer?" Mike said as they approached the stranger.

"Didn't I buy you boys beer before?" the stranger asked Mike and Tommy.

"Yep, you did. Two weeks ago," Mike replied.

"Same deal as last time?" the stranger repeated. "You give me eight bucks for two six-packs."

"Agreed."

Mike handed the stranger the money. A few minutes later, the stranger handed the boys a bag of cold beer. The objects in the bag looked and felt like two six-packs, so the boys were happy.

"Thanks, mister."

"Don't mention it. You never got this from me. Right?"

"Yep," the boys said as they walked into the dark alley with the prize.

***

The boys walked back to the shed through the back alleys of Damen Avenue and Dickens Avenue with two six-packs of cold beer. They were careful not to draw any attention to themselves from any wandering neighbors. They stayed in the shadows and were very stealthy on their way back. Once they got back to the hatchway in the alley, they used the ceremonial knock. The hatchway opened up. Mike handed the beer through the hatchway to Danny.

"What took so long?" Danny asked Mike.

"It took a few minutes. But we found the same guy we met two weeks ago. He didn't ask any questions and got us the beer."

"Good deal," Johnny replied.

As the boys pulled the beer from the bag, they noticed it was Budweiser beer instead of Schlitz.

"Hey, this is Budweiser," Danny said to the boys.

"We had Schlitz last week," Mike replied.

"Beer is beer. Give me one." Tommy pulled a beer from the plastic ring.

"Can we discuss something I found out today?" Mike blurted out to the boys.

"Sure, what's up?" Tommy replied.

"Remember how I told you guys I thought Ray Chambers could be a killer last week?"

"Yeah, we told you before we thought you were crazy," Danny replied.

"Well, I was only part right. The killer could be a Chambers, but not Ray; it could be Ricky."

"Who is Ricky?" Tommy asked.

"Ricky is Ray's younger brother who lives in the garden apartment below Ray."

"I didn't know Ray had a younger brother," Johnny remarked.

"I have seen him in the neighborhood before. I just didn't recognize him. He has a blue '66 Chevrolet Chevelle SS with bucket seats. A nice car," Danny replied.

"How did you find out about Ricky?" Tommy asked.

"I went to deliver the Friday afternoon paper to Ray's house and collect the weekly paper money, and he was not home. Just as I was about to leave, Ricky came out of the garden apartment. He made me wait in the foyer of his apartment so he could get his wallet. He paid the bill for Ray."

"So, what did you find out?" Johnny asked.

"Ricky had to go into the garage to get his wallet. So, I had time to wander into his front room. That's where I spotted the yearbook. You know, the Hamilton Technical High School 1966 edition."

"So what? Every student has a yearbook," Tommy replied.

"I opened the yearbook to page 228, where Wally Bass's picture was circled with an *x*, and below the photo he was marked dead. Then I found Kevin Burger, Joe Dirt, Paul Cagney, and Mike Conners. All the same way. A circle, an *x*, and marked dead."

"Shit, you stumbled into the killer's house," Tommy proclaimed.

"I found one more thing."

"What was that, Mike?" Danny asked.

"A photo of Karen Mille was falling out between pages 240 and 241, so I turned to that page. Her photo had been circled, but no *x* and no marking of 'dead' below the picture."

"What happened next, Mike?" Johnny asked.

"I heard Ricky coming back from the garage. So, I carefully put the yearbook back on the coffee table exactly the way I found it. I stepped back into the foyer and pretended nothing had happened."

"Weren't you nervous?" Tommy asked.

"Ricky gave me two bucks, and I got out of there as fast as my little legs could." Mike started to shake all over again.

"What are you going to do about this, Mike?" Tommy asked.

"I think I need to tell Larry at the newsstand and ask for some advice."

"Larry is a good guy. I like him," Tommy replied.

"I'll try to talk to Larry on Saturday if I get a chance."

"What about talking to the detectives?" Danny asked.

"I need to talk with Larry first," Mike replied. "I don't want to get Ray or Ricky in trouble for no reason."

"But Mike, what if you're right?" Tommy asked. "You may have poked a hornets' nest."

"Then I've got a target on my back, and I am going to feel some stinging."

"Let's just drink our beer, boys." Johnny tried to calm the boys down.

"Budweiser is the beer Harry Caray likes to sing with during the seventh-inning stretch at the Cubs games," Mike said as he made a toast with a can.

The boys finished their second beers and then quietly left the shed through the alley. Mike locked the hatchway behind the boys as they all left. Then Mike peeked out the doorway to exit through the yard. All four of the boys would meet up on the Dickens Avenue, pretending nothing was going on. It was just another Friday night in the city.

Chapter 53

Mike had decided to talk with Larry about what he had found at Ricky Chambers's house on Friday evening. The boys encouraged him to do so because they felt that he was a nervous wreck. Knowing someone is a possible killer is a grave burden to hold on to. Mike needed to get it off his chest, and Larry was probably the best person to do so with. He trusted Larry after all the conversations over the past couple of days. So, Mike would try to set something up with Larry for later in the day after the paper deliveries on Saturday.

***

As Mike arrived at the newsstand on Saturday morning, he saw the room was busy with all the paperboys. Each one was at a high table with a stack of papers in front of him. The papers were being rolled, rubber banded, and stuffed into the news pouches for today's deliveries. Mike saw Larry in the back office and went over to chat with him.

"Hey, Larry, can I talk with you later after the deliveries and collections today?" Mike asked.

"Sure. I should be here later today. But I will only be here until 2:00 p.m. I have some errands to run later today."

"Ok. I'll try to get here then," Mike replied.

THE GRUDGE LIST

"Is there anything I can help you with now?"

"No. I need to talk with you alone later," Mike replied.

"Ok, Mike, we can chat later today."

Mike went back to the stack of newspapers he'd started to roll earlier. He counted fifty newspapers for his customers. After the news pouch was stuffed and placed on the bike, Mike took off.

***

He made the deliveries and collected this week's bills from customers who had not been home on Friday. Ricky Chambers had paid the Ray Chambers bill. So that was one stop he knew he did not have to make. *Drive by and fling the paper at Ray's door and speed by*, he thought. *Don't stop; don't collect $200.* Mike was thinking of the game Monopoly as he said that to himself. He finished the paper route in record time, and all the collections were done for the week. Now to go back to the newsstand and drop off the collected cash to Larry.

***

Mike biked toward the newsstand with the final collections of the week. The song blaring through the radio was "Ob-La-Di, Ob-La-Da" by the Beatles. Larry Lujack was on and said the song was from the Beatles' 1968 White Album. Mike was enjoying the tune. As Mike got close to the building, he could see lots of paperboys there at the newsstand. They were all hanging around after their routes shooting the breeze. He knew Larry would not be alone for a while. So, he decided to turn in his money and come back later in the afternoon.

Mike left the newsstand and decided to go home and see if Tommy wanted to play ball. He would need to kill a few hours before the newsstand would empty out. As Mike arrived on Dickens Avenue, he saw that Tommy was already throwing the ball against the ledge of the building. It appeared that he was practicing for the next baseball game.

"Practicing, Tommy?" Mike asked.

"Yep. Just waiting for you, Mike."

"Are we playing today?"

"Sure, but I have to go see Larry and talk to him later in the afternoon."

"About the Ricky thing?" Tommy asked.

"Yep. About the Ricky thing."

The boys played ball for several hours. Tommy was winning 10 to 8 as they arrived at the bottom of the ninth inning.

"This is your last chance," Tommy said as he threw the ball to Mike.

Mike proceeded to hit the ball three times, and Tommy caught all three fly balls.

"I won today," Tommy said as he threw his mitt into the air.

"Yep. You beat me today. Can we do a rematch tomorrow?"

"We can."

"I've got to run now, Tommy. I have to see Larry at the newsstand."

"About the Ricky thing?"

"Yep."

***

Mike jumped on his bike and raced to the newsstand. He hoped that the office had cleared out of all the paperboys. He needed Larry alone to explain to him what he'd found out about Ricky Chambers and possibly get some advice on what to do about it.

Mike arrived at the newsstand just before 2:00 p.m. Larry was in the back office by himself. Mike walked back to Larry and looked around the office.

"What's up, Mike?" Larry asked.

"I need to talk to you about something," Mike answered.

"Sure. Tell me what's going on."

"I went to Ray Chambers's house on Friday to collect, and he was not home. His brother, Ricky Chambers, was home in the downstairs garden apartment and paid the bill for Ray."

"That's good," Larry responded.

"When I was waiting for Ricky to get his wallet, I noticed a yearbook on his coffee table."

"Oh."

"I peeked in the yearbook in the senior section. There were five pictures of students with a circle, an *x*, and 'dead' written below the name. The five names were Wally Bass, Kevin Burger, Joe Dirt, Paul Cagney, and Mike Conners."

"Mike, you're kidding me," Larry said.

"No, I am not." Mike raised his voice. "There was another name circled. The student was Karen Mille, and there was a photo of her. She was just circled. No *x* through the name, and she was not marked as dead."

"How the heck did you see this, Mike?" Larry asked.

"I wandered into his living room while he was in the garage looking for his wallet. The yearbook was on the coffee table in plain sight."

"Did Ricky figure out you'd looked in his book?" asked Larry.

"No. I don't think he saw me. I put the book back exactly as I saw it before and stepped back into the foyer. Then Ricky appeared from the garage and paid me for Ray's bill, and I left."

"Mike, you should consider yourself extremely lucky."

"I guess. I just couldn't get out of there fast enough."

"I think we need to call the detectives on this."

"I don't want to get Ray or Ricky in trouble because of something I saw," Mike responded.

"Let's talk with them to let them know what you saw."

Larry immediately picked up the phone to dial the detectives. He looked around for the business card and found it in the drawer. Then he dialed the number for the Jefferson Park precinct.

"I am trying to reach Detective Abbey Cato," Larry said as he spoke on the phone.

The desk sergeant said she would not be in until Monday. "Can I take a message and give it to her on Monday?"

"Can you have Detective Abbey Cato or Watch Commander Dane Hoy call Larry West as soon as possible when either one gets back in the office? She has my number already."

Larry hung up the phone and turned to Mike. "I'll give them an hour and then try to call back. The detective is not back in the office until Monday. I am hoping that the watch commander can help us out here."

"Ok."

"Don't say anything to anyone until we can get ahold of the detectives or someone at the precinct. Ok, Mike?"

"Sure." Mike nodded his head.

"Go home and lie low, Mike. Don't go near the Chambers house unless you're delivering the paper."

"I can do that." Mike left the newsstand and headed for his house on Dickens.

Larry was thinking to himself, *What did this little boy stumble into? Is Ricky Chambers or Ray Chambers a killer that is loose in the city? What are the detectives going to think about this? Is Mike safe delivering papers to the Chambers house?*

A lot of questions and no answers. It was going to be a long weekend for little Mike.

Chapter 54

He got into his blue '66 Chevrolet SS and drove to the Northwest Side of Chicago once again. Cruising up the Kennedy Expressway would take only twenty minutes. The exit for Narragansett was where he would get off. He headed south on Narragansett to the restaurant at the intersection of Gunnison Avenue. He knew she would be working at the restaurant until it closed early Sunday morning. The Pancake House was open until midnight during the week. During the weekend, they extended the closing until 2:00 a.m. Karen Mille was the manager and would have the last shift; he knew this from prior scouting trips to the restaurant. He parked his car in the corner of the lot, next to Karen's car, and waited till the closing hour.

He saw Karen exit the building at 2:15 a.m. all alone. She saw the car next to hers and thought, *Oh, he wants to talk once again.* As Karen got close to his car, the passenger-side door opened up.

"Hi, Karen. Can we talk?" Ricky asked.

"What do you want, Ricky?" Karen replied.

"Can we just talk a little bit in my car?"

Karen was hesitant to get into the passenger side of his car. She just wanted to go home after her shift.

"I brought you some Baileys and coffee, your favorite."

"I could use one," Karen replied. She got into the passenger side of the car and motioned with her hand. "Give me a drink."

Ricky poured a Baileys and coffee into a plastic cup that he had already put an ounce of chloroform in. He figured this would be enough to knock her out for a little while.

"Why did you not want to go out last weekend?" Ricky asked.

"We had a good thing going, and then you messed it up. You got drunk and were mean to me. I hate when you do that."

"I can change."

"I don't think so."

"Give me another chance?" Ricky asked.

"Why should I?"

"I love you."

"You're no good for me, Ricky," Karen said as she finished the drink.

"You're the one and only girl for me. Ever since high school, I knew you and I were meant to be together."

"You're crazy, and you always drink too much."

"Well, if I can't have you, then no one can."

"Now I know you're crazy," Karen said, beginning to slur her speech.

She tried to reach for the door handle to get out, but her hands did not seem to be working. At this point Ricky got the rag with more chloroform out and placed it over her nose. Karen struggled just a bit, but it was too late. Her limp body fell slightly forward in the passenger seat.

Ricky got the keys out of her purse and unlocked her car. He picked Karen up out of the passenger seat and placed her in the driver's side of her car. From his bag in the back seat, he retrieved a gun. It was a .22-caliber J-22 made by Jennings Firearms. He placed the gun in her right hand. He had ejected one shell from the magazine, as if Karen had fired it into her right temple. But the bullet that killed her would be fired from the Walther PPQ .22-caliber handgun by Ricky.

He placed a pillow on the right side of Karen's head and aimed the Walther. He fired a single shot, which was mostly muffled by the pillow. Karen's head snapped back against the window, nearly shattering the window. The bullet entered the right side and never came out of her skull. Ricky pulled the pillow away and could see a massive amount of blood starting to ooze out of her skull. He threw the pillow into the trunk of his car. He did not want to leave any evidence.

Ricky surveyed the crime scene before he left. It looked to him as if Karen had taken her life with a gunshot to the right temple. The J-22 had been purchased at a gun show in Wisconsin and would not be traced to him. The Baileys and coffee he had offered her were in his car. That evidence would be thrown away later in the morning. Her purse would need to be placed on the passenger seat, so he placed it there, facing Karen. He left the car keys on the floorboard of the driver's side of the car. One last look and he was gone from the parking lot of the Pancake House.

This was the sixth and final victim on the grudge list. All these victims had wronged him during an embarrassing time in his life as a senior at Hamilton Technical High School.

Wally Bass had stolen his lunch money and pushed him down on the floor, breaking his wrist.

Kevin Burger had snapped a towel at his leg during gym class, which had caused his leg to bleed.

Joe Dirt had hit him during a dodgeball game and broken his nose.

Paul Cagney had pushed him into a pond where a Canada goose had attacked him in the rear, and several stiches were required.

Mike Conners had jammed a baton into his hand during the 440 relay, giving him an injury to his index finger that required surgery.

He had asked Karen Mille to the prom, and she'd stood him up.

All these students had made his life in high school unbearable. Ricky had decided he was going to get even once they were all out of high school. He'd done what he had intended to do. They were all gone now. Ricky was the last one standing.

***

It was time to get back to Bucktown. Ricky quietly exited the parking lot of the Pancake House and headed back home. The Kennedy Expressway would be empty at 2:30 in the morning. He could take his time since there was little traffic on the road.

The list was now complete. He was proud of himself. He had killed six classmates and not gotten caught.

Chapter 55

The Gonnella bread truck was making the daily delivery of baked goods to the Pancake House at 5:00 a.m. on Sunday. The driver pulled up to the back door as normal. He knocked on the door because it was locked. He would open the door, roll the baked goods into the back room, and leave the invoice. This morning it was completely different. The door was locked, and there was no one to greet him. The delivery man knew something was not quite right this morning. He looked to the back of the parking lot and saw someone in the driver's side of the only car around. He walked over to get a better look, and that was when he figured out that he should call the police.

***

The police officer arrived within five minutes of the 911 call from the Gonnella driver. The crime scene was roped off with yellow tape: "Police Line Do Not Cross." Then a flood of police personnel arrived. The police, the detectives, the coroner, and the ME were all on-site, looking at the body of Karen Mille.

The watch commander on duty was called by the dispatch officer and in turn called Detectives Cato and Douglas to be activated and sent to the crime scene. Since they were both off duty, home, and sleeping, the watch commander called to wake them up. They both were told to get up and immediately go to the Pancake House crime scene to take charge. The detectives were up, dressed, and on the scene in twenty minutes.

***

At the crime scene of the death of Karen Mille, the detectives were reviewing the body in the car.

"Did anyone move the body?" asked Detective Cato of the officer on-site.

"No, ma'am," said Officer Torrance.

"Rick, this looks like a suicide on its face."

"Agreed," replied Cato.

"Let's get the ME's opinion before we make any conclusions."

"Officer Torrance, do we have the victim's name?" Cato asked.

"Yes. The deceased is Karen Mille. Her driver's license was found in her purse, which was lying on the passenger side of the car."

"Who found the body?"

"That would be the bakery driver this morning. He is over there."

"Did you get a statement from him?" the detective asked.

"Yes, we did. He is anxious to get going. He has a lot of early-morning deliveries to make. He also said he thinks the woman is the Pancake House manager but is not a hundred percent sure."

"If you have all his information, kick him loose. Can you follow up on the manager status?"

"Will do," said Officer Torrance as he walked over to the delivery guy and let him go.

As Detective Cato was looking at the victim more closely, she took some notes and wrote them down onto her six-inch-by-three-inch pad. The victim was Karen Mille, manager of the Pancake House, which was to be confirmed. Gunshot in the right temple. A J-22 handgun had been found in her right hand. Her purse was on the passenger seat. Car keys had been found on the floorboard. The driver's window had been smashed but not broken. The car was parked in the far back corner of the lot. *Looks like a perfect ambush situation.* Detective Cato thought that last item but did not write it on the pad.

"Hey, Rick, do we have enough on this case for now?"

"Yep. We should let the ME process the scene and get us a report."

"Do you want to go and get some breakfast?" Cato motioned that they should get out of there.

"Yes. I am hungry this morning," Rick replied.

"Let's not go to the Pancake House."

"Agreed."

"International House of Pancakes ok with you?"

"Sure. Anywhere but around here."

***

The two detectives drove away from the crime scene and headed for some breakfast. They had both seen death many times, and it had never affected their appetites.

Chapter 56

The detectives were in the precinct early Monday morning. The criminal investigations were not getting solved. More work was being added to the existing case load of Wally Bass, Kevin Burger, Joe Dirt, Paul Cagney, and Mike Conners. The Sunday case of Karen Mille was just another file, and it appeared that the detectives were floundering, with no results. There were no suspects who matched the fingerprint found on the previous cases. But Detective Cato thought that they were going to get a big break. She could feel something coming and just did not know where it was going to come from.

The detectives received the ME's summary report on the death of Karen Mille from the desk sergeant. The deceased, Karen Mille, had died of a single gunshot wound to the right temple. Death was instantaneous due to the blood loss from the head wound. Karen had been a twenty-two-year-old woman. She'd been the manager of the Pancake House. The gunshot was consistent with a .22-caliber gun, and a J-22 had been found on the scene. Her car keys had been found on the driver's side floorboard. A purse had been found on the passenger seat. Her Illinois driver's license identified her as Karren Mille. A blood toxicology report showed minute trace amounts of chloroform in her blood stream. A partial fingerprint had been found on the right side of the J-22 handgun. This fingerprint did not match the victim's.

The magazine had a seven-round capacity, and only one round was missing. The slug had been retrieved out of the victim's skull. The bullet had bounced around her head, causing several perforations of the membranes of the skull. The death of the victim had been labeled a suicide, pending the detectives' investigation.

After Cato and Douglas reviewed the report, they both agreed that the ME had thrown this case over the wall to them. They would be stuck investigating the case to determine if this was a homicide.

"Hey, Douglas, what do you think about this Karen Mille case?"

"I think my girlfriend just dumped it in our laps," Rick replied.

"So, she is your girlfriend now?"

"Kinda sorta."

"I've got an idea." Cato turned to Rick. "Let's take that single fingerprint and get the department to run it through the database."

"I think that's a good idea," Rick responded.

"Let me take the case file down to the fingerprint department to see what they can come up with."

"Sounds good." Rick agreed this was an appropriate course of action.

***

Cato walked down to the fingerprint department and turned the case file over to the desk sergeant on duty. The sergeant looked through the case file and copied the fingerprint sheet and handed the case file back to Cato. She was informed that it would take at least twenty-four hours because of the backlog of cases. The results would be available on Tuesday. Cato left and returned to her desk, where Rick was already waiting.

THE GRUDGE LIST

***

The desk sergeant walked over to Detective Cato.

"Hey, you have a message from Saturday. A guy by the name of Larry West wanted you to call him when you got back in the office, and it did not seem urgent. He did not leave his number. He said you already had it."

"Did he say what it was about?" Detective Cato asked.

"No. He said that it was important, and he requested that you or Detective Douglas or the watch commander call him back."

"Thanks," said Detective Cato. "You should have tried to contact me over the weekend." "Hey, Rick, we got a message from Larry West."

"What does he want this time?" Rick responded.

"Don't know. Says its important."

"Do you want to call him or go visit?"

"Why don't we go take a drive out there later today? This way we can do another drive by the Ray Chambers place," Detective Cato said with a devious smile.

"Trying to catch Ray with his pants down."

"Not a bad idea, Rick."

***

The detectives decided to drive to the Bucktown neighborhood Monday afternoon. They had paperwork to finish before getting out of the precinct. They intended to snoop around the house of Ray Chambers and see what the newsstand manager Larry West wanted.

Chapter 57

The drive from the Jefferson Park precinct to Bucktown did not take long. The detectives were trying to drive by Ray Chambers's house and catch him off guard. They did not know it, but he was downtown at his office today.

The detectives pulled up to the front of Ray's house, parked the car, and walked up the single flight of stairs to the second floor of the house on Hoyne Avenue. Ray was not home when they rang the doorbell. The detectives had struck out today. As they were about to leave, a door from below opened. Ricky walked out from the garden apartment.

"He is not home," said Ricky.

"Oh. Thanks," Detective Cato replied.

"You two missed him once again. He is at work today," said Ricky.

"Nice to see you again, Ricky. Do you know when Ray will be home?" Detective Cato asked.

"No. He is a reporter and does not have normal hours. He is always chasing down a story."

"That is a reporter's life."

"I guess."

"Can you tell him we stopped by again, and we will be in touch?" Detective Cato requested.

"Sure. I can pass the message along to him. When I see him."

"Have a nice day," the detectives said as they got into the patrol car and left.

The detectives drove down Hoyne Avenue and then turned onto Dickens Avenue, away from the Chambers house, and headed east. They noticed that the boy Mike was playing street ball at the same spot as they had witnessed last week. Mike and Tommy were playing with a rubber ball across the street. As the detectives approached, the boys had to stop to let the car pass. But the car did not drive by. The detectives stopped perpendicular to the boys' baseball game.

"Hi, Mike. How are you today?" Detective Cato yelled out the window.

The boys looked over at the patrol car. "Oh, hi, Detective Cato," Mike said as he approached the car.

"Who is winning?"

"We just started our game. It's in the first inning," Mike replied.

"If we were younger, we would get out and play with you two."

"Are you here to see Ray again?" Mike asked.

"Well, kinda sorta," Detective Cato replied.

"We saw him go to work early this morning. I don't think he is home right now."

"We already visited Ray's house. You're right. He went to work early this morning. We did talk to his brother Ricky."

At this point Mike started to shake. "You did?"

"What's the matter with you, Mike? You're shaking," said Detective Cato.

"Oh, nothing," Mike said as he pulled back from the patrol car.

"Go on and play, boys. We have to see someone around the corner." Detective Cato drove the patrol car away.

"Mike, are they going to see Larry?" Tommy asked.

"Yep. They are. I'd better go get my bike and get over to the newsstand. I have a funny feeling they are going to be talking about what I found out on Friday."

Mike left Tommy and headed for his house. He would get the bike out and ride as fast as he could to the newsstand. Since the detectives had a head start, Mike would be there shortly after they parked the patrol car. The detectives would be grilling Larry about what Mike had found out at Ricky's house and then told Larry. Mike was sure that they would want to hear it from him directly.

***

Mike arrived at the newsstand and saw that the patrol car was parked in front of the office. He left his bike next to the doorway and walked in to see Larry, Detective Cato, and Detective Douglas all in the back room.

There were no other paperboys in the office. The place was empty except for three adults and one kid.

"Mike, nice to see you. Come join us in the office," Larry said as he motioned for him to come over. "You remember Detective Cato and Detective Douglas."

"Yes, I remember them."

"Larry called and left us a message on Saturday. Said you may have information on something?" Detective Cato asked.

"Well, I saw something on Friday, and I don't want to get anyone in trouble."

"What was it that you saw, Mike?"

"I was collecting the weekly paper money for the customer Ray Chambers, but Ricky paid for the paper this week."

THE GRUDGE LIST

"So, what's so special about that?" Detective Cato asked.

"He had a yearbook on his coffee table. I peeked into it and saw something."

"What did you see, Mike?" Detective Cato asked gently.

"In the Hamilton Technical High School yearbook, in the senior section, he had five students circled, with *x*'s through their faces and the word 'dead' underneath their pictures. They were Wally Bass, Kevin Burger, Joe Dirt, Paul Cagney, and Mike Conners."

"Did Ricky see you look in the yearbook?"

"No. He was in the garage looking for his wallet. I put the yearbook back on his coffee table exactly how I found it."

"So, you're sure he did not notice you looked in the book?"

"I am sure he did not notice me peek."

"What happened next?" asked Cato.

"Ricky paid me two bucks for the $1.40 weekly paper bill, and I got the heck out of there. He said that Ray was at Lake Geneva until Sunday night."

"So, you have not confronted Ray or Ricky about what you saw in the yearbook?" Cato asked.

"I just told Larry about this."

"Did you tell anyone else?"

"Well, I told my boys."

"Who else?"

"That's it. Tommy, Johnny, and Danny. Larry too."

"Ok, let's try to keep this to ourselves."

"There was one more thing," Mike replied.

"What else did you see, Mike?"

"There was a photo of a student between the pages. It was falling out of the book. I turned to that page, and the photo in the book was of Karen Mille. The picture had a circle around it. There was no *x*, and there were no words below her picture."

"Mike, thanks for talking with us this afternoon. Why don't you go home and try not to talk about this to anyone? Let us get a chance to investigate if there is a connection here to what you found and what is going on." Detective Cato walked Mike to the door.

Rick looked at Abbey and said to Larry, "Do you think that Mike is making this up? Does he have an active imagination?"

"No, he is on the level. As I told you two before, Mike is one of my best and brightest paperboys in Bucktown."

Cato said, "You need to keep an eye on this kid. He could be in serious danger if this information is true."

Douglas said, "We need to investigate this as quickly as possible, Abbey."

Larry said, "I will go out of my way to watch Mike and try to keep him safe."

"As long as Ray and Ricky do not know Mike knows about them, he is most likely safe to deliver papers like normal. If Mike were to stop delivering papers to Ray Chambers, that is when they might suspect something. You and Mike need to operate as if nothing is going on."

"That is a tall order, Detective Cato," Larry replied.

"I know, but we need to keep this under the radar. We cannot let it out that we know about Ricky, or Ray for that matter. We need time to investigate them both."

Larry started to rub his index finger on the side of his head. "I have a headache about this."

"This is not easy for us either," Detective Cato replied.

"Let's get out of here, Cato, and leave Larry alone." Rick pointed to the door.

"Thanks for the information, Larry. We will be in touch." The detective reached for Larry's hand and shook it as a goodbye gesture.

As the detectives got into the patrol car, they both looked at each other. "Do you think the kid's story is legit?" Cato asked Rick.

"Don't know, but if I were a betting man, Cato, I would say yes."

"We need to get back to the precinct and take a really hard look at Ricky Chambers. We may want to ask the watch commander if an arrest should be made. Just in case the connection is too close to the possible victim."

"Agreed," Rick replied.

"Do you think the death of Karen Mille on Sunday was just a coincidence with what Mike said, that she had a circle around her picture in the yearbook?"

"Well, this coincidence just became a strong assumption of guilt. The little voice inside me is saying that all these things are connected somehow."

"Let's get back to the precinct and do some digging on Ricky."

"Agreed."

Chapter 58

Mike said farewell to his mom and once again got on his bike to head to the newsstand. It was Monday, and that meant the afternoon paper had to be delivered by 4:30 p.m. But there were fifteen minutes that Mike would use to scrounge around looking for pop bottles. He had to get his fix of some sweet candy before he did his paper route. He had to get his sugar buzz like any kid in the neighborhood. So, he set off to collect glass pop bottles, or empties, as they were called, along the streets and sidewalks in the neighborhood. For each empty bottle, the local stores would give you two cents. This was the refund set by the state of Illinois so that all glass pop bottles would be recycled. The radio on the bike was tuned to WLS 890 AM with Larry Lujack today. The song playing was "Burn Down the Mission" by Elton John. This tune was from the *Tumbleweed Connection* album, as the DJ would announce after the song finished. Mike sang along with the music and collected pop bottles. After cruising the streets and picking up the bottles, he had accumulated twenty in his news pouch bag. That was enough for him to go to the store to get forty cents' worth of candy. There were several mom-and-pop stores that took the returns for cash and then exchanged the cash for candy. This was a very lucrative market. There was the Red store on Dickens, the White store on Charleston, the Jenos store on McLean, and the Skippy's store on Webster. All the stores were mom-and-pop grocery stores where the owners lived on the second floor and operated a business out of the first floor. Mike's favorite store was the Red store. This was the one on his block, and they knew him very well. He could get some extras from this store owner because his mom would send him here during the week for groceries. He was a regular customer.

Mike wandered into the Red store with his bottles and placed them on the counter.

"So how many you got today, Mike?" the storekeeper asked.

"I got twenty bottles today," Mike replied.

"That's forty cents in returns. Do you want the cash or candy, Mike?"

"Candy of course."

"Pick out what you want, and I'll put it in a bag for you."

"Thanks."

Mike picked out an assortment of candies, and the storekeeper dropped them into a paper bag.

"Here are a couple of extra Twizzlers for you. You're such a good boy."

"Thanks, Mrs. Red."

"Call me Helen."

"Thanks, Helen."

Mike left the Red store with a bag of candy and knew this sugar buzz would carry him the entire length of the paper route for today.

Mike got back on his bike, and a new tune was on the radio. The DJ Larry Lujack had announced that the song to be played after the commercial was "Moon Dance" from the album *Moon Dance*, by Van Morrison. He proceeded down the middle of Hoyne Avenue, and there was Mary Crystal on her porch, watching him ride his bike.

"Mike, you be careful."

"Will do, Mrs. Crystal," Mike replied.

"Watch out for those pesky cars."

Mike waved at Mary and mumbled under his breath, "Doesn't she have anything better to do than watch me?" He continued on his ride to the newsstand.

***

Mike arrived at the newsstand as all the other boys were arriving. He took an open place at the high table where a stack of papers was waiting. He started to roll, rubber band, and stuff the news pouch with his papers. Once he counted fifty papers, he stopped. This would be enough for the Monday afternoon delivery. He was just about to leave when Larry motioned to him to come back into the back office.

"Hey, Mike, can you come back here?" Larry asked.

"What's up, Larry?"

"Have you had a chance to read the Monday afternoon *Chicago Today*?"

"No, I just got here and started to roll the papers for delivery."

Larry opened the paper on his desk to show Mike a news story. He flipped through the pages until he got to page 86. There it was. A story about Karen Mille, who had committed suicide Sunday morning in the parking lot of the Pancake House on Gunnison Avenue.

"I thought you would want to see this," Larry said as he looked at Mike.

"Oh my god! I am in deep trouble."

"No, you're not, Mike. We told the detectives about this on Monday."

"But this happened on Sunday."

"I know."

"We could have prevented this."

"We don't know that," Larry replied.

"Larry, we knew about this before it happened." Mike's body started to shake.

"Mike, you and I could not have known this was going to happen."

"But we could have done something about it."

"Don't beat yourself up about this. I called the detectives. They did not pick up the message in time."

"But Larry, this girl Karen is dead because we messed up."

"Mike, relax. Don't get so worked up about this. The detectives thought you had an overactive imagination. I told them the opposite of what they were implying. I told them you were a very bright boy and not to underestimate your smarts."

"But Karen is still dead. It's our fault."

"Mike, we couldn't know this was going to happen."

"Are we in trouble with the police?"

"That I could not tell you," Larry replied. "I'll call the detectives and talk with them in a couple of minutes."

"What do I do if I see Ricky or Ray?"

"Just fling the paper at them and ride your bike extremely fast past them. Don't stop and say one word. Just keep pedaling by."

"That I can do."

"Now go deliver your papers."

Mike left the back office and was shaking all the way to the doorway.

Larry was going to give Mike twenty minutes and then drive over to Hoyne Avenue. He would park his car across the street from Ray Chambers's house so he could keep an eye on Mike as he delivered his paper to the customer's doorstep.

Larry parked across the street and watched for Mike. He saw the paperboy riding down the street and flinging his papers. Mike threw the paper for Ray Chambers right at the door with amazing accuracy. He was safe today. At least one more day for the little paperboy.

Chapter 59

The detectives were in the precinct office early Tuesday morning. They knew that the watch commander was going to be looking for them. The first order of business was to get the results of the fingerprint submission from the Karen Mille case.

"Hey, Rick, I am going to run down to the fingerprint department to get the results on the fingerprint submission from Monday."

"That sounds like a good idea, Cato."

"You stay here and hold down the fort in case you-know-who is looking for us."

"You mean the watch commander?"

"Yep. He will want an update," Cato said as she left the desk.

Detective Cato walked down to the fingerprint department to get the Karen Mille fingerprint results. The desk clerk on duty saw her coming and handed her the file.

"Sorry, Detective—there were no matches found in the database for the print you submitted," Officer York apologized.

"You don't have to say you're sorry, Jane. I was hoping you gals could hit me a home run."

"By matching the print?" Jane replied.

"Absolutely," Cato replied.

"The person that partial right index finger belongs to is not in our database."

"Thanks, Officer York."

"You can call me Jane."

"Thanks, Officer Jane."

"You're welcome. Better luck next time."

Detective Cato returned to the bullpen, where Rick was anxiously awaiting her return.

"Was there a match?" Rick asked.

"Nope. Dead end. No match."

"Don't look now, but the watch commander is headed in our direction."

"Cato, Douglas, my office," Watch Commander Dane Hoy barked at the detectives.

The two of them walked over to the watch commander's office. As they entered, he pointed to the seats in front of the desk. They both knew that meant to park their butts in those seats. As they did that, Officer Hoy closed the door and sat down in his chair behind the desk.

"Well, what update can you provide me on your five victims and now six?" asked Officer Hoy.

"We just got the results on a fingerprint that was lifted off the J-22 handgun that Karen Mille killed herself with," Detective Cato replied.

"What did you find out, Detective Cato?"

"The fingerprint does not match anyone in our database. So, it's a dead end as of now."

"The chief is chewing my butt out on the lack of results on these unsolved cases. You two need to get some results." Officer Hoy was showing a bit of frustration in his voice.

"We do have a theory that we're working, but it's not fully baked," said Detective Cato.

"What theory?" The watch commander asked.

"Rick and I are reviewing a possible suspect the paperboy thinks is the killer. He saw pictures in a yearbook with circles around them and *x*'s over them and the word 'dead' listed below each picture."

"Did you two just make this shit up?"

"No, we did not. He also said that the sixth victim, Karen Mille, had a circle around her picture but had no *x* or 'dead' written below the photo."

"Who is this paperboy again, Cato?"

"His name is Mike Peters, and he delivers the *Chicago Today*. He found the yearbook in one of his customers' houses when he was collecting the weekly bill for the paper."

"Who was the customer?"

"The customer was Ricky Chambers. He is the brother of the reporter Ray Chambers."

"Oh. He is the reporter who has been causing the chief to breathe down my back on these cases. His paper has been printing rather inflammatory reports about the precinct," Officer Hoy said as he rolled his head.

"We thought that Ray Chambers was the killer, but the fingerprints did not match."

"What do you mean his fingerprints did not match, Cato?"

"Rick and I pulled some glass bottles out of his trash, and we tried to run the prints from the containers to see if they matched. But they did not."

"Nice trick, Cato."

"We thought so."

"Don't get ahead of your skis," the watch commander replied.

"We need to do some research on Ricky Chambers now," said Detective Cato.

"Because of what the kid saw?"

"Yes."

"Well, get out of my office and get to it," the watch commander said as he pointed to the door.

The detectives got up and left his office.

As the detectives sat down at their desks, the phone rang, and Cato picked it up.

"Hello, this is Detective Cato."

"Hi, this is Larry West from the newsstand."

"Hi, Larry. How can I help you?"

"We saw the news of the suicide of Karen Mille in the *Chicago Today* yesterday. The paperboy Mike thinks her death is his fault."

"It is not his fault, Larry. This was going to happen regardless of what he saw the other day."

"Well, that's somewhat comforting, Detective Cato, but Karen is still dead."

"Yes, I understand that fact, Larry. But Mike could not have done anything about it."

"Well, the little boy is feeling really bad about the situation."

"What if we come down there today and try to talk with him?" Detective Cato asked.

"I think that is a really promising idea. Your presence face to face with Mike to explain that he had nothing to do with it will go a long way to calm his nerves. The boy has been a nervous wreck the past couple of days."

"We will try to get down there later today and have a talk with Mike."

"Thanks. A conversation with the boy would calm him down."

"We can do that."

"How is the investigation progressing?" Larry asked.

"We are continuing to do some background checks and research on possible suspects. We are getting close."

"Thanks for this update, Detective Cato." Larry hung up the phone.

Detective Cato was stretching that update to Larry, and Rick knew it as well. The two of them knew they would need to have a conversation with a little paperboy later in the day.

Chapter 60

The detectives decided to go see Mike after lunch on Tuesday. They figured he would be playing in the neighborhood and that they should try to catch him before he had to go to the newsstand to deliver the papers. They cruised down Dickens Avenue, and there was Mike, playing street baseball with another boy. They pulled the patrol car alongside the boys and got out to have a chat with Mike.

"Mike, you got a minute?" Detective Cato yelled toward Mike and Tommy.

Mike looked at Tommy and then the patrol car. He slowly walked over to the detectives who were leaning on the patrol car.

"Hi, Detectives," Mike replied.

"We understand you feel bad about the death of Karen Mille," Detective Cato said.

"Well, I knew something about it, and then it happened. You two did not do anything about the information."

"Mike, how could you or Rick or I have known this was going to happen?"

"Well, it did, Detective Cato. It happened. Karen Mille is dead."

"Mike, please don't beat yourself up on this. No one could have known about what was going to happen to Karen."

"Did she commit suicide like the papers said, or was she murdered?" Mike asked.

"Rick and I are not sure. The crime scene appears to show a suicide, but we are not sure on this one."

"Well, when will you be sure if it was suicide or murder?" Mike asked.

"We need to investigate the crime and do our homework to find out," Detective Cato replied.

"Are you here to arrest Ricky Chambers?" Mike asked.

"No. We are here to question him and see if he has a reasonable alibi for Sunday morning. We have no evidence that would lead us to believe that Ricky Chambers killed Karen Mille."

"But I saw her picture in the yearbook with the circle."

"Yes, we know, Mike, but that's not hard evidence of a crime. Anyone could have done that."

"Done what?"

"Circled someone's picture in a yearbook."

"When are you going to talk with Ricky Chambers?"

"Right after we finish this conversation with you," Detective Cato replied.

"Rick doesn't say much, does he?" Mike asked.

"No. He is a very silent partner," Detective Cato replied. "That's the way I like my partner."

Rick just nodded his head up and down in agreement.

"I am still not happy with the two of you. How are you going to protect me if Ricky Chambers comes after me for snitching on him?" Mike asked.

"We are trying to keep you completely out of this Mike. I do not want you involved in any way," replied Detective Cato.

"But I am involved. I am the one who looked in Ricky's yearbook."

"Yes, we know, Mike. Can you just give us some time to investigate Ricky Chambers?"

"Well, I am going to avoid his garden apartment. If I see him and I am delivering the paper, I will just ride right by and not deliver Ray Chambers's paper."

"Mike, I think that would be the right approach to take until we can dig something up on him."

"You two get back to me or Larry just as soon as you know something."

"That we can do, Mike. You will be the first to know."

"Thanks. Hey, Tommy, let's get back to the game," Mike said as he turned his head.

"Thanks, Mike. Enjoy your game." Detective Cato and Detective Douglas got back in the car and drove off.

The detectives planned to swing by the residence of Ricky Chambers to ask him some questions. They were really trying to make sure he had a reasonable alibi for Sunday morning. Was Ricky Chambers the killer of Karen Mille, or had she committed suicide? This was the question they were asking themselves in the car as they drove west down Dickens Avenue. They knew the destination was right around the corner, on Hoyne Avenue.

The detectives pulled up in front of the residence of Ray Chambers and parked right in front of the house, on the east side of the street. They both exited the patrol car and went down the flight of stairs to the garden apartment. They rang the doorbell, but no one answered the door. Several more times they rang the doorbell, and again, no one answered. It was just their luck that Ricky was not home. Since the detectives did not have a work address for Ricky, a second visit back to the Hoyne Avenue address was going to be necessary. The detectives were just about to leave when Rick had an idea.

"Wait a minute," said Detective Douglas. "Let's try the second floor, where Ray lives."

They walked up the flight of stairs, and there was no answer there either. Ray Chambers wasn't home either.

"Let's head back to the precinct, Rick, and see if we can dig up a work address on Ricky Chambers."

"Sounds good, Cato."

**

The detectives got back in their patrol car and headed back to the precinct. They needed to do some investigative work on Ricky Chambers. There was a bit of pressure that the little boy Mike had placed on the detectives' shoulders for the victim Karen Mille. Cato and Rick discussed it and agreed that it was beyond their control. So, they left it alone for now.

Chapter 61

He got into his blue '66 Chevrolet Chevelle SS and drove to Lake Geneva on Tuesday morning. North on I-94 to I-41 and then to Highway 50 to Wisconsin was the route that Ricky had traveled so many times as a child. The distance was about eighty miles, and it would take only about an hour and a half to get there. He was going to his childhood cabin in the woods. The same cabin that his parents had left him and Ray after their tragic death.

***

The cabin was on Lake Geneva, just a few minutes from the downtown area. This was a secluded spot on a beautiful lake that was fed by several rivers and streams. The lake was well known for good fishing and contained largemouth bass, northern pike, walleye, and bluegill. The Lake Geneva area was once a hangout for George "Baby Face" Nelson and George "Bugs" Moran at the Lake Como Hotel. These were the stories the natives told the tourists to sell more memorabilia from the area. This lake was one of the deepest in the area, measuring 135 feet deep, which was a fact often told by Ricky's dad. This time of year, the summer traffic tripled in volume because of all the tourists visiting Lake Geneva, and Ricky felt like he could blend in and disappear.

His departure from the Hoyne Avenue residence on Tuesday morning was extremely fortunate for Ricky. He did not know that the Cato-and-Douglas team wanted to talk with him. The detectives did not know he was going away for a few days either. Ricky needed a few days to get away and was going to use the time to unwind and maybe go fishing on the lake. Since the cabin did not have any phone service, he'd told his brother Ray that he would be gone for a few days and would be back in the city next week. This was just like Ricky—taking off and disappearing.

Ricky had been let go from his job on Friday because of an angry outburst against another employee at the trucking company he was working for. He had always had a tough time keeping a job. His brother Ray knew this about his brother, and that was why Ricky was allowed to live in the garden apartment on Hoyne Avenue for free. His parents had left the house to Ray but with the condition that Ricky could live there for as long as he wanted. Ray was always the big brother watching out for his little brother.

Ricky had brought the Hamilton Technical High School yearbook with him to the cabin near Lake Geneva. He opened the book to make an update to the yearbook for Karen Mille. Her picture had a circle around it, and Ricky put an *x* through her smiling face. He also handwrote the word "dead" under her picture. He thought to himself, *What should I do with the murder weapon?* The Walther PPQ .22-caliber handgun would tie him to the murder of Karen Mille, and he did not want that to happen. So, he decided when he went fishing on Lake Geneva that the deepest part of the lake would be an ideal drop point for the handgun. No one would find it at the 135-foot depth of the lake. Even if a scuba diver found it, it would be impossible to trace it back to him. That was the plan that he was going to stick to. Then he thought about what to do with the Hamilton Technical High School yearbook. He would burn it in the cabin, and the ashes would destroy all the other evidence. The book and the gun would be gone from his possession, and no one from Chicago would be able to connect the dots. He thought that all this planning would cover his tracks for the deaths of Wally Bass, Kevin Burger, Joe Dirt, Paul Cagney, Mike Conners, and Karen Mille. They were all dead now, and he was the last one standing of this group of Hamilton Tech alumni.

Ricky started a fire in the log cabin later that night. The temperature was going to be cold for a summer day, so a fire would keep the place nice and toasty. He got out a beer from the refrigerator and pulled out the yearbook for one more walk down memory lane. The fire was burning brightly, and he placed two more logs on the hearth. The fire was roaring now, and there was enough heat to keep the cabin warm for the rest of the evening. Ricky opened the yearbook and read the names one more time.

Wally Bass broke my wrist. Dead.
Kevin Burger caused my leg to bleed. Dead.
Joe Dirt broke my nose. Dead.
Paul Cagney caused me to get stiches in my butt. Dead.
Mike Conners hurt my finger, which needed surgery. Dead.
Karen Mille stood me up for prom night. Dead.
All are dead, and my grudge against them and the debt they owed to me has been paid back in full.

Ricky closed the yearbook and tossed it onto the fire. The yearbook burned quickly and was reduced to ash in just a few minutes. He used the poker to stir the ashes of the book so that no evidence would remain. The paper book would be no more. Ricky would drop the Walther PPQ .22-caliber handgun in the deep end of Lake Geneva while he fished for walleye, which was his favorite fish. He would slip the gun over the side of the boat while no other fishermen were looking. A watery grave for the gun that had killed Karen Mille. The other stuff at the garden apartment would have to be disposed of as well. He would take care of that when he returned.

Ricky started to fall asleep and was thinking about beer-battered walleye on a hot skillet with a cold beer, dreaming the tasty-fish-for-dinner dream.

Chapter 62

Mike said goodbye to his dad and got out the bike to head to the newsstand. It was Tuesday, and Mike was running a few minutes late, but he had to deliver the papers by 4:30 p.m. He pulled the bike out from the back porch and started to walk through the gangway. Mike had left his radio on the porch and had to return to get it. Music was a requirement to do the paper route, he thought. He strapped the radio to the handlebars and turned it on. The station was preset to WLS 890 AM radio, of course, and Larry Lujack was on. The song playing was "Sweet Jane" by the Velvet Underground. Mike had thought about being a DJ at one time, but detective school was more appealing to him.

***

Driving his bike down the middle of Dickens Avenue and then to Hoyne Avenue was the normal route. Just on cue, there was Mary Crystal on her porch, watching him ride his bike.

"Mike, you be careful."

"Will do, Mrs. Crystal," Mike replied.

Mike waited for what she was going to say next.

"Watch out for those pesky cars." This was like clockwork.

Mike waved at Mary and mumbled under his breath, "That old woman. She needs to get a hobby or something."

He continued on his ride to the newsstand.

***

Mike arrived at the newsstand and assumed a perch on one of the high tables where stacks of the Tuesday *Chicago Today* were waiting like giant square statues. He started to roll, rubber band, and stuff fifty papers into his news pouch. This was the number he needed for his customers today. Larry was in the back office on the phone and looked as if he did not want to be bothered. Mike finished his rolling operation and then exited the newsstand to get his paper route started.

Mike got on the bike, and once again another good tune was on the radio as he proceeded down Webster Avenue. Larry Lujack had just announced that after this commercial the next song was "Proud Mary" by Creedence Clearwater Revival. Mike was thrilled that another of his favorite songs was on the radio. The band CCR, as it was nicknamed, was one he wished he could get to see if they had a concert in Chicago. He would have to sneak out to see them or ask his older brother Henry to take him. Either way, the band was a good one, and he enjoyed their music. As Mike was delivering the papers to his customers, he started to think. The little voice inside him was starting to talk to him.

Just go up to Ray Chambers and ask him about the victims in the stories. Just like you did when you went to the precinct on the Northwest Side, when you talked with Watch Commander Dane Hoy. Have a conversation with Ray Chambers. Ring the door, deliver the paper, and ask the question. Just do it.

The little voice inside Mike got louder and louder until he started to talk to himself. "Just shut up in there," Mike yelled at his little voice inside. He continued with his paper route and just listened to the music. Another song was blaring through the radio, and this got his focus off the little voice inside him. "Roadhouse Blues" by the Doors had just come on. As Mike started to sing the words of this song, his little voice stayed quiet.

Mike was finishing his deliveries, and he knew that Mary Crystal was waiting. The second-to-last paper stop was Ray Chambers, then Mary Crystal. He decided to deliver Mary's paper next instead of Ray's and then make his last stop. Mary was waiting for her paper as usual.

"Thanks for the paper," she said as Mike hand delivered the paper on the porch.

"You're welcome."

"You're such a nice boy."

"Thanks, Mrs. Crystal."

Mike proceeded to the house of Ray Chambers. He rode up to the house, grabbed a paper, and walked up the flight of stairs. He rang the doorbell, and no one answered. He was just about to leave when Ray opened the door.

"Is something wrong, Mike?" Ray asked.

"Here is your paper, Mr. Chambers."

"You normally throw it up the flight of stairs during the week and keep going. Is something wrong, Mike?" Ray asked.

"No. I was just wondering how your stories are going."

"What stories, Mike?"

"About those people who committed suicide."

"Oh, those stories."

"How do you know so much about the details?" Mike asked.

"I have a secret weapon, Mike."

"Oh. What is it?"

"I'll tell you, but you will need to keep quiet about it," Ray replied.

"What is it, Mr. Chambers?"

"It is a police scanner radio."

"What?"

"I bought a police scanner radio. When I hear of something going on, I listen to what the cops are saying and then get over to the crime scene."

"But how do you know so much about the crimes?"

"Mike, keep this between us. The cops aren't too bright. They talk about the crime scene on a certain frequency. My scanner is tuned to that frequency. Everything they tell the dispatchers, ME, morgue, watch commander, and other detectives, I can hear it."

"So, you listen in on them."

"Yep. They don't even know I am listening. I hear everything they are talking about on the police scanner radio."

"So that's how you get the information on the crime scenes before the other reporters."

"You're bang on, Mike. Please don't tell anyone."

"I thought that maybe you were involved with the crimes."

"Mike, whatever gave you that idea?" Ray asked.

"You just knew too much."

"No, it's the scanner," said Ray. "I use a Bearcat Model 3 with eight channels and most times the police use the first channel."

"That is pretty clever, Mr. Chambers."

"Mike, please call me Ray."

"Ok. Thanks, Ray. Here is your paper. I've got to go."

"Remember, Mike, this is our little secret."

"Yes, I'll remember, Ray."

"Nice talking with you, Mike."

"You too."

Mike was relieved after he left the house of Ray Chambers. Ray was using the police scanner to beat the cops at their own game to get the crime scene information. But Mike's little voice was saying, *What about Ricky Chambers?* That was the wild card he could not explain.

Chapter 63

The detectives were back at the precinct on Wednesday morning. They needed to find some background information on Ricky Chambers. He had eluded them every time they had gone over to the garden apartment to interrogate him. The man was never home. The detectives made a phone call to review what they had on Ricky with Mary Wright, and this went straight to a voicemail system. She would call back later during the day and leave a message that Ricky could be a possible suspect in their investigation based on the facts of the case.

"Hey, Douglas, how is the background search going on Ricky Chambers?" Detective Cato asked.

"Give me a couple more minutes, and I'll share with you what I have."

Detective Douglas was on the phone with the police department that did the background checks on any individual in the United States. This department could provide just about any public information about a person, and sometimes confidential information as well.

"Hey, Cato, here is what I found out about Ricky Chambers."

"Do tell."

"Ricky was working for a trucking company on the Northwest Side. He was fired on Friday because of an anger problem with another employee. He has had several jobs and can't seem to hold onto any of them. He lives in the garden apartment with his brother, Ray Chambers,

THE GRUDGE LIST

who lives on the second floor. He is twenty-one years old and single. He graduated from Hamilton Tech High School in 1966. No arrests or tickets. He is clean."

"Rick, is this another dead end?"

"Don't know, Cato."

"We need to find him and have a conversation in person at his house. We need to catch him at home."

"Agreed."

"Let's try to call the brother and flush him out."

"You mean use Ray to get to Ricky?"

"That's exactly what I mean," Cato replied.

Detective Cato had the number of the *Chicago Today* office where Ray worked. He thought to call Ray first and see if he knew when Ricky would be home. Ray answered the call. He was at his desk this morning.

"Hello, this is Ray Chambers."

"This is Detective Abbey Cato from the Chicago Police Department."

"Hi, Detective. What can I do for you?" Ray replied on the phone.

"I need to have a chat with Ricky Chambers, your brother."

"Can I tell him what this pertains to?"

"Routine investigations. We need to ask him a few questions," Detective Cato replied.

"I can give you his number at the apartment, but he is not home this week."

"Oh. Is he out of town?"

"Ricky went fishing. We have a cabin on Lake Geneva, and he is there for a few days."

"When do you expect him back?" Detective Cato asked.

"I think he will be back Sunday or Monday of next week. Can your questions wait until then?"

"Yes, they can. They are just routine questions on an active investigation we are looking into."

"I'll give you his number at the apartment, but he doesn't have an answering machine or service. You need to just try and catch him."

"Can you leave him a handwritten message in his apartment, Ray, that we really need to talk with him? Can you give him our number here at the precinct?"

"I sure can. I'll go into his apartment and leave a handwritten message on his coffee table that he needs to contact you as soon as he gets back home. This way you can expect a call from him just as soon as he sees then note."

"Can I ask you, Ray, why Ricky went to Lake Geneva in the middle of the week?"

"Well, it's kind of embarrassing. He lost his job on Friday at the trucking company he was working for."

"Can you tell me what happened?" Detective Cato asked.

"I don't know all the details, but Ricky told me he lost his job again."

"Does this happen often?"

"He kind of has anger-management issues," Ray replied.

"Has he reached out for professional help?"

"No, he can't afford it."

"Ok, can you relay the message that the detectives are trying to reach him?"

"I'll relay the message just as soon as he surfaces. I cannot call him at the cabin. There is no phone."

"No phone," replied Cato.

"When my parents owned the cabin, they did not want to spoil the experience. So, they never put a phone in there. If you needed anything, you had to go into town and use the general store's phone."

"That seems a little primitive in this day and age, Ray."

"I know, Detective Cato; it does seem weird. But when you are trying to unwind on the lake, you don't want annoying salespeople calling you. You want to enjoy Mother Nature for all it's worth."

"If that's your cup of tea, Ray, then do it. I would install a phone."

"Thanks for that bit of advice, Detective."

"Free of charge. Can you relay the message to Ricky and give him the number?"

"Will do," Ray said as he ended the call.

"Rick, do you think he will relay the message?" Cato asked.

"Yes, I think he will, but not for a few days," Rick replied.

The two detectives went back to doing paperwork and trying to dig up anything else on Ricky Chambers at the precinct. They were all dead ends. There was nothing on Ricky that they could put their hands on. Both of them thought that something was simply wrong with Ricky. Two and two were adding up to five. More investigative work would be needed to push these cases along. They both ducked out of the precinct before the watch commander started to look for them.

"Let's go get some lunch."

"Sounds good, Cato."

"Where to?"

"Let's go to Super Dawg for a hot dog."

"Sounds good to me," Rick replied as he rubbed his stomach.

"You're always hungry, Rick."

"Yep, always."

Chapter 64

Mike pulled his bike from the back porch and made sure the radio was fastened to the handlebars. His mom was working the shift from 3:00 p.m. to 11:00 p.m. at the local hospital, and his dad was taking a nap. There was no one to say goodbye to him and tell him to have a nice paper route. He turned the radio dial to the on position, and the station was still preset to WLS 890 AM radio. As Mike walked through the gangway, the music was blasting out a tune. The song was "Border Song" by Elton John, as Larry Lujack announced at the end of the song. Mike prized his bike and his radio as the only possessions a boy needed.

***

Mike rode his bike down West Dickens Avenue, made a right turn onto North Hoyne Avenue, made a left turn onto West Webster Avenue, and finally made a right turn onto North Hamilton Avenue and then arrived at the newsstand. He did not see Mrs. Mary Crystal on her porch today. The streets seemed incredibly quiet, and he encountered very few cars. This eerily quiet neighborhood made Mike recollect the scanner that Ray was using to get to the crime scenes. He needed to reveal this item to Larry and get his opinion on the likelihood that it was the source of the reporter's news.

He arrived a few minutes earlier than normal. The newsstand was empty except for Larry. He was in the back office on the phone. Larry waved his hand to Mike to come and join him in the back office. Mike went back there and waited until Larry was off the phone.

"Thanks, Mike, for coming into the back office."

"Not a problem, Larry."

"How is it going today?" Larry asked Mike.

"Fine."

"I did not hear from the detectives at all this week."

"Their lack of response makes me nervous," Mike replied. "I need to relax and take it easy today."

"I agree with you. Just try to keep it light and easy. Otherwise, you will be a basket case."

"Larry, I have to tell you what I did yesterday."

"What did you do? Are you in trouble?"

"No. I talked to Ray Chambers yesterday at his house."

"You did what?" Larry looked shocked.

"I knocked on Ray's door yesterday and asked him about the crime stories he was following. I pretended to be a dummy and just asked some questions."

"I guess since he did not kill you, Ray is not the murderer."

"No, Larry. Ray is not a murderer. Not that I know of. He seems to be an ok guy."

"Well, did he tell you how he gets all the details of the crime scenes before anybody else?"

"Yes, he did. He uses a police scanner. He said it was a Bearcat Model 3. He also said something about how it had eight channels, and the police were using channel one. I don't know what that means."

"So, he is listening in on the police on one of their channels?"

"Yep. He also said that the police are not too bright."

"Did he elaborate on that last fact?"

"He said the frequency the police use is the same one he is tuned into. He hears everything they talk about at all the crime scenes. This includes the dispatcher, detectives, ME, morgue, and watch commander. They don't even know he is eavesdropping."

"So that's how he is getting the scoop on all these stories."

"Yep. He also said the police don't know he is listening and that I need to keep quiet about this."

"Mike, I agree with Ray on this. You'd better not say anything about this to anyone. This includes the boys."

"He is a very clever reporter," Mike replied.

"He is, and a persistent one at that, Mike. We need to keep his secret for your protection and mine."

"What about Ricky?" Mike asked.

"The detectives have said nothing about Ricky."

"The subject of Ricky never came up with Ray yesterday," Mike said as he returned a frown to Larry.

"Ricky never came up when you were chatting with Ray?"

"Nope. Not one word," Mike replied.

"Then maybe Ricky Chambers is the true killer," Larry replied to Mike.

"I was hoping you would have some news from Detectives Cato and Douglas."

"They have not called back yet, Mike."

"Well, I am going to stay away from Ricky's garden apartment just in case."

"I think that's a good idea, Mike. Keep your distance from him."

"Well, I have to get to the paper route for today." Mike left the back office and went to a spot near the high table where a stack of papers was waiting.

Larry just nodded and said, "Get the Wednesday edition out, Mike."

Mike started the rolling, rubber banding, and stuffing process once again. Fifty papers were to be placed in the news pouch and delivered by 4:30 p.m. The paperboy's job was to deliver his papers like clockwork to the happy readers of the *Chicago Today*.

Chapter 65

Ricky was up early on Thursday. His motto was "The early bird gets the worm." It was a fishing day on Lake Geneva. He was looking forward to catching some walleyes and frying them up in a beer batter with a little butter and garlic. The early-morning hours would be free of boaters, and the lake was as smooth as glass. A perfect day to go fishing.

He had a small fishing boat left to him by his parents. It was an eighteen-foot Grumman boat with a seventy-five-horsepower Johnson outboard motor. It was stored in the tiny garage that was on the property. He hooked the trailer up to the car and eased down to the landing slip that was nearby and adjacent to the lake. He backed the boat into the lake, which was about fifty feet from the storage garage, and boom, time to go fishing. He put the trailer and car away, grabbed the cooler, and got into the boat for a morning fish. The Walther PPQ .22-caliber was inside his coat.

Ricky pushed off from the shore and fired up the seventy-five-horsepower Johnson outboard motor. The boat glided along the glassy surface like a knife cutting through butter. The sun was just starting to rise, and it was a beautiful day to go fishing. Since it was Thursday, the tourists and the damned water-skiers would not be up. In the summertime, on Fridays, Saturdays, and Sundays, there were too many water-skiers ripping up the water and scaring all the fish. Monday through Thursday early morning was the best time to go fishing on Lake Geneva. As Ricky motored the boat out to his favorite spot, he had to make a stop at Black Point. This was the deepest part of the lake at about 135 feet in depth. This was where he would make a deposit of the Walther PPQ .22-caliber handgun, the one he had used to kill Karen Mille last weekend. He was approaching Black Point now and did not see anyone around. He pulled he gun out of his coat and quietly slipped it into the water. The gun sank like a rock going down to the bottom of Lake Geneva. The evidence was now gone, and Ricky could relax. It was time to go to Williams Bay, where the walleye fishing was always good. He motored the boat across the lake until he reached a spot in the middle of Williams Bay. He cut the motor, and the boat was left to drift with the wind. He used his favorite fishing pole to drop a jig into the water, and the fishing for walleye started in earnest. After about one hour's time, Ricky had caught ten fish. He threw four back because they were a combination of northern pike and largemouth bass. The six leftovers were decent-size walleye for eating, and he put them in the fish cooler. Fish for dinner and a cold beer were all that Ricky was thinking about. The early-morning fishing trip was a success. It was now time to get back to the cabin. The lake started to come alive with other fishermen and damned water-skiers. The water-skiers were the reckless water invaders who scared away the fish and caused lots of boating accidents.

Ricky started up the seventy-five-horsepower Johnson outboard motor and slowly cruised the lake back to the cabin. He had pulled out six decent-size walleye from the lake and was going to get his fill of fish for dinner. As the fishing boat glided to the boating slip adjacent to the cabin, Ricky cut the motor and let the boat glide to the shore. He jumped out of the boat where the slip was to secure the boat with a rope on the corner cleat. He would use the trailer to crank the boat forward out of the water onto the structure on wheels. The boat would be put away and the fish would be put away in the refrigerator.

***

Ricky decided to go into town and get some supplies. He needed some more beer and some batter supplies for his fish. He would make a call to his brother Ray as a routine check-in. Since it was still early in the morning, he would call the house phone number first. If there was no answer on this number, he could try the office. He would use the general store phone since there was no phone installed at the cabin. Why his parents never put one in was a mystery to Ricky. Since he did not have the money, a phone would never be installed at the cabin.

Ricky dialed the home number for Ray, and after the fourth ring, Ray picked it up.

"Hello."

"Hey, Ray, just checking in. This is Ricky."

"Ricky, how is the fishing up there?"

"I went this morning and caught six good walleyes."

"I wish I could have joined you," Ray replied.

"You can always come up. You know where the place is."

"I know. The job for the paper is getting in the way."

"Oh, right, that."

"One of us has got to keep a job."

"Thanks, big brother."

"You're welcome, Ricky."

"I can save you some fish if you come up on the weekend."

"That would be nice."

"Can you make it up?"

"Let me see what I can do, Ricky. I have a deadline with the editor, and he is riding me pretty hard to get the stories in on time."

"Just come up for Saturday and leave early on Sunday."

"That sounds good. I'll do that."

"We can both go fishing together."

"You're on. Oh, by the way, I have a message from some detectives."

"What detectives?" Ricky asked.

"The detectives Cato and Douglas have been trying to reach you to ask about some investigations. They said it was some general stuff and they really wanted to talk to you."

"What did you tell them about me?"

"I told them that you were on vacation in Lake Geneva and would not be back until next week."

"Thanks, Ray."

"They left a number for you to call."

"Can you leave it in the apartment? I'll call them when I get back next week."

"I can do that. I'll leave it on your table in the dining room."

"Thanks, Ray. You're a good brother."

"Sure, Ricky. Catch more walleye for me. I'll see you on Saturday."

"Will do," Ricky replied.

Ricky was now worried about the detectives. What did they want with him? Had they found some evidence? How had they found him? Lots of questions and no answers. *Oh well, I am not going to call them until I get back to the apartment*, Ricky thought as he left the general store in Lake Geneva.

Chapter 66

Friday was here again, and that meant that Mike would get enough money from the paper route, including tips, to get the hockey stick. He could not participate with the boys in the street because he did not have the equipment, but after Friday he would be part of the team.

***

Mike pulled his bike off the back porch, and before he had it through the doorway, he turned on the radio. Larry Lujack was on this afternoon and had just announced the song to be played after the commercial. It was "No Matter What" by the band Badfinger—a good tune for a Friday afternoon as Mike walked to the street. The streets were quiet once again, and riding down the center lanes of the streets was the way to get to the newsstand. As Mike proceeded down Hoyne Avenue, he did not see Mrs. Mary Crystal on the porch. This was two days in a row, and he wondered if something was wrong. The collection stop would answer the question of what had happened to her.

Mike arrived at the newsstand and took a spot next to the high tables at the stacks of newspapers nearest the doorway. All the paperboys were already there rolling, rubber banding, and stuffing the papers into their respective pouches. Mike was late this day, and he knew it.

THE GRUDGE LIST

"Hey, Mike, you got a minute?" Larry yelled from the back office. Larry motioned with his hand for Mike to come back and see him.

"What's up, Larry?" Mike asked as he got to the back office. "You wanted to see me?"

"Mike, I have not heard from the detectives. They kind of went silent."

"So, they have no new information about the killer or killers?"

"Yep, that is correct. They have no new news."

"They don't know about Ray and his police scanner?"

"I did not tell them, Mike," Larry replied.

"I did not say anything to them either," Mike replied.

"They are trying to find Ricky. He seems to have disappeared."

"I have ridden by the Chambers house and the garden apartment several times this week, and it appears to be quiet, like no one is home."

"Mike, keep a low profile and stay away from Ricky's place."

"I have to collect this week from Ray."

"Yes, I know. Please be careful."

"I will," Mike responded.

"Oh, by the way, you have a new customer to be added to your route."

"That makes number fifty-one."

"Yep. The customer's name is Helen Hunter, and she lives on Hoyne Avenue just past Mary Crystal. So, make sure you roll and deliver fifty-one papers today."

"Do I collect from her today for just one day?"

"No, don't bother. Today is a freebie for her."

"I'll just introduce myself as her paperboy and ask where she wants the paper delivered."

"Mike, that's a fantastic idea. Always customer friendly, you are. I like that in a paperboy. You're going to go far in this world."

"I try to give the people what they want. I hope she is a good tipper."

"You will know next week when she pays you."

"I'll add her to my paper route."

"Now get rolled and wrapped and deliver the Friday edition of the *Chicago Today*."

"See you later," Mike replied.

Mike finished the rolling process and stuffed the fifty-one papers into his news pouch. He headed out to deliver the papers as he had done so many times in the past. One delivery and one collection after another. Since he was delivering the papers a little later than normal, his collection rate was going up. A lot of customers were just starting to get home. So, Mike was hitting them at the right time. Just after work and just before dinner.

Mike was getting to the end of the paper route, and around the corner on Hoyne Avenue was Ray Chambers's house. He rode his bike to the stairway, grabbed a newspaper, walked up the stairs, rang the bell, and waited just a few seconds. Just as he was going to turn to walk down, the door opened, and there was Ray Chambers.

"How much do I owe you this week?" Ray asked.

"Your bill is $1.40 this week."

"Don't I owe you for last week?"

"Your brother Ricky paid me last week."

"Here is two bucks. Keep the change."

"Thanks, Mr. Chambers."

"Mike, I told you to call me Ray."

"Thanks, Mr. Ray."

"If in the future I am not home when you collect, you can always go see Ricky downstairs, and he will take care of you."

"Can I ask you something, Ray?"

"Sure, what's up?"

"Did you both go to Hamilton Technical High School?"

"Yes, we did. Ricky was one year behind me."

"Was Ricky in the class of 1966?"

"Yes, he was. How did you know that?"

"I peeked in his yearbook that was on the coffee table last week."

"Yep. We both have yearbooks from good old Hamilton Tech."

"Ricky's had some pictures circled, with *x*'s through the faces of the students' pictures."

"Oh. Everyone does that if it's someone they don't like."

"You may want to ask Ricky about his. I have to get going now. I have more papers to deliver and collect on."

"Ok, you finish your paper route," Ray replied.

***

As Mike walked down the flight of stairs, Ray thought to himself, *What is that boy talking about? Ricky's yearbook with circles around student pictures. What is he getting at?* Ray made a mental note to ask Ricky about this strange encounter with the paperboy.

Mike finished his route with Mary Crystal and the new customer Helen Hunter. Mary was just feeling a little sick and was not hanging out on the porch. She was inside with a flu bug, wrapped up in her pj's. But she was ok and just a little under the weather. Mike was relieved. He missed that old woman yelling at him from her porch to watch out for those pesky cars.

Chapter 67

Ray had a tight deadline on a couple of stories for the paper on Monday. He would accept Ricky's invitation and drive up to the cabin on Friday night and travel back home on Sunday morning. A lot of work had to be completed for the Monday release on three big stories Ray was working on. He could finish it on Sunday during the day at the house on Hoyne Avenue. So, Ray decided to drive up on Friday after the traffic lightened up on I-94 and then return early in the morning on Sunday. A day fishing on the lake with Ricky on Saturday would be a nice break in the work routine.

Ray made the drive up north to the cabin and followed the same route that Ricky had taken earlier this week. North on I-94 to I-41, then west onto Highway 50 to Wisconsin. Ray's deceased parents had willed him the cabin with the stipulation that Ricky could use it and even live there for as long as he liked. Ray was ok with the wishes of his parents. He kind of felt as if he owed it to them to take care of his little brother. Since Ricky was the only family that Ray had in this world, Ray was fiercely protective of anything that happened or was going to happen to him. "Protective angel" was the term his mom had used once when she was alive. His dad had just said, "Make sure you take care of your little brother." Ray missed his parents so much now that he was an adult. Ray thought about the death of his parents that fall night when a drunk driver killed both of them late at night on the Kennedy Expressway, going the wrong way in the city. They were both declared dead at the scene. The wake was one of sorrow and a lot of crying. The sons should not have buried the parents when Ray was in college and Ricky was struggling to find a job. *Life is so unfair*, he thought, rolling the memories around in his head.

Ray finally arrived at the cabin on Lake Geneva. A drive late at night on Friday took only about ninety minutes. It was a pleasant drive up, and he knew he could unwind for a day and a half. Maybe. Ray was going to slowly ask about the yearbook when they went fishing on Saturday morning. He was in no mood to stir Ricky up and set off his anger issues just after arriving at the cabin. He would do it on the lake Saturday, and gently.

"Ray, you finally made it," Ricky said.

"Yep. The drive-up was not too bad. The traffic was actually light for a Friday evening. You know all the Chicago people travel to Wisconsin to get away from the city heat on the weekend."

"The summer pattern to Lake Geneva from June to August is always one of congestion and traffic."

"Are we going fishing tomorrow morning?" Ray asked.

"You bet. We will have to get up early to avoid the invaders."

"The invaders, Ricky?"

"You know, the damned water-skiers."

"Oh yeah, those weekend shits."

"They cause the fish to scatter, and it's not worth fishing," Ricky replied.

"Ok. What time do you want to get up?"

"Just before dawn," Ricky replied.

"That will be the one-hour window in the morning when the lake is quiet, and we can catch some walleye."

"You're correct, big brother. That will be the best time to fish."

"Let's turn in."

"Sounds good." Ricky turned the lights off, and they both went to their respective bedrooms.

***

The two brothers woke up an hour before dawn on Saturday, just as planned. They packed a thermos of coffee and threw some snacks into a backpack. They loaded a cooler with ice from the refrigerator for the fish. They pulled the Grumman fishing boat out of the garage with the help of the car and gently rolled it down the hill to the slip on the lake. They left the car and trailer next to the slip because Ricky wanted to go fishing only for about an hour. The lake would be crowded with the weekenders, and the fish would definitely not be biting with all the traffic stirring up the water.

They pushed the boat off from the slip and cranked up the seventy-five-horsepower Johnson outboard motor. The motor purred like a kitten.

"Dad really took care of this boat." Ricky looked at Ray.

'When was the last time we went fishing, Ricky?"

"I can't remember when the last time was that we were both together in this boat."

"I know. I have been really busy working and covering a lot of stories for the paper."

"Yep. I have not seen much of you, Ray. You're always out of the house early in the morning and not back until late at night."

"My job as a reporter keeps me very busy."

"Well, it's nice to see you on the lake with me today."

"Where are we headed?"

"Williams Bay is where we are going. I caught a lot of nice walleyes there the other day."

"Ricky, isn't that spot usually busy for the fish?"

"Not early in the morning."

"Sounds good. Let's go get some walleyes." Ray pointed toward Williams Bay.

Ray cut the motor, and the boat drifted toward the inlet. There was no wind this morning, so the boat just glided through the water effortlessly. As both Ray and Ricky cast their rods into the water, they could see every splash around them. It did not take long before both of them had fish on the line. Ray caught a nice walleye, and Ricky caught a nice northern pike.

"Ricky, are you keeping that snake?" Ray asked.

"I'll throw this one back. I know how you hate to clean these."

"I only like the walleyes," Ray replied. "I'll clean them too."

"Let's see how many walleyes we catch in the next hour," Ricky said.

"Why just the hour, Ricky?"

"The invaders will be on the water in about an hour."

"Oh, I almost forgot about those water-skiers," Ray replied.

"I hate them. They cause the fish to go goofy."

"Ok, let's stay out for the hour and then go back to the cabin."

"Sounds good."

"I got another one. It's a walleye. That's number two for me."

"I'll catch up," Ricky replied.

In one hour, the fish count was four walleyes for Ricky and five walleyes for Ray. They each had a northern pike, which they returned to the lake. Overall, it was a good day for one hour's worth of fishing on Lake Geneva during the cool June summer day.

"Time to head back, little brother."

"Agreed. We have a cooler full of walleye, and that's plenty of fish for now."

"Hey, thanks for paying for the newspaper last week. I owe you for it."

"No problem. The paperboy came by, and you weren't home. So, I took care of it."

"Thanks. I'll reimburse you for it."

"You don't have to, big brother."

"I know money is tight with you losing your job last week."

"It was very untimely. That guy had it coming."

"What do you mean?"

"Oh, nothing," Ricky replied.

"Did the paperboy look in your yearbook?"

"What are you talking about?"

"When the paperboy came by yesterday for the collection, he said he peeked in your yearbook last week and saw x marks on some pictures of students."

"He must have been mistaken," Ricky replied.

"The paperboy said he saw some x marks on some pictures, and I told him everyone does that for fellow students they dislike."

"I don't know what he is talking about," Ricky responded.

"Oh, he must be mistaken."

"Yes, the paperboy must be mistaken, big brother."

"Let's get back to the cabin and get some breakfast," Ray said as he looked away.

Ray fired up the seventy-five-horsepower Johnson motor and headed for the cabin. Not a single word was spoken until the boat was in the slip. Ray knew that something was wrong, and his little brother was hiding a secret from him. A confrontation was coming, but Ray did not know when to pull the trigger. Ricky was prone to anger bouts, and he loved his little brother immensely. He would do anything to watch over him and protect him. Ray's little voice was talking, and he did not like what it was saying about his little brother.

Chapter 68

The scheduled Friday night hangout at the Boys' Clubhouse was pushed to Saturday because Mike's parents were having some neighbors over on the back porch for a Friday night get-together.

Mike changed the signal to one knock followed by two knocks followed by three knocks for Saturday. This was the normal signal to get into the Boys' Clubhouse. As Mike waited inside, he knew the boys would not be too much longer. The knocks came in a few minutes, and all three boys were inside the shed.

"How is everyone tonight?" Mike asked.

Tommy said, "Ok."

Danny said, "Fine."

Johnny said, "Ditto."

"Danny and Johnny, it's your turn to get the beer. Tommy and I got it last week," Mike announced to the group.

"Everybody cough up two bucks," Danny replied, and he collected the money from all four of them.

"Let's go get the beer," Johnny said as he turned to Danny.

***

Johnny and Danny hung out in the liquor store alley on Damen Avenue waiting for the right person to buy them beer.

"Hey, mister, can you buy us some beer?" Johnny said as he approached a stranger.

"Didn't I buy you beer last Friday?" the stranger replied.

"You may have bought the beer for our friends on Friday," said Johnny. "Yep, that's when you bought for Mike and Tommy. They are our friends."

"Same deal as last week?" the stranger asked.

"We give you eight bucks for two six-packs," said Johnny.

"Sounds good. Do you still want Budweiser?" the stranger asked.

"Yep. That would be fine," said Johnny.

A few minutes later, the stranger walked out into the alley and handed the boys a bag of cold beer. There were two six-packs of something, but the boys did not check.

"Now remember. You don't know me," the stranger said as he made the handoff to them in the alley.

***

The boys returned to the Boys' Clubhouse through the back alleys. They gave the official knock, and the hatchway opened. Johnny handed the bag of beer through the opening to whoever grabbed it inside.

"What kind of beer did you guys get?" Mike asked.

"The stranger said it was Budweiser," Danny replied.

"I like Budweiser better than Schlitz," Tommy barked.

"Let's just have a beer, boys." Mike grabbed a beer from the plastic ring.

"So, anything happening with Ray Chambers, Mike?" Tommy asked.

"I went to collect from him yesterday, and I kind of asked him about Ricky and the yearbook."

"You did what?" Tommy replied with a shocked look on his face.

"I asked Ray about Ricky's yearbook with the x markings through the student pictures. That's it."

"What did Ray say about Ricky?" Tommy asked.

"Ray said that all the students do that to those they don't like in school," Mike replied.

"I don't think so, Mike," said Danny.

"I think Ray is pulling a fast one on you, Mike," Johnny said.

"Well, if he did, I didn't tell him I saw the word 'dead' at the bottom of the pictures."

"What else did Ray say to you, Mike?" Tommy asked.

"That's it. Then I left. I told him I had more papers to deliver and collections that I had to make."

"So is Ray the killer, Mike?" Tommy asked.

"I don't think so. I really think that Ricky, his brother, has something to do with this. Just a gut feeling that something is not adding up over there on Hoyne Avenue."

"What have the detectives said about Ricky?" Danny asked.

"Nothing. I asked Larry what the latest was, and he said they kind of went silent," Mike replied.

"We, the boys, need to keep an eye on you, Mike," Tommy announced.

"I appreciate the thought. Do you really think that Ray Chambers or Ricky Chambers would harm me for knowing something?"

"If what you said about Ricky is real, then Ray may know something about it, and then he is an accomplice." Tommy stated the obvious.

"You may be right, Tommy. Do I need to go into protective custody, like witness protection or something like that?"

"Mike, we can watch you. The boys will be your protection," Tommy replied.

All three boys, Tommy, Johnny, and Danny, said something to the effect of "We will take care of you."

"Thanks, guys. I know I can count on you three."

"This is the Boys' Clubhouse, and we are all members," Tommy announced.

"You all took an oath to keep our secrets safe and this clubhouse quiet no matter what." Mike pointed his finger at all three of the boys.

"Can we drink our beer now?" Johnny asked.

"So, what is your plan, Mike?" Tommy asked.

"Larry told me to lie low and avoid Ricky. Go the other way if I see his smiling face."

"Mike, that is kind of tough since we all live in the same neighborhood," Danny replied.

"I am going to count on you three to watch my back. If anything is not right, you are to run to Larry and let him know."

"We can do that," Tommy replied.

"Thanks."

The boys continued with their conversation about sports and other things. The beers went down well because they were cold on a warm Saturday night. Mike was worried about the next few days, and it showed on his face. The boys decided to make a pact and keep an eye on Mike. He was their friend, he was a fellow paperboy, and he was part of the Boys' Clubhouse.

Chapter 69

It was Saturday night once again, and Rick had a hot date. The date was with Michelle Lynn, and the place was Luigi's, the Italian restaurant.

Rick had arrived at Michelle's place at 7:00 p.m. He had already made a dinner reservation at Luigi's in advance for 7:30 p.m. As Rick rang the doorbell of Michelle's house on the Northwest Side, he was thinking he'd forgotten something. So, he ran back to the car to retrieve the dozen roses he had purchased just before he drove over to Michelle's house. As Michelle opened the door, she saw Rick running away from the doorway and back to his car. She started to think, *What's going on? Did I scare this guy off our date?*

Rick came sprinting back to the door to say, "Sorry about that. I forgot something." Then he presented the roses from behind his back to Michelle.

"Are those for me?" Michelle asked.

"Yes, I got them especially for you," Rick replied.

"They're beautiful."

"Just as beautiful as you are, Michelle."

"Let's take them inside, and I'll put them in water." Michelle pushed the front door open, and Rick walked inside.

"Is Luigi's for dinner ok?" Rick asked.

"That's my favorite place," replied Michelle.

As Michelle went into the kitchen, Rick sat down in one of the easy chairs in the living room.

"I'll just be a minute to get these beautiful flowers into a vase and some water."

"Take your time. The reservation is for 7:30 p.m."

"You're getting to know me too well, Rick!"

"Just trying to make my date happy."

"You're doing a great job."

"Do you want a drink?" Michelle asked.

"Sure. But if I remember, last time, I drank alone. You wanted your Chianti at the restaurant."

"You have a good memory, Rick," replied Michelle.

"I'll just pour myself a drink while you're working on the flowers."

"Sounds good. I need to trim the stems on the roses to fit the vase anyway."

"Anything new at the ME's office this week?" Rick asked.

"No, not really. Just the same old same old work. More bodies and more reports."

"Do you feel like you're making a difference in the Cook County Medical Examiner's Office caseload?"

"You know, Rick, sometimes it's a grind, and other times it is rewarding. You just have to take the good days with the bad days."

"You sound like my partner."

"Who, Abbey?" Michelle asked.

"Yep. She said the same thing you just said to me last week."

"Us girls got to stick together."

"Don't I know it."

"Now that I think of it, something did happen last week."

"What was that?"

"You know, we had to let one of the technicians go unexpectedly, I think it was on Thursday."

"Let go? I thought your office was shorthanded," Rick said.

"We are short staffed. No one wants to work in the morgue in Cook County. It's too depressing."

"So, who did you let go?" Rick asked.

"A technician by the name of Patrick Duffy. He was selling the ME summary reports on the victims that came through the office to the local newspaper reporters."

"Do you have names of the reporters that Patrick Duffy was selling the reports to?"

"Yes, we have one."

"Only one?" Rick asked.

"It seems that this guy Patrick Duffy was selling the reports for fifty bucks to any reporter who would pay for them. He tried to sell the information to the *Chicago Tribune* and the *Daily News*, and those reporters turned him down. One reporter at the *Chicago Today* did buy the reports."

"Michelle, please don't tell me that the one reporter was Ray Chambers from the *Chicago Today*," Rick said.

"How did you know who it was?" Michelle asked.

"He has been under investigation for doing some shady things. This goes right up there with what has been happening lately."

"The ME's department fired Patrick Duffy on the spot under one condition."

"What condition?"

"That he does not disclose who he was selling what to. Otherwise, they were going to prosecute him and put him in jail."

"So, you let him go and he gets no jail time."

"That was not my decision. I would have thrown the book at him. But my boss said that Cook County could not afford the bad publicity."

"So, your boss is burying the incident."

"Apparently, he is doing just that. He is not referring this to you guys for criminal prosecution."

"Well, he should have. This Patrick is a scumbag."

"He sure is. He was profiting off my work, and he was right under my nose. My boss was kind of mad that I did not catch him."

"Who caught him?"

"A corrections officer was walking by him in the cafeteria and saw money being exchanged between him and a reporter."

"So, he had a little enterprise going on until he got caught."

"Yep. Patrick Duffy would not say how many reports he sold or how many reporters he sold them to."

"So, you really don't know what the magnitude of this crime is," Rick replied.

"Nope, we do not," Michelle answered.

"I'll let Detective Cato know about this on Monday, just in case we need to turn up the heat on Ray Chambers."

"Do what you want with the information. I am not to talk about it to anyone per my boss's instructions."

"But I'm different, right?" Rick asked.

"Aren't you my boyfriend?"

"That's up to you."

"You are," Michelle replied.

"Now can we go to dinner? I'm hungry."

"Let's go," Michelle replied.

Rick finished his Maker's over ice, and she locked the front door as they headed to Luigi's for a nice dinner.

Chapter 70

Ricky decided to return to the apartment on Hoyne Avenue on Monday despite telling his brother he was staying in Lake Geneva for a few days of fishing. He had a goal of disposing of all evidence he'd used for any of the murders. This way if the police wanted to show up and search his home, there would be nothing to link him to any of the crimes. He was careful to drive the speed limit down the highways in Wisconsin and Illinois. Attention to him or his car was not in the cards. Ricky just wanted to get home and box up all the stuff and then get rid of it.

***

Ricky arrived at the apartment midmorning on Monday. He knew that Ray had a few stories he was working on and would be at the office downtown. He could sneak into the apartment, gather the stuff, and go back to Lake Geneva for some rest and relaxation. As Ricky entered the apartment from the back alley, he parked the car in the garage as usual. After walking back from the garage, he quietly walked up the back stairs to the second floor, where Ray lived. He looked in the back window and did not see anyone inside. The car that Ray was driving was also gone from the front spot. So, he thought the place was safe to enter.

Ricky unlocked the door of the garden apartment's back entrance. He grabbed a box from the closet and started to search for the stuff that he had used in all the crimes. He placed rags, chloroform, a hunting knife, handcuffs, bullets, a cooler, and assorted other items in the box. He then took the box to the garage and placed it in the trunk of his car. The thought was to dispose of them in Wisconsin where no one would find them. Once the box was loaded into the car, Ricky came back to the garden apartment to clean. He polished every surface with a simple solution of water and vinegar in a spray bottle. He had seen this on a show once and thought this would remove most evidence that the police would look for just in case they came with a search warrant. An hour later all the surfaces had been cleaned, and the place was immaculate. Now it was time to get back to Lake Geneva and dispose of all the stuff in the box.

Ricky drove back to Lake Geneva and headed for the cabin. Just across the border, he stopped at the welcome center. This was where he would drop the cooler into the garbage can. He did not see anyone around, and he threw it into the dumpster. He proceeded to the cabin to finish the disposal plan.

***

Once at the cabin, Ricky separated the rags from the other stuff. These were placed in the fireplace and burned. Since some of the rags still had chloroform on them, they burned hot, and Ricky walked outside because of the fumes and smell. Next would be all the other items.

Ricky put the box of remaining items in the boat and decided the bottom of the lake was going to be the burial ground for this stuff. He trailered the boat down to the slip for a midafternoon fishing trip and launched the boat. The destination was Black Point, where all the good walleye fishing was on the lake. No one would even think to look for evidence from a crime scene there at the bottom of the lake.

He motored the Johnson seventy-five-horsepower boat to the spot in Lake Geneva called Black Point. He pulled the fishing rod out, and he pretended to cast the lure into the water. He looked around and saw there were no other fishermen to the stern of the boat. He placed the fishing rod between his legs to hold it. He slipped the hunting knife, handcuffs, and box of bullets into the water next to the boat. The items made no splashes, and they dropped to the deep end of Black Point and were now gone from Ricky's possession. There were three bottles that had chloroform in them and also needed to be disposed of. He emptied the bottles over the side of the boat into the lake. Once the bottles were empty, he placed them back in the box. He hung around for a few minutes to pretend he was fishing for the sake of a good appearance. A few more minutes, and he motored the boat back to the cabin.

The only thing left in the box of stuff was three empty chloroform bottles. These he would take to the general store in the town of Lake Geneva and dispose of in the garbage. Ricky would pick up some supplies, and this would then conclude the disposal of all evidence. Ricky would be free of all the items that linked him to Wally Bass, Kevin Burger, Joe Dirt, Paul Cagney, Mike Conners, and Karen Mille.

Monday night, back at the cabin, Ricky was feeling relieved. He had bought some beer from the general store in Lake Geneva and was frying up some of the walleye he had caught earlier that week on the outside barbecue pit. The beer was nice and cold, and the walleye were fresh off the lake. Ricky had a smile on his face from ear to ear. His thoughts went to how he had pulled this off and there would be no evidence that could link the murders to him. As he watched the lake, drank the beer, and ate the walleye, Ricky was satisfied that the grudge list was complete. His honor was avenged, and he was the last one standing. He was the winner, and they all were the losers. They were all dead.

Ricky now needed to figure out what he would say to Ray. He knew Ray had figured some of this out, and he worried that his brother-to-brother relationship would be in serious jeopardy. He did not have an answer for this, and his little voice was talking to him. He did not like what it was saying. *You're a bad person.*

Chapter 71

Lauren Powers was the current principal of Hamilton Tech High School. This was her first year as the principal of a huge high school on the north side of the city. Lacy Jones was her secretary and an exceptionally good one. She had the pulse of the high school and knew everything. Lacy was tasked by Principal Powers with finding out anything she could about Wally Bass, Kevin Burger, Joe Dirt, and Paul Cagney. Two additional students were added to her list. Mike Conners and Karen Mille were the fifth and sixth victims that the *Chicago Today* had reported as recently deceased. Principal Lauren Powers found the two additional names in the 1966 Hamilton Technical yearbook and added them to the list for Lacy to review.

Lacy was able to confirm that all six students were from the class of 1966, and all had graduated as seniors that year. A further review with the faculty revealed that the six students had hung out together and were members of the ski club. There were a total of ten students in the ski club: Wally Bass, Kevin Burger, Joe Dirt, Paul Cagney, Mike Conners, Karen Mille, Joe Shapiro, Ben Harper, Al Gannon, and Ricky Chambers. Six members were dead, and four members were alive. Lacy could not make a connection other than that they were all members of the Hamilton Tech High School ski club in the class of 1966. *Is it possible that the club is being exterminated?* Lacy thought.

Lacy knocked on the door of principal Lauren Powers's office.

"Principal Powers, do you have a few minutes to talk about those students the detectives were asking about?"

"Sure, what did you find out about them?" Principal Lauren Powers asked.

"There were ten students in the ski club. Six are dead and four are living."

"We need to turn this information over to the police," Principal Powers replied.

"I have not found out anything else about these students that may be helpful. So, I am kind of at a dead end on this." Lacy was tapping on the desk.

"Don't do any more review on these students. We will turn over what we have to the detectives and let them sort it out," Principal Powers looked out the window.

"You're the boss, principal," Lacy replied.

"I'll make the call to the detectives and let them know about what you found."

"Thanks. Here are the notes I made about the students."

"Lacy, you did an excellent job of digging on this. I hope this will be helpful to the detectives."

"This is not going to be good for Hamilton Technical High School," Lacy said as she shook her head.

"I know what you mean. This is an unbelievably bad look for the school," Principal Powers replied.

"Your kid goes to school and joins the ski club and winds up dead."

"I agree with what you're thinking."

"We could have a panic on our hands," Lacy replied.

"We will need to try to keep this quiet."

"*Mum* is the word." Lacy left the principal's office and closed the door.

Principal Powers needed to talk to the detectives. She wrestled with the idea of letting the board of directors of the school know as well. She would call a special meeting for later in the day if she could get all the directors assembled. Then she would call the detectives about what Lacy had uncovered about the deceased students.

Principal Powers checked her schedule and saw that there already was a board of directors meeting today at 4:00 p.m. This was a lucky break. She could tack on this information about the students at the end of the planned meeting. This way the board could not criticize her for not informing them of any bad publicity for the school.

The board was informed at the afternoon meeting, and no special communications were released. There was some healthy discussion among the board members, and there were concerns about the news. But the board had to allow Principal Powers to release the findings to the police. The detectives had a job to do, and the school had a responsibility to turn over this information.

Principal Lauren Powers called the detectives at the Jefferson Park precinct on Wednesday morning. She had the number from the visit they'd made to the school a few weeks ago.

She dialed the number for Detective Cato from her office.

"Hello, this is Detective Cato."

"Hello, this is Principal Lauren Powers. You visited us at the school a few weeks ago."

"How are you, Principal Powers?" Cato asked.

"I want to pass along some information that we found out about those students," Principal Powers replied.

"I am listening carefully. What did you find out?" Cato asked.

"We have determined that there were ten students in the ski club at Hamilton Technical High School in the class of 1966. Six students are now dead. Four students are alive."

"Can you give me a breakdown of those students, Principal Powers?"

"Sure. The six students who are dead are Wally Bass, Kevin Burger, Joe Dirt, Paul Cagney, Mike Conners, and Karen Mille. The four students who are still alive are Joe Shapiro, Ben Harper, Al Gannon, and Ricky Chambers."

"Thanks, Principal Powers, for this information. Can you tell me how many people know of this right now?" Detective Cato asked.

"Our board of directors; Lacy Jones, who is my secretary; and I know. That's it."

"Can they please keep a lid on this for now? This way we can perform our investigation into the crimes and find the killer or killers."

"We will try. But eventually it will come out into the open."

"We need some time to find the guilty party and arrest that person," Detective Cato replied.

"Lacy, the board, and I will try our best to keep a lid on this here at the school. The police will need to do their part to keep quiet as well."

"Principal Powers, you have my word on this."

"Thanks. Let me know as soon as the detectives have any breaks in the case. We are sitting on a stick of dynamite, and it's about to blow up the school."

"I know how you feel. Hang in there, and we will do our best to discover the truth about these crimes and bring the criminal to justice."

"Thanks, Detective Cato."

Principal Lauren Powers thought that soon the entire world would know about the dead students and their connection to the school. Lauren was thinking to herself, *What mess did I just get involved in?*

Chapter 72

The detectives decided to visit the garden apartment of Ricky Chambers after dinner on Wednesday night. They were having no luck with a return phone call from Ricky or Ray, so an on-site visit was worth a shot. The detectives drove their patrol car to the Chamberses' residence and parked right in front of the building. As they got out of the car, they noticed a light on in the garden apartment.

"Bingo," Detective Douglas said to Detective Cato.

"I do believe Ricky Chambers is home," Detective Cato replied.

"Let's go check on him."

"Let's do that."

"I am going to the back door," Rick replied. "Just in case he gets a little squirrely."

"That's a good idea," Cato replied.

Detective Cato walked down the flight of stairs and rang the doorbell of the garden apartment. No one answered. He rang it again. No one answered it. He rang it a third time, and there was movement toward the door.

"Who is it?" Ricky asked.

"Detective Abbey Cato of the Chicago Police Department."

"What do you want?"

"We would like to ask you a few questions," Detective Cato replied.

"Just a minute." Ricky left the room.

A minute went by, and nothing. Another minute went by, and then the door opened. Detective Douglas was in the apartment with Ricky.

"What is going on?" Detective Cato asked.

"Ricky was trying to exit through the back door," Detective Douglas replied.

"You want to tell us why you were trying to take off, Ricky?" Detective Cato asked.

"I thought you guys were pulling a prank on me."

"We just wanted to ask you some questions." Detective Cato stared at Ricky.

"What kind of questions?" Ricky asked.

"Do you know anything about the murders of Wally Bass, Kevin Burger, Joe Dirt, Paul Cagney, Mike Conners, and Karen Mille?"

"Those students in the paper who died?" Ricky returned a glance to Detective Cato. "No. But my brother is writing about them. That is just awful."

"So, you don't know anything about them, Ricky?" Cato asked. "How did you know that they were students?'

"Uh, it was mentioned in the newspaper that they were students," replied Ricky.

"Were you a student at Hamilton Technical High School in 1966?"

"Yes. I was a senior at Hamilton Technical. So, what about it?"

"Were you in the ski club at the high school?"

"Why yes. I was. So, what is it to you two?" Ricky replied.

"It seems that out of ten students in the club, six are dead and four are alive. We have reason to believe that the club is being exterminated."

"That's crazy talk, Detective Cato," Ricky responded.

"We are just following up on all the leads in our investigation. Since you are one of the living, we believe your life could be in danger," the detective stated in a stern voice.

"My life is in danger?" Ricky asked.

"There are four remaining students from the club: Joe Shapiro, Ben Harper, Al Gannon, and you, Ricky Chambers."

"So, you think the killer is coming after me?" Ricky asked.

"It's possible. The killer could be coming after all four remaining students. We just don't know," Detective Cato said.

"Well, I am going to keep an eye out for myself," Ricky replied.

"Do you have a yearbook, Ricky?" Detective Cato asked.

"No, I did not buy one when I graduated."

"You sure you don't have a Hamilton Technical High School yearbook from 1966?" the detective asked once again.

"No, I don't," Ricky replied.

"We have it on good authority that you do have a yearbook and it was sitting on that coffee table." Detective Cato pointed to the living room.

"You must have me confused with my brother Ray. He has a yearbook. I never bought one. I considered it to be a waste of money."

Ricky was thinking to himself about how the detectives could know about the yearbook. Could it be the paperboy who'd looked at it and told them Ricky had such a yearbook? Ricky would keep this idea quiet. *That dammed paperboy.* Ricky was replaying this thought in his head.

"Ok, Ricky, we will ask your brother about it."

"Now can you two get out of here? I have some errands to run."

"Would you mind if we looked around, Ricky?" Detective Cato asked.

"Yes, I would. Now please get out of my apartment."

"Ok, Ricky. But we will be back," Detective Cato said with a stern voice.

As the two detectives left the garden apartment of Ricky Chambers, Detective Rick Douglas pointed to the upstairs apartment. Cato nodded her head. The detectives walked up the flight of stairs to the apartment of Ray Chambers. They had one question to ask Ray. Had Ricky bought a Hamilton Technical High School yearbook in 1966? It seemed like a simple question to ask and an easy answer to obtain. When they rang the doorbell, Ray Chambers was not home. This would be a question they would have to ask over the telephone or the next time they saw Ray Chambers. The two detectives knew Ricky was lying. They just needed to corroborate their hunch on this.

As the detectives walked down the flight of stairs from Ray Chambers's apartment, they could see Ricky staring through the curtains of the apartment below. He was watching them intently. The detectives nonchalantly avoided looking at Ricky. They knew that he was watching them, but they did not want to let him know this fact.

"Let's get out of here, Rick. This guy stinks." Detective Cato had that look saying that he was the killer on her face.

"He is as guilty as sin." Detective Douglas nodded his head.

"We need to get a search warrant from a sympathetic judge," Detective Cato replied.

"But with what evidence, Cato?"

"We may have to get creative."

"You make it sound like we need to break the law," Rick said.

"No. Just bend it a little."

The detectives got into the patrol car and left the garden apartment of Ricky Chambers. All the time they were getting in the car, they could feel his beady eyes staring through the window and stabbing them in their backs.

"This guy is dirty, Cato."

"I am in agreement with you, Rick."

Chapter 73

Ray arrived home at 10:00 p.m. Wednesday evening after chasing some stories that did not pan out. He saw that the lights were on downstairs as he parked his car in front of the house. So, he thought that Ricky had returned early from Lake Geneva. He seemed to remember that Ricky was not going to come home until Friday. Ray rang the doorbell of the garden apartment to see if Ricky was still up. One ring and no answer. Two rings and no answer. Three rings and no answer. Ray was thinking that if he did not answer the door, he had left the light on and was not home. Ray would check once more in the morning before he went to work.

***

Thursday morning Ray checked the garden apartment, and the light was not on. So, Ricky was probably not home and had left the night-light timer on. Ray thought about using the spare key he had, but this was only to be used for emergencies. He would check the garage to see if the car was there. They had flipped for who would get the garage, and Ray had lost the flip. So, Ricky always got the garage for his Chevy. Ray got the street space in front of the house. The garage was empty, and no car was in sight. So, Ray concluded that the light he'd seen on

Wednesday night had to be the night-light with a timer. Later today he would try one more time to contact Ricky from his office downtown at the *Chicago Today* building. Ray seemed to remember that Ricky had said he would be back on Friday but was not sure.

***

Ray had missed Ricky by just a few minutes that morning. Ricky was having breakfast out at the local IHOP restaurant. He was going down to another trucking company in the West Loop area for an interview for a job later in the morning. The owner of the trucking company had wanted to talk with Ricky early in the morning. The owner was leaving after Ricky's interview for a four-day vacation.

***

As Ricky left the IHOP restaurant to drive to the interview, he thought that a conversation and confrontation with Ray were coming. Ricky thought about whether he would do it tonight and then get out of town. He would see how the interview went and then make the call later in the day.

***

Ricky went down to the ABC Transit Company in the West Loop area of the city, off Randolph Avenue. The owner had set the interview for 9:00 a.m. on Thursday. Ricky arrived on time and sat down with the owner. The interview lasted about thirty minutes, and the owner was happy with Ricky. The ABC Transit Company was going through a growth phase and had a hard time attracting and retaining truck drivers for any period of time. Ricky landed the job, and the owner wanted him to start next week on Monday. Ricky was happy to get back to work, so he accepted the offer. He would be driving once again, but this time with ABC Transit Company. Ricky could now relax a little bit. But he knew that a confrontation with his brother was going to happen. Maybe later today.

Ray had tried to call the number for Ricky during the morning hours but got no answer. He tried once again after lunch, and Ricky finally answered the phone.

"Ricky, are you home today?" Ray asked.

"Yes, I came back early last night," Ricky replied.

"I thought I saw your light on last night, and I rang your doorbell, but you did not answer."

"I did not get home until late," Ricky replied.

"Can we talk tonight, Ricky?" Ray asked in a quiet voice.

"What about, big brother?"

"I need to talk to you later tonight."

"I'll plan to be home."

"Ok, I'll plan to come down to see you after dinnertime."

"That will work. I'll make sure I'm home."

"I can't get away until then," Ray replied.

"Hey, I just wanted to tell you. I went on an interview this morning."

"That's great. Did you get the job?" Ray asked.

"Yes, I did. I start Monday working for ABC Transit Company."

"That's great, Ricky. We will talk tonight. Ok?"

"Sounds good, big brother. Talk with you then."

Ricky knew that tonight was when all the shit would hit the fan. Ray would want to know about all the stuff that had been going on.

He would have to come clean about what he had done over the past two weeks. He would have to tell Ray, his big brother, that he had done some really bad things, and he was not proud of them. He had been holding a grudge against those six students, and now they were all dead by his hands.

Chapter 74

The watch commander was looking for the detectives once again. Officer Hoy was pacing in his office and looked out his window into the bullpen of detectives.

"Where are Detectives Cato and Douglas?" Officer Dane Hoy asked the office through the doorway. The desk sergeant came over and informed him that they were going to the judge's office to get a search warrant signed.

"When they get back, tell them I want to see both of them in my office," Officer Hoy replied.

***

Meanwhile, in the judge's chambers of Katie Garrett, two detectives were requesting a warrant on Ricky Chambers. This judge was known as a tough son of a bitch. She required really hard evidence before she would sign a search warrant on a private citizen. Her chambers were located in the Cook County building on Twenty-Sixth and California, on the fourth floor.

The two detectives had approached the judge's clerk in the office adjacent to the judges'.

"We are here to request a search warrant on a case," Detective Cato said as she looked at the clerk.

"Do you have an appointment with the judge?" the clerk, Amy Lockheart, asked.

"No, we do not," Detective Cato replied.

"Let me see if the judge will see you today." Miss Lockheart walked into the judge's office.

A few minutes later, the clerk came out and let them into the judge's chambers.

"The judge will see you now." Miss Lockheart pointed to the open door. "The judge has only a few minutes before court. So, make it fast."

"We will do just that. Thanks, Miss Lockheart," Cato said as they walked into the judge's chambers.

"Detectives, what can I do for you?" Judge Katie Garrett asked.

"Judge, we would like you to sign this search warrant for a suspect in one of our criminal investigations," Detective Cato said as she handed her the completed warrant.

"I don't sign anything unless I am completely briefed on what's in it," the judge replied.

"We have evidence that a Ricky Chambers has killed someone in one of six criminal investigations we are reviewing."

"Is it one or six?"

"We are not sure if the one person is responsible for one death or all the deaths of Wally Bass, Kevin Burger, Joe Dirt, Paul Cagney, Mike Conners, and Karen Mille."

"I have been following the news articles in the local paper. All the victims seem to be from one high school."

"That is correct, Judge. All six deceased individuals were from the Hamilton Tech High School class of 1966. We believe that they were part of the ski club at the school. There were ten students from the club. Six are dead and four are living."

"You think that the club is being rubbed out?" asked the judge.

"We really don't know, Judge Garrett."

"What hard evidence do you have on this Ricky Chambers that makes you want to toss his place for your investigation?"

"We think he is the killer or maybe involved in the crimes in six cases that we are working on."

"Ok, Detectives, what evidence do you have? Please explain why I should sign the search warrant."

"We have the testimony of a paperboy that he saw a yearbook with the names and faces of the deceased. Each one was circled and crossed out with an *x*, and the word 'dead' was written under each picture."

"Detective Cato, are you telling me a kid saw something in a yearbook and you think this person Ricky Chambers did it?"

"Yes, we do, Judge Garrett."

"Did you two smoke something before you got here?"

"Judge, we did not make this up. We suspect that this person Ricky Chambers committed the crimes. There is also the brother, who is a reporter, and he seems to have the details of the crimes before anyone else does."

"Who is the reporter brother?"

"The reporter is Ray Chambers from the *Chicago Today*."

"I never saw his name on the news articles."

"We believe the editor is keeping his name out of the print. Sort of like a ghostwriter situation. No names, just the details."

"So, the stories come out of the paper with no reporters' credentials. That is an interesting development. Have you pressed the editor on this?"

"We have, Judge. The editor is shielding the reporter and claiming a free speech position by hiding him."

"Of course he is."

"We have all kinds of evidence on all six victims. We just do not have a common thread except for the paperboy and the yearbook."

"Give me the search warrant. I'll sign it, but with one stipulation."

"What's that, Judge Garrett?"

"You can search only what is in plain sight on the premises. No opening of drawers, cabinets, or locked areas."

"Judge, can this include the garage as well?"

"I'll agree to that. But only plain sight."

"Thanks, Judge. If we find something, we may be back for another search warrant."

"I realize that Detective Cato. But your prima facie evidence is a bit thin, and I don't want a lawsuit against me. I kind of like my job here as a judge."

"That's why you're the judge." Detective Cato nodded.

Judge Katie Garrett signed the search warrant for the premises of Ricky Chambers. This warrant was effective for twenty-four hours only, beginning on Friday. So, the detectives would plan to execute the search warrant on the house of Ricky later in the afternoon on Friday.

***

The detectives returned to the precinct late Thursday afternoon with a search warrant in hand. As they entered the building and passed by the desk sergeant, a message was passed to them. The watch commander wanted to see them ASAP.

"Hey, Rick, I think we need to go see you-know-who."

"The watch commander?"

"That is correct, Rick."

The detectives walked over to Officer Hoy's office, and just before they got there, he barked at them, "Where the hell have you two been?"

"We had to go see a judge about a search warrant."

"Did you get it?" Officer Hoy again barked at them.

"I have it here in my hand, and we are going to execute it tomorrow."

"Well, it's about time you two made some progress on these cases."

"We are trying."

"The chief is breathing down my ass. I am getting tired of getting chewed out."

"Sorry about that," Detective Cato replied.

"Ok. Get out of here and put someone behind bars."

"Will do." Abbey turned to Rick. "Let's get out of here."

"We are going to nail this guy tomorrow." Rick looked at Abbey.

"I do believe you're right, Rick. The little voice inside me is saying the same thing."

Chapter 75

Ray dreaded the confrontation with Ricky that was planned for Thursday night. He wondered if his little brother was capable of killing some of his former fellow students. His mind was going in a lot of different directions. As he was thinking about the last six stories he'd covered, the little voice inside him said there was no way that Ricky could have done any of those crimes. Ray decided to get out his Hamilton Technical High School yearbook. A stroll down memory lane was in order to quell his feelings.

He went searching through some boxes in the closet and found the yearbook. The yearbook he had was from 1965, when he was a senior, and his brother Ricky was a junior. He thumbed through the pages and found Ricky in the junior section. He looked for himself, and his smiling picture was in the senior section of the yearbook. Now he looked for the six students he had reported on in the past two weeks. There he found them: Wally Bass, Kevin Burger, Joe Dirt, Paul Cagney, Mike Conners, and Karen Mille. They were all juniors at Hamilton Technical High School. Could this be a coincidence, or was there more to the story than Ray had reported on? This was a question his little voice was asking him, and he did not want to answer it. He would have to confront Ricky and ask him some questions. As Ray was flipping pages, he stumbled onto the ski club page. He noticed that there were ten students pictured and mentioned on the page in the yearbook. The six dead students were in the picture. There were four other students that he had not heard of, with the exception of one. They were Joe Shapiro, Ben Harper, Al Gannon, and Ricky Chambers. Was there something more to this story that Ricky might be involved in, or was Ray just thinking the worst of the situation? Ray was determined to find the underlying explanation. He headed downstairs to talk with Ricky.

***

Just after dinner, Ray walked out the back door and down to the back entrance of Ricky's apartment. He knocked on the door, and Ricky was sitting in the kitchen as if he was expecting Ray.

"Hey, Ricky. How are you tonight?" Ray said, easing into the conversation.

"Fine, big brother. What's up?"

"Oh, I am just checking in on my little brother."

"That's nice of you. But you don't have to check up on me."

"So, you landed the job at the trucking company?" Ray asked.

"Yep, the owner hired me on the spot. I start next week."

"What company did you say it was, Ricky?"

"The company is ABC Transit Company on Randolph Avenue."

"So, you're going to be driving once again?" Ray asked.

"Yep, I'll be driving the big forty-foot transports once again."

"Did you ever call the detectives from last week? You know that message I gave you."

"Oh yes. They stopped by yesterday."

"Oh, so they talked with you."

"Yep. I talked to Detective Cato and Detective Douglas yesterday.

They just had some routine questions about some former students from the Hamilton Tech ski club. I think they came here to tell me I needed to watch my back."

"Why would they do that, Ricky?"

"It seems that six of the ten students in the ski club are deceased. I am one of the four still alive. They were concerned for me and the other three remaining students."

"So, they think that somebody is going around killing students from the ski club?"

"That's their theory, big brother."

"I'm so relieved," Ray replied.

"What do you mean?"

"I thought you maybe had something to do with those former students."

"Whatever gave you that idea?"

"Just a little voice inside me saying that my brother was involved."

"You don't have to worry about me. I can take care of myself. If there is somebody exterminating the ski club, I'll get him."

"You don't need to take matters into your own hands, Ricky."

"I just mean I can take care of myself, big brother."

"I know you can."

"Is that what you wanted to talk to me about earlier?" Ricky asked.

"Yep, that's what I needed to ask you about," Ray replied.

"You have been out getting stories, and you're out at all hours of the night. Do you want to go fishing again at the cabin this weekend?"

"That sounds great, Ricky. A little fishing for the Chambers boys."

"It will be busy this weekend because of all the summer invaders."

"You're right. But we can get up early and catch some more walleyes."

"I would like that, Ricky. Let's do that. I can meet you up there late Friday night. I have some more deadlines to hit for the paper."

"That sounds good, big brother. You know I start the new job next Monday."

"Yes, that's right."

As Ray left Ricky's garden apartment and walked out the back entrance, the nagging little voice inside him was not done. There was something wrong, and Ray was feeling uneasy about the conversation with Ricky. He decided that he would need to keep tabs on his little brother and take a bigger interest in what he was doing. This way he could protect him and keep the promise he'd made to his mom and dad. He'd told them on their deathbeds that he would always watch over his little brother. That was a promise he was not going to renege on.

Chapter 76

It was Friday morning in Ricky's garden apartment, and the replay of yesterday's conversation with his brother was fresh in his mind. His brother had not pushed him too hard when he'd brought up the theory that the ski club was being hunted. The detectives had kind of confirmed this theory and lead him to believe that he was the one in danger. He had dodged a bullet, but his luck was about to turn on him. Ricky did not feel safe at the house, and he knew it was only a matter of time before the detectives came back. This time it would be with a warrant. So maybe the right thing to do was to get out of town and lie low. Travel to the cabin where there was no phone, and he could see anyone coming up to the property a mile away. His little voice was screaming at him, *Get out of Dodge*. This one time he would listen. He would wait until Ray left for work and then slip out after the rush hour, around 10:00 a.m. This way the traffic would be light and the trip to the cabin would be only an hour and a half. A breakfast at IHOP would be a welcome stop before he left the city for the weekend. But what about the job he had committed to starting on Monday? Ricky would call the owner and ask if he could start the following week. Maybe after a week, things would quiet down.

THE GRUDGE LIST

Ricky packed a few things into his '66 blue Chevrolet Chevelle SS and then drove out of the alley behind Hoyne Avenue. He would circle the block to see if that kid Mike was around. A little bit of unfinished business needed to be dealt with, Ricky was thinking, *I am going to get me a paperboy.* This way there would be no witnesses to the year-book-picture incident. As Ricky circled the block on Hoyne, he saw Mike on his bike, riding right down the middle of the street.

***

Mrs. Crystal yelled at Mike, "You'd better watch out for those pesky cars, Mike."

"Thanks, Mrs. Crystal, I will." Mike continued to ride his bike.

Mrs. Crystal yelled to Mike, "Watch out, Mike! That car is coming too fast."

Mike turned his head and could see that a blue Chevy was barreling down Hoyne Avenue right at him. He made a ninety-degree turn between two parked cars and headed to the sidewalk as the Chevy nearly ran him over. The car proceeded to speed off and turn right on Webster at an extremely fast rate of speed.

"Are you ok, Mike?" Mrs. Crystal came running down her staircase toward the sidewalk.

"I think I am," Mike replied.

"That car almost ran you over." Mrs. Crystal wagged her finger at Mike. "I told you to watch out for those pesky cars."

"Did you see the license plate?" Mike asked.

"Yes, I did. It was an Illinois plate with the numbers 311 136."

"I am going to tell Larry to report that car to the police."

"I think that is a good idea," Mrs. Crystal replied.

"I think I am going to go home and rest."

"That's a good idea, Mike. You go home and try to put this behind you. You may want to stay off the streets for a little while."

"But Mrs. Crystal, I like to ride the streets," Mike replied.

"Maybe next time that car will get you."

"Maybe." Mike was brushing off the near miss.

***

Ricky had just realized that he'd tried to kill a little paperboy with his car this morning. No one had really seen him, so he considered himself safe, for now. He proceeded to drive south on Damen Avenue to the corner of Madison Street, which was the destination before he got out of town. A visit with the local waitress at the IHOP, and then he would scamper out of town. As he drove down Damen Avenue, there was a tremendous amount of fog in the air for a cloudy day. The visibility was severely limited, and he had to slow down as he drove to the restaurant.

Once at the restaurant, Ricky loaded up on coffee, pancakes, and the good-looking waitress. He chatted her up, and she shut him down. She was not interested in him, but he was interested in her.

***

After breakfast it was time to get on the road. The time to get to Lake Geneva would be only about an hour and a half. But this fog was causing some severe visibility issues with the traffic. Ricky pulled his Chevy onto Damen Avenue and headed for the Eisenhower Expressway. Once on the Eisenhower, he would hook up with the Kennedy Expressway and then head north to Wisconsin. As he got off the Damen Avenue ramp to the Eisenhower Expressway, he could barely see the lane markers that divided the lanes. He proceeded down the Eisenhower Expressway through the Hubbard Tunnel, and it was completely fogged in. The visibility was only a few feet. What made matters worse was that the lights in the tunnel were not working. It was pitch dark on the expressway. Ricky could hear only a few cars on the roadway and was getting nervous. All of a sudden, he saw a truck in front of him. He felt like a deer in the headlights. The truck had its high beams on and was traveling at a high rate of speed. Before he could react, the '66 Chevrolet was turned into an accordion, with Ricky in the middle. He knew that this was the end, and his fishing days were done. He would not make it to Lake Geneva. He would not fish with his brother for walleye. He was now departed to the next world.

The police were on scene at the accident in the Hubbard Tunnel in just a few minutes. A transport truck had been going the wrong way and had plowed into a Chevy head-on. The driver of the Chevy had died instantly. The body was mangled in the wreckage, and extricating it required the jaws of life. The truck driver was hospitalized for a severe concussion, broken bones, and other injuries. The truck driver was cited for traveling too fast and going the wrong way on the expressway. The ME was called to the scene to make an ID of the mangled body but could not do so. The body would need to be autopsied at the coroner's office, and a positive ID would need to be made. The Chevy had a 1970 Illinois license plate, number 311 136, and was registered to a Ricky Chambers. So, for now the victim was listed as the registered owner until the ME could positively match the crushed body to him or someone else.

Chapter 77

The detectives decided that 11:00 a.m. on Friday would be the time to execute the search warrant on the premises of Ricky Chambers on Hoyne Avenue. They would surprise the resident inside and possibly bust down the door. The plan was subject to change depending on what the inhabitant did.

As the detectives arrived at the house on Hoyne, they parked right in front, in the space that was designated for Ray Chambers's house. Detectives Cato and Douglas walked down the flight of stairs to serve the search warrant on Ricky Chambers. As they rang the doorbell, Rick thought about what had happened last time. Ricky had tried to run out the back door. So, Detective Rick Douglas decided to cover the back door once again, just in case Ricky got squirrelly again. After three rings and no answer, Abbey called Rick back to the front of the house.

"Hey, Rick, I don't think he's home today."

"I think you're right, Abbey. How do you want to go in?"

"How are your lock-picking skills, Rick?"

"I can open this lock in just a minute."

"We have the search warrant. I really don't want to bust the door down. So can you pick the lock?" Detective Cato asked.

"I sure can. Give me just a minute."

Rick was good at picking locks. It was a specialty that he'd acquired through the years.

"Got it. This Schlage lock was a piece of cake."

"Thanks, Rick. Now let's go in and look around," Detective Cato replied.

***

The two detectives were alone in the house, searching for anything in plain sight. Ricky was nowhere to be found, so the search warrant could not be handed to him. They taped a copy of the warrant to the inside door, which was normal procedure when no one was home. As the detectives moved from room to room, they both noticed how clean the air smelled. As if someone had known they were coming and wiped everything down. After a one-hour search of the premises, the two detectives found nothing. No gun, no knives, no drugs, no incriminating evidence. The search of the Ricky Chambers residence was a bust. The detectives would need to apologize to the resident once they saw him in the flesh. But just before they left, Detective Douglas got a bright idea.

"Hey, Cato, there is a glass on the counter, and it looks like Ricky was going to wash it."

"So, what are you thinking, Douglas?"

"Looks like Ricky's fingerprints are all over the glass. Let's take the glass and lift his prints just in case."

"That's not a bad idea, Rick."

"We will need to be careful not to tell anyone we did this."

"What do you mean?" Cato replied.

"Stealing a glass from a murderer."

"You mean a suspected murderer."

"Sorry. Innocent until proven guilty."

"Exactly."

The detectives bagged the drinking glass as evidence and then left the garden apartment of Ricky Chambers. They found nothing that would incriminate the resident as they followed the intent of the search warrant that Judge Katie Garrett had signed for them. The warrant stated, "Search and seizure of contents only in plain sight." Abbey and Rick felt a little hamstrung but followed the law. By taking the drinking glass to dust for fingerprints, they were bending the rules just a little bit. They knew this item might not be used in a court of law because of the illegal method they were using to obtain it. The piece of evidence would be submitted to the fingerprint department later in the day. They both knew they would not get the results until Monday. There was a standard twenty-four-hour turnaround on all evidence submitted to that department. Since it would be late in the day on Friday before they could get back to the precinct, the twenty-four hours would turn into seventy-two hours for the results.

Chapter 78

Friday was, of course, a delivery afternoon and a collection day for Mike the paperboy. The tips and his pay over the past two weeks had been enough to buy a new glove, ball, hockey stick, and puck. With the new catcher's mitt, he could play a better game of street ball over the weekend. With a new hockey stick and puck, he could play with boys in the street as well. Mike was on top of the world. But why had someone try to run him down with a car on his bike on Hoyne Avenue? This was a question that he would pose to Larry at the newsstand, and he would ask what course of action needed to be taken against the motorist.

***

Mike pulled out his bike from the back porch and turned on the radio. Larry Lujack was on this afternoon, and the tune was "Friend of the Devil" by the Grateful Dead. As he got on his Sting-Ray, Mike decided to play it safe. He rode the sidewalks all the way to the newsstand since he had almost been run over that morning. As he passed by the house of Mary Crystal, he heard her yell at him.

"So, you're staying on the sidewalk today," Mary Crystal yelled toward Mike.

"That was a close call this morning, Mrs. Crystal."
"I warned you about those pesky cars."
"You sure did."
"Go get my paper."
"Sure, Mrs. Crystal." Mike rode away and stayed on the sidewalks.

***

Mike arrived at the newsstand in just a few minutes. All the paperboys were there rolling and rubber banding the Friday afternoon edition of *Chicago Today*. Larry was in the back office, and Mike had to talk with him. So, before he did his part to get the papers ready for the customers today, he barged in on Larry.

"Hey, Larry, got a minute?" Mike asked.
"Sure thing. What's up?"
"A car almost ran me off the road earlier today."
"What?" Larry asked.
"I was riding my bike down Hoyne Avenue this morning, and a car came barreling down the street. If Mrs. Crystal hadn't yelled at me, I would have been hurt."
"Did you or Mrs. Crystal get the license plate?" Larry asked.
"Mrs. Crystal got the number and gave it to me. I did not see the number."
"Are you all right, Mike?
"Yep. I made a right turn between two parked cars, and the Chevy sped off down Webster Avenue."
"Give me the plate number, and I'll call this in to the police."
"The car was a blue Chevy with plate number 311 136 and with Illinois plates."

"I'll call this in to the detectives and ask them what they want to do about it."

"Ok. Sounds good." Mike went to one of the high tables to roll and rubber band the papers.

"Hey, Mike, don't forget to deliver fifty-one papers today."

"You got it," Mike replied.

"You'd better watch yourself out there, Mike." Larry looked on.

Larry picked up the phone and called the number for Detective Abbey Cato at the Jefferson Park precinct. The desk sergeant picked up the phone and answered that the detective was gone for the day and asked whether he wanted to leave a message. Larry left a message for Detective Cato to call him in regard to a near miss auto accident involving one of his paperboys. The desk sergeant said he would give her the message as soon as she got back to the precinct. The message would be misplaced by the desk sergeant and not get to Detective Cato until Monday, when she was back after the weekend. The desk sergeant didn't know this and neither did Larry.

***

Mike left the newsstand Friday afternoon with fifty-one papers to deliver and a mission to collect on as many customer accounts as possible. He was on edge and constantly watching his back since he had almost been run over by a car that morning. So, he decided to stay on the sidewalks as he delivered the papers and collected the money. This turned out to be a safe strategy for a Friday.

It took nearly an hour to finish the deliveries and collections. As Mike rounded the corner onto Hoyne Avenue, there was the Chambers house. This was the third-to-last house on the Friday route. Mike decided to ring the doorbell only once, and if Ray Chambers did not answer he would leave quickly. There was no answer, and no lights were on. So, it was safe to bet that Ray was not home. Ricky was not going down to the garden apartment to knock on Ricky's door to collect. He would wait for Ray Chambers to be home on some other day. Mike ran down the flight of stairs and then finished the last two deliveries and collections. He proceeded back to the newsstand and turned in the collections to Larry.

***

As Mike got back to the newsstand to turn in his collections, Larry was there in the doorway almost waiting for him.

"How did your route go today?" Larry asked.

"It went all right. No incidents or accidents," Mike replied.

"I left a message with the detectives about your near miss with the car."

"What did they say?"

"The desk sergeant said he would pass the message on to Detective Cato when she got back to the precinct."

"So, nothing is going to happen to that driver."

"Nothing for now, Mike," Larry responded.

"Great. What happens if that driver comes back?"

"Stay off the street." Larry raised his voice.

"I'm going home now." Mike got on his bike and rode away.

The song "Green River" by Creedence Clearwater Revival was on the radio as Mike was pedaling down the sidewalk. As Mike made his way back home, he turned his head right, left, and center, scanning all the time for cars and other objects that might try to get him.

He made it home in one piece.

Chapter 79

The ME, Michelle Lynn, was working a rare Saturday to help with the staff shortage at the Cook County Medical Examiner's Office. There was only one body that needed an autopsy that day, and she was hoping for a peaceful and quiet day.

Michelle pulled the body from the storage slab in the morgue and wheeled the remains to her operating bay in the examiner's lab. This individual had been mangled by a truck, and firefighters had removed the body from the smashed Chevrolet car using the jaws of life. Since the body parts were just that, she was stumped about where to start the examination to determine who the deceased was. After a few attempts to piece through the wreckage of the corpse, she noticed a wallet smashed into the pelvic area of the deceased. A little tug here and push there of the mangled body, and out dropped the bloody wallet. As she slowly unfolded the billfold, a license was exposed. The license was that of one Ricky Chambers, age twenty-one, blue eyes, weight 170 pounds, height 5☒10☒, home address on Hoyne Avenue. This information confirmed the occupant of the car with the license plate of 311 136 in the initial findings by the on-scene officer. Michelle had a positive identification on the body parts on her examiner's table. The details of her report would indicate that a male by the name of Ricky Chambers had died an instantaneous death during an encounter with a transport truck going the wrong way in the fog in the Hubbard Tunnel. Ricky Chambers had been in the wrong place at the wrong time.

The news of the identity of Ricky Chambers would be passed along to the police so they could make the next of kin notification as soon as Michelle Lynn was done with the autopsy. She remembered that Rick Douglas was working on a case involving this individual and that Ricky Chambers was the brother of Ray Chambers, the reporter. She would give Rick a heads-up on this development so he could take some action on this case.

***

The Chicago Police Department called Ray Chambers to try and inform him of his brother's accident, but there was no answer at his home number. The watch commander knew the detectives working the related case and made a special request of Cato and Douglas to work on Saturday. Detectives Cato and Douglas were assigned to make an on-site notification to Ray Chambers of the loss of his brother.

***

They went to see him at his residence on Hoyne Avenue on Saturday afternoon, and no one was home. They left a note for Ray to call the detectives at the precinct by slipping it under the doorway. Since the detectives were in the neighborhood, they drove over to the newsstand to try to catch Larry.

***

At the newsstand, Larry was in the back office, and the newspaper boys were already gone for the day. The detectives parked their patrol car out front and walked in on Larry at the newsstand.

"Hey, Larry, how are you?" Detective Cato asked.

"Detectives, nice to see you. What brought you down to my neck of the woods?" Larry asked. "Is this about the near miss on Mike? You know the message from Friday?"

"What message from Friday," said Detective Cato. "I don't remember a message from you but, we have some news."

"Oh?"

"Ricky Chambers is dead. He died in a car accident on Friday morning."

"What happened?"

"I can't tell you anything more than that. We are trying to make the next of kin notification, and we were unable to contact Ray Chambers. He does not appear to be home."

"Mike did not collect the paper route money from him yesterday. He may be at his cabin at Lake Geneva."

"That could be where he is. I think he told us there is no phone up there. So, we will have to wait until he gets back if that is the case."

"Can you tell me what happened?" Larry asked.

"Ricky Chambers appeared to be involved in a crash with a truck traveling the wrong way in the tunnel. The truck slammed into his car, apparently killing him on the scene. We have not been able to reach Ray Chambers, his brother, so please do not say anything about this."

"I understand."

"Please keep quiet on this. This news has not been released to the public."

"I will keep it quiet," Larry replied.

The detectives left the newsstand where Larry was in the back office all by himself. They wondered if he would tell Mike about the departure of Ricky Chambers.

***

As the detectives were driving out of the neighborhood, they decided to go east on Dickens Avenue. They rolled down the street, and there was Mike, playing street ball with another boy. The boys had to stop to allow the car to pass them, but Detective Cato stopped right next to Mike. Both detectives got out of the car and walked over to Mike and Tommy.

"Hi, Mike, how are you?" Detective Cato asked.

"Are you here about that car that tried to run me over yesterday morning?"

"What car?"

"The Chevy that barreled down Hoyne Avenue and almost got me."

"We were not aware of any car that tried to run you over," Detective Cato answered.

"Larry said he called you two and left a message with the license plate."

"Do you remember what the plate number was?" Detective Cato asked.

"It was a blue Chevy with an Illinois license plate: 311 136."

The detectives looked at each other in disbelief. The plate number that Mike had given them was from Ricky Chambers's car, and he was now dead. Had he tried to run Mike over just before he met his demise? That was a very strange coincidence.

"We are going to tell you something, and you need to keep this quiet."

"Tell me what?" Mike asked.

"Ricky Chambers was killed in a car crash on Friday morning. He was identified by the ME on Saturday."

"Oh my God."

"Please keep this quiet. We have not been able to contact the next of kin, which is Ray Chambers. He seems to have disappeared."

"He is probably up in Lake Geneva at his parents' cabin. He told me once he goes there to unwind. There is no phone up there."

"That would explain why we are having trouble contacting him."

"He will probably be back for work on Monday."

"Thanks, Mike. We will keep an eye out so we can notify him. Whatever you do, do not say a word to anyone. We have just told Larry your newsstand guy and you. That's it. We need to notify the next of kin."

"Ok, I'll keep quiet on this."

"We will let you know when we contact Ray Chambers."

"Thanks."

The boys went back to playing street ball.

***

The detectives got back in their patrol car and drove out of the neighborhood. They did not tell Mike that the license plate he'd mentioned, 311 136, just happened to be the plate of the late Ricky Chambers. They would inform him of this fact after they contacted Ray Chambers. They were both thinking to themselves that the little boy had dodged a bullet from a serial killer.

Chapter 80

The Friday night hangout at the Clubhouse was moved to Saturday night for the second week in a row. Mike's parents were once again entertaining neighbors on the back porch on Friday evening. Friday or Saturday to hang out with the boys did not matter to the gang as long as there was beer.

Mike left the signal as one knock, two knocks, and then three knocks for the Saturday evening get-together. There were no nosy neighbors around this week to intercept the signal. It was Mike and Tommy's turn to get the beer, and they were reminded of this fact by Johnny and Danny.

"Everybody cough up two bucks," Mike announced to the other boys.

"Here you go." The boys handed over the money.

"Ok. We will be right back," Mike replied and looked at Tommy.

Mike and Tommy hung out at the liquor store on Damen Avenue for a full thirty minutes. It seemed a little bit slow, and they were having no luck getting a volunteer to get the beer. Then, all of a sudden, the same guy from two weeks ago appeared.

"Same deal as last week?" the stranger asked.

"Yep," Mike said as he handed him the eight bucks.

A few minutes later the stranger walked out into the alley and handed the boys a bag of cold beer.

THE GRUDGE LIST

"Was Old Style ok for you boys?" the stranger asked.

"Sure."

"Now remember. You don't know me. You never saw me before," the stranger said as he disappeared into the alley.

***

The boys returned to the Boys' Clubhouse through the back alley, being careful that no one saw them or was wise to their mischief. The ceremonial knock was given, and the bag of Old Style was handed through the hatchway.

"What took you guys so long?" asked Danny.

"No one was buying beer for us," Mike replied. "Everyone should grab a beer," he proclaimed.

"So, Mike, tell Johnny and Danny about that near miss with the car yesterday."

"Hang on, Tommy—does everyone have a beer?" Mike asked.

"Yep," Tommy replied.

"The detectives told me early today that Ricky Chambers was killed in a car crash on Friday."

"No shit. How awful," Tommy replied.

The other two boys looked shocked.

"What happened, Mike?" Danny asked.

"The detectives did not say much. They told me he was dead of an apparent car crash. They also said to keep it quiet."

"Why keep it quiet?" Tommy asked.

"Because the next of kin, Ray Chambers, could not be found."

"Is he the reporter who has a cabin on Lake Geneva?" Johnny asked.

"Yep. I collected the weekly money from Ray a long time ago. That was when he told me he had a cabin up there from his parents and there was no phone. So, my guess is that he can't be contacted until he comes back to Bucktown."

"That is going to be one ugly bit of news about his brother," Tommy replied.

"It is going to hit him hard that his younger brother is dead. He must have left for Lake Geneva Friday after work. I tried to collect the weekly money on Friday and Saturday, and he was not home."

"So, Mike, what about this car that nearly hit you yesterday?" Tommy asked. "Tell us about your encounter with the car."

"Well, I was driving down Hoyne Avenue yesterday morning, and a car came barreling down the street. Mrs. Crystal yelled at me, and as I turned around, I could see this car was going to run me over."

"So, what happened next?" Tommy asked.

"I made a ninety-degree turn between two parked cars and headed for the sidewalk. The Chevy took off and went right on Webster so fast I did not even see the driver."

"So did you get the license plate number?" Tommy asked.

"No, I did not. But Mrs. Crystal saw the whole thing. She got the plate number, and I took it to Larry the newsstand manager. He called it in to the detectives. They said they would look into it."

"You dodged a bullet, Mike," Tommy proclaimed.

"I sure did."

"What was the plate number?" Danny asked.

"I remember it very well. It was an Illinois plate with the number 311 136."

"I swear I have seen that plate around the neighborhood," Johnny yelled.

"You have? Where?" Mike asked.

"I seem to remember seeing that license plate somewhere on my route when I was delivering papers last week," Johnny replied.

"Well, if any of you boys see it again, let me know so I can get the cops after the driver. Now give me another beer. This can is empty." Mike motioned for a second can of Old Style.

"Let's drink to Mike. Ricky is dead, and Mike dodged the car." Tommy raised the can of beer up into the air.

"That's a little bit twisted, Tommy. But I'll drink to being here with you boys on a Saturday night at the Boys' Clubhouse. The best place in town."

The boys continued the celebration into the night until the two six-packs of Old Style were gone. Mike was alive, and they were happy to be together after a long week of things happening in the neighborhood. Maybe now things would get back to normal and the boys could concentrate on playing street ball and street hockey.

Chapter 81

Mike had to get up early on Sunday morning. The paper delivery today would require several trips back and forth to the newsstand and would take over an hour to complete. The Sunday paper could not be rolled and had to be hand delivered to each customer's house. This truly was the one day that none of the paperboys liked.

***

Mike pulled his Sting-Ray bike out from the back porch and made sure the radio was attached to the handlebars. He turned the radio on as he was walking through the gangway between the houses. The DJ on WLS 890 AM radio he was unfamiliar with; he just announced the four songs to be played. It sounded as though the DJ was trying to take a break and put on a string of songs of uninterrupted music. The songs were "Closer to Home" by Grand Funk Railroad, "Green-Eyed Lady" by Sugarloaf, "Naturally" by Three Dog Night, and "Mississippi Queen" by Mountain. Mike would appreciate the lack of commercials as he rode his bike to the newsstand.

Driving down the center of the streets was a tradition with Mike, and he knew that the cars would not be out and about. The Friday incident was already in the back of his head, and he felt safe on the road. The trip to the newsstand proved to be uneventful, and Mike arrived unscathed.

***

He strolled into the newsstand, and there were already a few paperboys present. Larry was in the back office and called to Mike as soon as he entered through the doorway.

"Hey, Mike, can you come back into the office?" Larry asked.

"I'll be right there—give me a minute," Mike responded.

Mike walked back into the office, where Larry was looking at something in the paper.

"Mike, did you see the headline on page 1 of the *Chicago Today* Sunday edition?" Larry asked.

"No. I just got here. I have not even had a chance to look. What's on the front page?"

"Well, you'd better look right now."

The front page contained the following headline in bold letters:

"RICKY CHAMBERS DIES IN HUBBARD TUNNEL CRASH."

The story went on to report on the fact that a transport truck had gone the wrong way in the Hubbard Tunnel in a dense fog and crashed head-on into Ricky Chambers's car, killing him instantaneously. The news report also went on to say that the parents of Ricky Chambers had died in the same Hubbard Tunnel a little more than three years ago. The tunnel had claimed two parents and one son inside three years. The paper concluded that the Hubbard Tunnel was the deadliest place on the highway in the Chicagoland area. Apparently the lights in the tunnel had been malfunctioning and were not on at the time of the crash. It was a very tragic accident that Ricky Chambers would never recover from. He was pronounced dead at the scene. The truck driver who had caused the accident was admitted into the hospital with non-life-threatening broken bones and a concussion.

"This is what the detectives could not talk to us about yesterday." Larry looked at Mike.

"Oh my. This is a tragic accident," Mike replied.

"The son and the parents die in the Hubbard Tunnel almost three years apart. This is a sad news story, but it sells papers," Larry said as he pointed to the headline.

"How do I deliver the paper to Ray Chambers's house?" Mike asked.

"Well, I am sure he has been notified, Mike."

"I thought he was still away at his cabin on Lake Geneva."

"The detectives must have contacted him before they released this news story," Larry said to Mike.

"I am not so sure, Larry."

"This would be a real tragedy if the news reporter hears that his own brother died from the same newspaper he works for without a police notification." Larry just rolled his eyes. "They could not have done this to one of their own reporters."

"Is this how the newspaper business works?" Mike asked.

"No. It has to be a mistake," Larry replied.

"Well, it is a big one."

"I agree with you on this, Mike."

"I'll go deliver the papers now."

"That's a good idea."

"If I see Ray Chambers, I'll let you know. He still has not paid me for last week's bill," Mike said as he left the newsstand with a bag full of the Sunday edition.

"Thanks." Larry waved to Mike as he walked out the doorway.

Mike delivered all the papers for the Sunday edition with no accidents or incidents. The home address of one Ray Chambers was empty. This customer was not home when the paper was dropped on his doorstep. Mike did notice that the Friday edition, the Saturday edition, and now the Sunday edition were all sitting on the doorstep waiting to be picked up.

Chapter 82

Ray was up at the cabin on Lake Geneva the whole weekend. He had left from the office on Friday night. The plan was to go fishing with Ricky on Saturday and Sunday, but his little brother did not show up. Ray was thinking that Ricky probably had a good reason for standing him up. A discussion with him would be stern and demanding.

Ray did enjoy his time up at the cabin during his brief departure from work. The absence of a phone was a welcome feeling so he could unwind and relax. The only downside was that if there was an emergency, no one could get in touch with you until you plugged back in. Ray did not go into town and use the phone, so no news would reach him until he returned to civilization on Monday.

***

Ray decided to go home Sunday night and knew he would be in the commuter traffic making its way back to the city. The drive from Lake Geneva would take about two hours with all the heavy traffic that headed south from Wisconsin to Illinois. But after a while he arrived at his house on Hoyne Avenue.

***

Ray parked his car in the designated spot in front of the house. The apartment downstairs had a light on, so maybe Ricky was there. Ray went down and knocked on the door. No one answered the repeated knocks. He'd probably left the timer on. Ray walked to the back of the house to check the garage to see if Ricky's car was in the garage. There was no car in the garage. *So where is Ricky?* The thought went through Ray's head. He walked up the back stairs and unlocked the door; he thought maybe his brother had been arrested or something. He went to get the emergency key for Ricky's apartment. The front door was unlocked, and Ray walked into Ricky's place. Nothing appeared to be out of order. There was a slip of paper taped to the front entrance door. It was a search warrant that was dated Friday. Detective Cato's and Detective Douglas's names were on the piece of paper with a phone number to call if there were questions. Ray locked up the garden apartment and was going to go upstairs to his residence to call the detectives from the search warrant notice. As he walked up the flight of stairs to his home, he noticed the Friday, Saturday, and Sunday papers were sitting on the door stoop. He grabbed all three papers, unlocked his front door, and went into his living room. As he picked up the phone to dial the detective's number from the warrant, he looked down at the Sunday paper's front-page headline.

"RICKY CHAMBERS DIES IN HUBBARD TUNNEL CRASH"

Ray dropped to his knees holding the Sunday paper and started to read the article about his brother. The newsprint went on to say that Ricky Chambers had been killed in a car accident on Friday. A transport truck had been going the wrong way and smashed into Ricky, killing him instantaneously. The article also listed a couple of contributing factors: the fog and that the lights in the tunnel had malfunctioned and were not on. At the end of the story was a notation that the parents of

Ricky Chambers had been killed by a drunk driver in that same tunnel three years ago. A tragic family accident in the Hubbard Tunnel.

Ray tried to call the detectives but got only the desk sergeant at the police precinct. The sergeant relayed the same information about Ricky that was already in the newspaper. Ray was asked to come down to the morgue to identify and claim the body at his convenience. Ray agreed to do this first thing Monday morning.

Ray had so many questions to ask Ricky that now would never be asked or answered. Was he the killer? Had Ricky Chambers killed Wally Bass, Kevin Burger, Joe Dirt, Paul Cagney, Mike Conners, and Karen Mille? Why had Ricky done this?

A dead man answers no questions and gives no one any closure. Ray would need to confide in the detectives and try to figure this out. But would they be willing to talk to the brother of a killer?

Chapter 83

Rick Douglas went down to the fingerprint department to get the results from the drinking glass that the detectives had stolen from the Ricky Chambers residence on Friday. The fingerprint department had been backed up on prints to process, so Monday was the earliest they could get the results. The detectives had labeled the print as a John Doe when they'd submitted it for analysis.

As Rick went to the desk for the fingerprint department, Officer Jane York saw him coming toward her.

"Detective Rick Douglas, how are you?"

"Fine, Officer York. Got my report on that print?" Detective Douglas asked.

"Yes I do. I have good news and bad news," Officer York responded.

"What are you talking about?" Rick asked.

"That print you had us run through the database does not match anyone on file. That's the bad news."

"What's the good news?" Detective Douglas asked.

"That print for John Doe matches the evidence for the five earlier submissions."

"What do you mean, Jane?"

"The print you submitted for five other cases—Wally Bass, Kevin Burger, Joe Dirt, Mike Conners, and Karen Mille—matches the John Doe fingerprint."

"You're kidding," Rick replied. "You just hit me a home run."

"Get me a name for the fingerprint of John Doe, and you got your killer."

"I already have a name, but it's going to be hard to prove."

"Why is that, Rick?" Jane asked.

"The person with the fingerprint is deceased."

"That's unfortunate. You can't really prosecute the dead," Jane responded.

"A bit of a dead end. No pun intended." Rick grabbed the fingerprint report.

Rick walked up to the bullpen with the fingerprint results and sat down with Abbey to discuss.

"Hey, Abbey, I have the results of that fingerprint we submitted off the drinking glass we took from the Ricky Chambers residence on Friday."

"And what were the results?"

"A home run," Rick replied.

"You're kidding."

"The print off the drinking glass matches five out of the six cases we are working on."

"You mean that the paperboy was right!" Cato proclaimed.

"That paperboy was right on the whole time. We should have pushed harder when Ricky Chambers was alive."

"Rick, what the hell are we going to tell the watch commander about these six cases?" Abbey asked.

"No idea. How do we go after a dead man?"

All of a sudden, a voice floated over the bullpen of detectives.

"Cato, Douglas, my office right now," the watch commander yelled across the floor.

Detectives Cato and Douglas walked into the watch commander's office and closed the door.

"Well, what is the latest on the six crimes you two are investigating?" Officer Dane Hoy asked.

Detective Cato said, "We have a fingerprint match of John Doe to five of the six cases we are reviewing. We also have a witness who saw a vehicle on the other case."

Dane Hoy said, "Spell it out. Do you have a suspect or not?"

Cato said, "We have a fingerprint match from a drinking glass we grabbed in our search on Friday of the apartment of Ricky Chambers. The print matches the five crimes we are investigating: the deaths of Wally Bass, Kevin Burger, Joe Dirt, Mike Conners, and Karen Mille. We also have a witness for the Paul Cagney case who saw a '66 Chevy with Illinois plate 311 136. The plate and the fingerprint belong to Ricky Chambers."

Dane Hoy said, "So go arrest him."

Cato said, "We can't, he is dead. He died in a car-and-truck crash on Friday."

Dane Hoy said, "Is this the same guy that was killed in the Hubbard Tunnel?"

Cato said, "He is the same guy. Ricky Chambers."

Dane Hoy said, "The news story said he died in the tunnel and his parents died in the same tunnel three years ago."

Cato said, "The father, the mother, and the son all died in that tunnel."

Dane Hoy said, "How the hell are we going to prosecute a dead man? The blowback on this from the public will be terrible."

Cato said, "This is why you are paid the big bucks. What do you want us to do about this?"

"Let me talk to the chief about all this and get back to you."

"I just want you to know we lifted the drinking glass from the premises of Ricky Chambers to get the fingerprint."

"You stole the glass from the apartment?"

"We bent the rules a little bit," said Detective Cato.

"Shit, a judge would throw this evidence out," said Officer Hoy. "What were you thinking?"

"We should have been listening to the paperboy a little bit harder," said Detective Cato. He was right the entire time he talked to us. We underestimated the twelve-year-old, and we should not have."

"We should hire that paperboy," said Officer Hoy.

"I agree with you, Officer Hoy. When he gets a little bit older, the police department should hire him."

Chapter 84

Mike pulled his Sting-Ray bike out from the back porch and made sure the radio was attached to the handlebars. He turned the radio on, and Larry Lujack was on as the DJ of the day on the call sign of WLS 890 AM radio. The set of songs being announced was "All Right Now" by Free, "And It Stoned Me" by Van Morrison, "The Midnight Special" by Creedence Clearwater Revival, and "Get Ready" by Rare Earth. Mike appreciated the lack of commercials as he rode his bike to the newsstand. Music was blasting from the radio, and one paperboy was singing to the tunes.

***

Mike drove down the center of Hoyne Avenue. As he passed by the home of Mary Crystal, she yelled at him from her porch.

"Didn't you learn your lesson the other day, Mike?"

He just waved at her and kept riding by.

"I warned you about those pesky cars, and you did not listen to me last time."

"I know, Mrs. Crystal." Mike waved at her.

"Go get my paper."

"Sure, Mrs. Crystal."

***

Mike arrived at the newsstand and took a spot at the high table, where a stack of papers was waiting for any paperboy. He rolled the papers, rubber banded them, and counted out fifty-one for his route. He stuffed them into his news pouch and placed the pouch on the handlebars, and then poof, he was off for the delivery.

The delivery of fifty-one papers on a Monday in the summertime for the *Chicago Today* was the life of a paperboy, and Mike really enjoyed his summer job. Riding his bike while slinging papers and listening to the radio was what Mike enjoyed so much. While riding, he thought about all the things that had happened and the people and things he had encountered during the last couple of weeks:

The murder of six students.

Ray Chambers, the *Chicago Today* reporter.

Ricky Chambers, a killer brother.

Detectives Abbey Cato and Rick Douglas.

Larry, the newsstand manager.

The Hamilton Technical High School yearbook.

The Boys' Clubhouse.

Playing street ball and street hockey with Tommy, Danny, and Johnny.

Then it dawned on him. "I was able to solve these murders before the detectives. Maybe I have found out early in life about what I really want to do. I want to be a detective just like those guys on the TV show *Dragnet*. Sergeant Friday was such a cool guy for a cop. That's what I want to do when I grow up."

Thank You

I would like to thank my wife Deborah who is my greatest supporter, a source of inspiration, and one of my harshest critiques. She often refers to me as Ricky even though that is not my real name.

Thanks to Shirley Moy for reading my first draft and helping me with developing a writing style. I made lots of grammatical mistakes and she was there to help me along this journey.

Thanks to the boys on Sunday for giving me a little push to keep going.

Thanks to my fellow golfers at Willow Creek Golf Course for being receptive to my babbling about the Grudge List book while I was writing it.

A special thanks to the team at Palmetto Publishing for getting this first book off the ground.

Chris Bryda is a first-time author of The Grudge List. This project has been a dream of his for three years.

He is retired from the software consulting business which he operated for 24 years. When he is not writing books Chris is playing golf and riding his racing bike on the Swamp Rabbit trail.

Chris lives with his wife Deborah in Greer, SC.

Milton Keynes UK
Ingram Content Group UK Ltd.
UKHW011836160724
445364UK00015B/135/J